BLACK JUJU

BLACK JUJU

TIM CURRAN

WEIRD HOUSE

ISBN: 978-1-957121-89-5

Text and Afterword © 2024 by Tim Curran

Cover and interior artwork © 2024, by M. Wayne Miller

Interior and cover design by Cyrusfiction Productions

Copy edited by F. J. Bergmann

Editor and Publisher, Joe Morey

Weird House Press
Central Point, OR 97502
www.weirdhousepress.com

CONTENTS

ILLUSTRATIONS

PART ONE: THE HUNTED

1

When night came, Maggart was still in the cemetery up on the hill, the branches of dead trees rattling about him, a low wind moaning through the old tombstones. The grave had been dug, squared off, and like a yawning mouth, it waited to be fed. Yet he sat there by a low brush fire, the shadows dancing around him, his heart barely beating in his chest. Across from him was the box made ready for the grave. He had built it himself out of cedar scraps. It was not a lovely coffin by any means, but it was functional. It was only a matter now of easing it into the grave and covering it with earth.

But every time he made to do so, he stopped. He sat back down by the fire and packed his pipe, remembering the boy and his mother, the farm and the life he would never know again. When he buried the box, he would be burying all of it and he just couldn't bring himself to do it.

So he sat there.

Waiting.

Perhaps hoping it was all a terrible nightmare he would wake from and tell himself oh by God, it was just a dream. That's all it was. Just an awful dream. And then the sun would come up and he and the boy would tend to the livestock and labor in the fields and they would come back at nightfall and his wife would have a fine spread of roast chicken, potatoes, and biscuits with honey. Life would be sane and his existence would have meaning again.

He opened his eyes and the fantasy dissolved. He was in the graveyard, the firelight making marble stones and leaning, simple wooden crosses flicker with an orange glow. The box was still there. And in the distance, a lone wolf howled in mourning.

There are things a man must do, he thought. *Things that hurt him deep inside, but must be done.*

Yes. Enough. He had to get this done with.

He tapped out his pipe and looked out across the fields of the dead, anxiety rising in him. He was not a man who believed in spooks and spirits, but for one moment he thought he saw glowing, dead-white eyes watching him from the shadows. Then they were gone. His imagination had taken a trick of the light and turned it into a wraith. He looked up at the sickly wedge of the moon above. The stars.

Breathing low in his throat, he stood up, worked the kinks from his back and placed his hands on the box. He realized at that moment that he'd never told the boy how much he'd loved him, and the idea of that was painful.

Enough. He was going to shove the box carefully into the hole and that would be that.

A stick cracked behind him and he started. He swung around, reaching for his scattergun, and saw a woman standing there. In the guttering firelight, she looked to be high yellow, with her dark skin and European features. She wore a simple calico dress, her black hair swept over one shoulder and her eyes just as black as original sin.

"What do you want here?" he put to her. "This is a private affair. Get off with you."

"Your lamb, your poor sweet lamb," she said and her voice was sweet and kind, nearly musical. He could feel it move along his spine like delicate fingers. She took another step forward. "Your lamb so stiff and cold."

She was a creole woman, and her accent was that of the West Indies. Maggart had never hated anyone, man or woman, based upon their skin color. This sense of fairness in the face of the adversity that had been his life and his upbringing was something he prided himself upon. Yet, for a reason he could not comprehend, he did not like her. Her charming accent was like rich chocolate, and she was not unattractive, yet something about her repulsed him to his core.

"I told you to get," he said.

"But I've come to help you. To give you back that which you love the most."

He had the scattergun on her, but something in her eyes told him that he would never use it. It suddenly felt heavy and greasy in his hands. His eyes blinking, his heart squirming like a grub, he felt the gun slide from his fingers and thump on the ground at his feet.

"You … you …" He attempted speech, but the words would not come and his mouth no longer knew how to form them.

"Hear my voice, Mister Maggart: If you do what I ask, in the manner I prescribe, I can give you what you want. I can make your boy alive again. But only if you do what I ask."

He tried to shake his head because it was a horror what she suggested. It was blasphemy and devil's work. If he allowed it, it would damn his soul to hell.

"Do you want him to be alive again?" said the voice.

Again, he tried to shake his head, but his mouth betrayed him. "Yes," it said.

"Are you sure? Much will be asked of you."

"Yes, oh please, yes, bring him back to me."

"Open the box then."

He was trembling. "Please, not that…."

Her eyes burned into him. "Open it. There are things I must do to the boy. And when I am done, I will tell you of those things you must do…."

By then, his will was not his own, and his hands moved of their own accord. They took up the claw hammer and pulled the nails one by one. Tears streaking down his face, his teeth chattering, Maggart opened the lid, cringing as the black, fetid smell of death blew into his face. The boy laid there like a broken doll. Something that had never lived.

The creole woman opened a hide bag she carried with her and took things out. Saying foreign words that were guttural and sacrilegious, she laid her hands on the corpse. And as she did so, it began to move.

2

The heat. The damn oppressive heat.

On the bad days, it got to Sam Bouchard and made him think of other places, febrile landscapes where the cane grew hot and dry, and things rustled in the knife-edged shadows. Then the sweat would run from his pores with a yellow stink, dampening his clothes and leaving a dew of salty moisture on his face. The breath would be sucked from his lungs, and his hands set to trembling. His fingers would be white rubber, palsied and useless. He could not even un-leather his Colts if death came rooting at the door.

He was no good on days like that.

His head rioting with unclean memories and the stink of pig-shit and pig-blood and pig-rot, he would crawl away and hide like a sick dog, praying nobody would come for him. Nobody with pistols in their hands and murder in their heart. Nobody who wore the grotesque face of a twisted fetish-beast. And nobody with eyes like red glass and a green rottenness where their souls had once been.

§

After Guadeloupe, there was peace for a time. There was sanity.

But Sam was careful, always careful.

He made his way up from New Orleans on the dodge, keeping a close eye on what was behind and what was ahead. Looking for enemies with old scores to settle. But that was the way a man like him operated: if you made a living with a gun, you played things careful. You kept your eyes open and your pistols primed.

He'd been cool and easy at first, thinking he'd left all that demented hoodoo business back on the island, but then in Baton Rouge it all came back to him. With teeth. He'd been living with a Cajun prostitute named

Maddie Borcheaux at a riverfront brothel. They'd grown up in swamp country together, had a good time talking about how the world was surely changing and eating crawfish and red beans, oysters and artichokes, drinking French wine.

Sometimes, Sam just liked to look at her.

Maddie was tall and graceful, her face smoothed from the finest unblemished porcelain, her slanting feline eyes such a shade of blue they would take his breath away. Her hair was red fire and its heat made his knees weak. When they were out in public, it was done up in a severe bun. And when they were alone and in one another's arms, it was let down in long scarlet tresses of secret glory. She was a creature of deep, burning emotions. When she loved, it was with an infinite passion that was bright and hot; and when she hated, her ire was fine and cold.

By nature, she was inquisitive.

In her line of work, she came across men (and women) from all walks of life and she always plied them with questions. She wanted to know who they were and where they had come from and what it felt like to walk in their shoes. In essence, she wanted their lives and stories and secrets. She wanted to hold these things close to her heart and guard them. So, one night after a fine dinner of blackened catfish and shrimp étouffée, she put her cerulean eyes upon Sam and said, "Tell me, Samuel. Tell me about something which you have done, something that you are not proud of, something you have never told anyone before."

"Must I?" he said, everything clutching tightly inside of him.

"Yes. I want to know those things others do not. I want to be made one with you."

Had anyone else other than dear Maddie said such a thing he would have probably laughed in their face. But he did not laugh. Her words rang true and reached deep into his heart. There was a sincerity to her that made him ache inside, and a decency that all the high-priced whoring in the world could not blemish. Lighting a home-rolled cigarette, he walked to the window and stared out at the traffic upon the river.

He thought: *Tell her something true. You do not dare lie to her. Tell her about the awfulness in your soul. She thinks you are strong; show her your weakness. How you shiver and sweat at night. Of the terrible fear that is on your soul.*

She watched him.

She was asking him to lance a little of the pain inside himself that she instinctively sensed. Like a leeching in the days of yore, a little bleeding might do him wonders. Smoking, he walked about the room, circling the dining table and studying the prints and tapestries on the walls. She did not interrupt him with words; she just watched him move as if he were chasing the thoughts in his own head. His movements fascinated her. It was as if his soul, his ghost, moved first, his meat and bones hurrying after it to catch up before they were left behind in a whirl of sleek kinetic energy. Was this how a hunted man moved? Was this the furtive, careful grace of prey? Moving quickly, waiting, breathing, tensing, then moving again once it was certain danger was not close at hand?

Finally he sighed, then stepped before the window again. He told her that several weeks previous, he had been riding in the Sulphur River country of Arkansas, among the great pine thickets. For days, he had felt someone behind him, closing in, watching him by day and hunting him by night. He did not know who it was. At least, he was not willing to tell her who he thought it might be.

So preoccupied with what was behind him, he paid little mind to what was ahead of him. Then, one day, jittery from lack of sleep, laid bare by jumping nerves and secret fears, someone stepped out from behind a sweetgum tree. It was a boy with a cap-and-ball pistol, a big old Colt Patterson .36 with a rusty barrel and a battered grip that looked as if someone had been pounding nails with it. He was dirty and desperate, no more than thirteen or fourteen. He had the .36 in both hands and said he needed Sam's horse and he was willing to kill to get it. He claimed he didn't want to hurt anyone, but this was an emergency. He needed to get to Texarkana, that it was a matter of life and death.

"Son," Sam told him. "I need my horse. I can't give it to you."

"If you don't, mister, I'll kill you."

Nothing Sam said made any difference to the boy; he wanted the horse. Sam figured only one of three things were going to happen—the .36, given its condition, would misfire; or it would blow up in the boy's hands; or he would shoot Sam clean out of the saddle with that cannon, spreading his insides for ten yards.

"Now down off that saddle," the boy told him. The tone of his voice made it quite obvious he would barter or banter no more.

Sam climbed from his mount and the boy, being more than a bit inexperienced in the ways of the world and men with guns, climbed up, trying to steady the horse and keep the .36 on Sam at the same time. He took his eyes off him for a brief second in that moment, one of Sam's Colt Peacemakers filled his hand and the boy realized he was in a terrible predicament.

"Now drop that weapon, boy, or I'll put you to earth right here," Sam told him. "Don't make me shoot you, and don't try your luck, because I rarely miss."

Indecision clouded the boy's eyes. The freckles on his cheeks stood out like spots of ink against his face which had gone decidedly pale and bloodless. He blinked. Sweat beaded his upper lip. He had a decision to make and it involved either his own death or that of the rider.

"Drop it, boy," Sam said. "I won't ask again."

By that point in his career, Sam knew all the signs of someone with a gun in their hands that was about to make a terrible, lethal mistake. The boy's eyes shifted. His mouth tightened. His shoulders bunched. His gun hand trembled. He let out a sigh that was supposed to sound disarming and lowered the barrel of the .36 a few inches. This was instinctive behavior. It was to let his quarry—Sam—know that he hadn't meant any harm in the first place. Playing possum and feigning innocence.

So what happened next was no surprise.

The boy brought the gun up quickly to fire, but as he did so, Sam threw himself to the side and fired two rounds at his adversary. As luck, and maybe skill, would have it, both slugs found their mark. The boy got off one shot that was well wide of its mark just as a hole appeared in his throat and another appeared just an inch forward of his left ear. They both did a considerable amount of damage, the first taking out the boy's voice box in an eruption of gore as the second went into his brain, bouncing madly through his skull, and ejecting from the back of his head with a goodly amount of bone chips and gray matter.

The boy hit the ground, as harmless as eighty pounds of well-marbled meat. He did not so much as twitch. It was an awful thing. Sam went down to his knees, knowing he'd had no choice but feeling a deep-gnawing guilt regardless.

"I could have given the boy my mount," he told Maddie, "but then I would've been a dead man. There would have been no way to escape on foot the one that was following me. He was getting closer and closer."

He considered burying the boy. It would have been the decent thing to do. Already, a dozen or so flies were investigating his wounds. By the next day, he would be a grim sight in that heat. As Sam searched for a good patch of loose earth to inter the corpse, he heard a horse snort from the treeline. The one who was following him was very near, waiting in the dark and twisted shadows of the piney woods. He told Maddie that he could have stood and fought, but something inside him shriveled from the very idea. This was not a fight he could win. He knew it then; he knew it now. Leaving the boy, he climbed back onto leather and thought he heard a low, wizened cackling, a sound of cold triumphant laughter as if the rider waiting in the narrow shadows was amused by what had taken place.

"I was a coward," he admitted to her. "First, I killed that boy. Maybe there wasn't another way, and maybe I wasn't brave enough to look for it. I don't know. But I do know that the rider dogging me seemed to be getting stronger as I grew weaker."

"That makes no sense," Maddie said to him.

"No, it doesn't. But as I rode out of there, I could feel his power, his wrath, and his hatred."

"Who was he?"

But Sam refused to discuss it further. She wanted an admission, she wanted to see the world through his eyes and now she had. At least a glimpse. He dared offer her no more than that. As the days passed, the subject was not broached again. Maddie let it lie. His pain was too deep. Though she did wonder if it was because he killed the boy, or because that other, the rider, had seen him do it and seemed delighted by the idea … *almost,* she thought, *as if Sam did exactly what he thought he would.*

Many days later, such things were forgotten, at least in casual conversation. Sam and Maddie enjoyed each other. They drank well, ate well, and loved well. They laughed and they carried on, and there was no happier, carefree couple in the Quarter.

One night in bed, surrounded by warm pillows and sunken into the feather mattress, a sprawl of delicious nakedness and twined limbs, Maddie said to him, "You are an insatiable creature, Samuel Bouchard."

He smiled, and it felt good, felt right. "I have been known to favor my vittles."

"That is not what I mean, and I think you know."

Sam lit a cigarette, his mind fuzzy and worn to a polished luster from the lovemaking. "It is your fault, my sweet wickedness. How many men have you seduced and brought here, teaching them your wild ways?"

"Many," Maddie admitted. "But I only remember loving the one."

"And the one only remembers loving you." He blew smoke out his nostrils and listened to the wagon traffic out on the street. "You make a man feel like a man, my wickedness. And once he feels that way … what else is there?"

"You are a meat-eater, Samuel Bouchard," she said, pressing his hand to one pert breast. "I sense a streak of wolfish hunger within you."

"Let me gorge myself then."

Maddie began to laugh. "You will die naked in bed, used up and breathless, but I think you will die happy."

§

After the madness of the West Indies, Maddie was exactly what he needed. By degrees, they fell in love. And what wasn't there to love about her? There was sunshine in her heart and laughter in her eyes. Maybe her ways were not pure and virtuous, but there was a loyalty and an honesty to that woman that put any high-stepping society woman to shame. So against his better judgment, Sam fell in love with her, until he was so smitten, he felt like a sixteen-year-old again. He'd float through his days, smiling, knowing his lizard-skin boots would last a lifetime because his feet never touched the ground. Mornings, he'd wake next to her and feel her in his blood and in his soul, and he'd want to drown in her. And what was even better than this constant, life-affirming high was that he knew that Maddie loved him, too. And knowing this, he wanted to carve their names in trees and shout his love from rooftops.

This love was insanity, it was a sweet addiction, it was a fever that would not release him, and he slept soundly in its heat. He loved Maddie so much, he wanted to crawl inside her. He wanted to sleep inside her skin and feel the beat of her heart and breathe with her lungs and feel her blood coursing through him.

He even started thinking marriage, God help him.

§

One pleasant night they shared a fine spicy meal of fried oysters, seared chicken, sausage gumbo, and stuffed bread washed down with a bottle of Montrachet red. It was like being home again, and Sam could not recall being happier than he was at dinner and then in Maddie's bed later.

"You spoil me, my wickedness."

"Ha! Always you call me wicked," she said to him, a lust that was unconquerable in her eyes. "Am I so wicked to spoil you? Am I so wicked to let you have me? So wicked to fill your belly with good food and imported wine? Show me the wickedness in that, Samuel Bouchard."

He laughed, becoming accustomed to such merriment, to a life where there was joy and contentment and no need of pistols in his hands. "Somewhere, Maddie, there is a preacher praying to the Lord above, trying to cleanse his mind of an image that haunts his dreams and turns his heart black with lust. And that image is you, my fine wickedness."

Maddie kissed him and traced her long fingers over his chest, moving them in gentle whorls over the scars of battle and gunplay that were many. "How many have tried to kill you, Samuel Bouchard? How many have hated you? And I alone love you."

"I never sought a fight."

"Not in the war?"

The war. It clouded his mind. He saw men dying, men who had been friends and men who had been enemies and all of them now just men, not good or bad or evil, but men whose lives had been poorly spent by politicians on both sides who pitted life against life. "I had no choice. We killed some Yankees and some Yankees killed us. That was our job on both sides—to kill. We did it, I think, well. Perhaps too well at times. Now that the blood has run cold and the smoke has cleared, we only have our memories, and maybe that's the worst thing of all." He rolled a cigarette with fingers that trembled slightly. These were things he did not want to talk about, yet he knew he must. There was a scab on his soul and it had to be picked so that the bad, diseased blood might run clear again. "When I think about it, I see the terrible waste it was. I wonder what could have been accomplished if together we had built instead of destroying, worked instead of hating." He chuckled. "Maybe the years have made me soft. Maybe your love has made me naïve."

"And maybe inside there is a fine man with a finer heart who cannot hate and cannot abide those who do," she pointed out.

"I wish I were that man."

Maddie, who could not tolerate violence of any sort and found warfare a fool's game, thought about what he said for a long time and then, into his ear, whispered, "How many, Samuel? How many souls?"

Had anyone but she asked this they would have gotten to know the Sam Bouchard who lived by guns and instinct … but Maddie? No, there was an honesty to her question and it was the sort of thing Sam asked himself as he lay in bed nights, sweating and fearful from nightmares of killing. "I don't know. I really don't know and I think … I think …"

"Tell me."

"I think that's what worries me the most."

Maddie said, "You have nightmares. You tremble and cry out in your sleep. Is it … is it the dead coming back for you?"

"Often."

"They do not rest easy, or maybe you do not."

3

He was a man alone and he traveled with a coffin-shaped box in the back of an old creaking buckboard. He wore a heavy gray overcoat dirty with the years, frayed denims, and hobnail boots. No one who met Maggart ever learned what his Christian name was, and maybe they were afraid to ask. His face was sallow and cleft, the shaggy beard that hung to his chest steel-gray, his eyes just as black as obsidian. There was an old hate in his heart and a blackness in his mind that would never see light. He was a grave man on a grave mission, and those who met him looked away quickly because the hate in his eyes was smoldering and hot.

There's death in that one, they'd think and, maybe, if they were of the faith, they'd cross themselves. *Murder. Pain. Ugliness. Tragedy.*

As Maggart moved from town to town, he asked questions and expected answers. There was a man he was looking for that was responsible for what was in the box in the wagon, lying in state. He planned on finding him and making him pay for his sins. What those sins were, he would not say, but those who stared long enough into the black agates of his eyes, realized that they did not want to know.

Though he could have kept moving from sunup to sundown, and perhaps right through the night, the horses needed to rest from time to time. They required watering and feeding. So each evening, he stopped, usually by a creek or river if he could find one, sometimes in the high prairie grass or at the edge of a nameless town. He ate simply—boiled beans with molasses, sometimes just hardtack—and his sleep, what there was of it, was uneasy. Often, he woke in the night, beneath the stars, and went over to the box in the wagon. Removing the buffalo rug that covered it, he would place his callused hands on it, feeling the cool, unfinished cedar and something deep inside him would weep.

It was then, he would remember the boy.

He'd been a pale, thin child, sickly, and his mother had doted over him as mothers do. As he grew, he got stronger and the stronger he got, the more help he was around the farm and the more independent he became. Maggart could clearly see the man he would become and it filled his heart with pride that he had accomplished one thing in this life, had one thing to boast of: his son.

Then one night, when things seemed to be going good and the fields had taken to seed and the livestock were growing fat and healthy, his wife woke him.

"Terrible pains, just terrible pains in my insides," she told him, her breathing ragged and her face glistening with sweat. "Been coming and going these past weeks, but now ... oh sweet Jesus ... now it's a constant."

That's when the illness first sank its teeth into her. Or, at least, it was his first true indication of it. And like a ripple in a pond, it did not dissipate, it only grew larger. And as it increased, she lessened until she was no longer the bright, vibrant woman he'd known. She was, in fact, a stranger. Where before she'd led the family with care and wisdom, two eager hands baking pies and churning butter and knocking out stacks of Johnnycakes with hot molasses on chill mornings, she became a withered thing, rheumy-eyed and gray-lipped, her blood running cold. By that point, she couldn't even get out of bed any longer. She lay there, rotting, steaming with fevers, talking with people long dead, alternately crying and laughing madly with hysteria.

And as she sought her grave, Maggart's world went quite literally to hell. The crops died in the fields. The livestock sickened. The horses died. A terrible plague had been visited upon his family. The local midwives and healers could do nothing for his wife, so one day, he took aside the boy and said, "You need to get to Texarkana and get a real doctor. Don't care how you do it, but you got to fetch one," he said, pressing the Patterson .36 into his hands. "You find a horse. Steal one if you got to. Then you ride hard and bring that doctor for your mother. You understand, boy?"

The boy nodded, scared, but proud that his father trusted him with such an important task.

"I'd go, but I don't dare leave your mother. It's up to you. If we don't get her a real doctor, she's gonna die."

He watched the boy run off down the trail that day and he never saw him again. Not for many days. Not until after his wife died and then he went looking for the boy and found his corpse. And that's when the creole witch found him, at the boy's grave, and said terrible things which were the sweetness he had hoped for, even though he knew, by scripture, that it was wrong, that his immortal soul was damned.

Now Maggart's life, the one he had known and cherished, no longer existed. It had been blown out like a candle flame. His existence was day upon day riding from town to town, always searching, asking questions, seeking the elusive spoor of his quarry. All he had left was what was in the box, and that slept in the cold darkness, waiting, forever waiting.

Your lamb, your poor sweet lamb, so stiff and so cold.

Maggart heard a sob come from his mouth and he hated his weakness, but the sound of that voice in his head was like a key that opened the despair and heartbreak he had locked away so carefully, so securely. He didn't like to think of her and the blasphemy she had impressed upon him, how she was always inside him now, just beneath his thoughts, pushing him on, directing him to that thing she wanted so badly.

He pressed his hands against the box, slivers poking into his palms. A voice in his head told him that it wasn't too late, that he could turn back onto the path of righteousness ... but then he thought of the boy in the box. His future, his life, all that he held sacred was in there. His heart wanted to burst with grief. If he continued on this path, it would burn his soul to cinders, yet he knew he could not turn back now.

If you do what I ask, in the manner I prescribe, I can give you what you want. I can make your boy alive again. But only if you do what I ask.

In his mind, he could see her face—it was like a cold moon obscured by wisps of fog. Then it clarified and her black eyes looked deep inside him, deranged with hatred.

Maggart covered the box with the buffalo rug and went back to the fire which burned low. He stared into its flames a long time. And as he did, he thought of Samuel Bouchard.

4

The tent-show revival was run by a man with the dubious name of Preacher Divine. He drew an interesting assortment—sodbusters and farmers, lowly thieves and pickpockets and drunks. A couple whores ran a shanty just up the road and their clientele tended to visit the tent show after their lilies were duly pressed. As always, the vagaries and hypocrisies of the human animal were amusing.

Inside, souls were being saved and Preacher Divine—a peg-legged, one-eyed savant who claimed to have been ravaged by the Devil in the form of a shark when he was a sailor years before—was preaching the gospel as he saw it. His tongue was well lubricated and his brand of snake oil always found customers. And that was the important thing. Preaching the gospel was his life's work. God spoke through him. He was the Lord's vessel. Regardless, at his core he was a practical man who kept a wary eye on the collection plate. Most nights it was not much, but now and again the pickings were quite remunerative, particularly in those places where there was sickness, despair, and hopeless lives. People often gave more than they could afford, but they were buying not just a ticket to the afterlife, but the Lord's blessing that would save them, help them walk the proper path, and lead them out of the darkness of their miserable, crowded lives.

So, adjusting his eyepatch (a nervous habit he did continuously), Preacher Divine saved souls and preached the Word, grinning inside as the collection plate filled and he knew he would have more than enough that night for a good meal, a bottle of the Devil's brew, and perhaps, just perhaps, enough left over for a turn with a painted lady.

When the large man came in out of the rain, he stopped speaking. The words seemed to dry up on his tongue. A bead of sweat rolled down the side of his face. He felt a strange uneasiness inside, a touch of fear. He did not understand it. The large man was no different than any other. He was dressed in a wet oilcloth slicker and a rain-dripping, pinch-crowned hat.

There's a darkness to him, he thought without really meaning to think anything. *I can feel it.*

Preacher Divine tried to speak again as his flock became restless, but he stuttered. His mouth had never been so dry. With a shaking hand, he sipped water from a tin cup, though what he needed was a taste of whiskey.

He shook it away, recovering himself.

"Make no mistake," he said in a deep baritone, "that the Devil is here among us. He hides in the lusts and carnal sin of each and every one of us. He is in our hearts. He hangs like a bloodsucking tick from the very soft white underbellies of our souls. He makes us think impure thoughts and contemplate dark deeds of the flesh."

A few people nodded. A couple of old ladies in bonnets, their lives playing out and bringing them closer to their maker each day, called out vociferous amens. A soldier giggled. A farmer broke wind.

Preacher Divine swallowed repeatedly, mopping sweat from his brow as his eyes passed over the stranger again. "But how ..." He swallowed again. "How, I say, does one deny the machinations of the Dark Lord? How does one turn away from wickedness and original sin?" He held up his dogeared, well-thumbed Bible. "With this book, I say to you! With the holy writ! It is our armor against iniquity! Only by studying the scriptures, knowing them, believing them, and yes, oh sweet God above, yes, *practicing* them can we free ourselves from the kingdom of Satan and be delivered into the caring, loving hands of the Lord most holy!"

His ragtag congregation, as it were, was getting worked up now. They were getting loud in their righteous condemnation of sin and the devious ways of the Prince of Darkness. And as they grew excited, so did Preacher Divine. He fed off them. Sometimes the Word was not enough. This was truly the addiction he craved—to be listened to, accepted, sainted by their wide-eyed adherence to all he said. Yes, he was the beacon of the Lord shining a light into the murky byways of their lives, lighting the path so that their spirits would be renewed.

"What do you see before you?" he asked them, making a conscious effort not to look at the stranger. "A minister? A student of the scripture? A righteous man? Yea, most certainly! But, my good friends, you also see a man who was once a sinner! A godless, drunken, whoring sailor who turned his face from God! It is true! Lord have mercy upon my soul, but it is true!" He lowered his head in shame, adjusted his eyepatch, then made a low sobbing in his throat. It was strictly theater, but he knew how to play his audience. "But though I turned away from Him, He did not turn away from me! One night, my ship went down in a terrible storm. We were adrift upon wreckage for many days ... and it was there that Satan found us! How I remember it! Satan, I say, the Lord of the Underworld! The Devil of the Deeps! He came as a great, horrible shark that killed many of us, maimed others! The beast took my leg! And then ... and *then*, I say, the Lord sent a ship to rescue our poor, ravaged souls! I survived! Many of us survived! But only through the intervention of the grand Lord of Hosts!"

They were beside themselves now. He had them firmly in the palm of his hand. Time to work them, squeeze more coins out of them.

"Why do I tell you this sad tale? Why do I burden you with the sins of my former life?" he asked them. "Because ... oh, sweet God, because I reach out a hand to you! Sinners, rejoice! The Lord has not forgotten you! If you but cast a look in His direction and pray unto Him, He will lift you from the gutter to a higher plane!"

The collection plate was filling nicely now. Ah, this was good, this was fine. This was true divinity. Yet, despite all of it, he still felt uneasy because the stranger would not take his awful, burning eyes off of him. They made sweat bead his face, stirred his guts, made him tremble with a slow-moving terror.

Now he stepped forward until he was but ten feet away, standing before the faithful in their chairs. By Christ, not now. Preacher Divine was about to end his sermon with the killing blow—hellfire and thunder and, finally, forgiveness to all. But this man ... *dear God, his eyes.* They would not stop looking at him and, worse, looking *into* him.

"Tell us, Preacher! Tell us of your sin! How you beat back the Devil and his demons! Tell us how you freed yourself and saved your soul!" the stranger called out, getting everyone worked up. "Lead us through your sins so that we can recognize our own!"

Everyone was crying out for the same now.

Preacher Divine felt like an animal in a cage. Something inside him paced back and forth. It wanted to escape, to flee this place, because the power had shifted now. The stranger had it and he felt weak inside as it was drawn from him.

"I ... I ... I ..." he stammered. Terrible thoughts gathered in his mind like storm clouds. They darkened his soul. Words were coming from his mouth and he could not stop them. Something was taking possession of him, working him like a hand puppet, playing him like a ventriloquist's doll. *What is this? Oh God, what is this?* It opened his mouth and made him speak the truth: "I bathed in sin! I swam in it! I was a fish in a black, horrible river of lust and depravity! I ... I bought a thirteen-year-old Indian girl from her parents! I admit it! I had knowledge of her! I raped her every night! I made her do things banned by the Good Book! She was my slave and we fornicated again and again! And ... and ... and when I tired of her, *I strangled her with these very hands! I strangled her as I ... I ... I filled her with my seed!*"

Now the congregation had gone quiet. The uppity Bible-thumping old ladies in the first row sat with their mouths hanging open. One of them fainted. Another man asked, "What in the fuck is going on here?" Now people were getting angry. Hands were balled into fists and fingers trembled on guns. People were calling out for a lynching. They wanted to hang Preacher Divine, beat him, burn him alive.

He fought valiantly against the force that had taken him over, but it was hopeless. His strings were pulled and he responded in kind. He shook. He drooled. Tears poured from his eyes. He tossed his bible aside and raised his hands above his head.

"*I am the Devil and I stand before you! I, who have raped young girls! Murdered men for money! Laid with the wives of farmers! I drink! I whore! I spurn the Lord!*" Now he began to cackle with madness. "*Evil came to me in the form of a rutting she-goat and we ... we ... we fucked! Yes! Yes, oh goddamned yes! I fucked that demon animal nightly and I liked it! I loved it! That filthy, squealing animal! We SUCKED! We FUCKED! It was she who whispered into my ear how I could rob each and every one of you with this self-righteous horseshit! It was she who—*"

But that was as far as he got. Chaos ensued. People scrambled from the tent and those that didn't went after Preacher Divine, beating him to the ground and kicking him until he lost consciousness.

It was much later when he opened his swollen eye, a broken and bloodied creature with shattered ribs and snapped limbs, most of his front teeth missing. The first thing he saw with his blurry vision was the stranger hovering over him.

"You ..." he said. "You ..."

It hurt even to speak. It was agony to move. He tried to lick his lips, but his mouth was dry. All he could do was blink his one good eye, his entire world split asunder as was his body.

"My name is Maggart," said the stranger. Though his eyes were black as the grave, his voice was not without pity. "I have been compelled to bring you to ruin and expose the sins of your heart." He pulled out a skinning knife. Light played off the blade. "Now I must take you as sacrifice because she wills it. Do you understand? She *wills* it."

As Preacher Divine struggled, Maggart told him he had made a bargain with the creole witch and he dared not refuse what she asked. Because if she wanted it, then he wanted it because he could only think about what was in the box and the pain associated with it.

"The boy, Preacher. The boy. She would make him live again."

But Preacher Divine did not understand any of it. He tried to form words with his mouth, but then Maggart jabbed the knife into his throat and his life spurted into the dirt.

5

"In the war I saw ghosts," Sam said to Maddie one day.

It was no joke and he told her so. He had never been so completely serious as he was at that moment. Laughter was miles from him. And, looking into his eyes, Maddie could see that. For the briefest instant, she saw those ghosts, too, breaching the veil of the next world with skeleton key fingers, hungry, so terribly hungry for what they had left behind or what was taken from them. For the salty marrow of life they wished to suck with puckered and scabrous lips. She blinked several times, for these images chilled something to white ice in her soul.

Sam looked off into space. "I was with the First Louisiana Cavalry at Chickamauga. It was considered a victory for our side, but with two solid days of fighting and eighteen thousand men of the CSA lost … well, I guess that's open to debate." He shook his head. "Regardless, this is where I saw my first ghost. Like I said, we fought for two days, two ugly and bloody days. By nightfall of the second day, Kelly Field was pitted by artillery, cratered and blasted. Corpses, whole and in part, were littered everywhere, as were the wounded and the dying. You cannot, I think, imagine such a scene … the bodies sprawled, heaped everywhere, the powder smoke hanging thickly in the air, the stink of blood and death just horrendous. When the rains fell, we thought they would wash away the stink and blood, but it only made things worse. The puddles that spread over the ground were red, red with blood."

He took his time in the telling, feeling it important that Maddie see what he saw and feel what he felt.

"I took two rifle balls that day … one in the belly and one that grazed my neck. Both wounds bled terribly. By nightfall, I was still lying in the field with the dead and dying. Stretcher bearers from both sides were trying to collect their wounded, but there were so many, Maddie, so damn many." His fingers traced the scar at his throat, remembering, remembering. "With night there came a chill, and a thick fog enveloped those killing fields. I was feverish, I suppose, and weak from blood loss. And sometime after sundown I saw the ghosts."

Sam told her he was tangled in a heap with seven or eight other Confederate corpses. His head was resting on the belly of a man whose guts had been quite literally shot out, his legs trapped beneath two other cadavers that were burned black from shell burst (both, amazingly, still had their gray CSA caps on their heads and one still gripped his Enfield rifle). Sam had been slipping in and out of consciousness for many hours since the battle, often crying out in a weak voice. When he next opened his eyes, it was fully dark and that's when he became aware of some unusual sounds. These were not the moaning or coughing or gagging of the dying, the skittering of rats that had come out to feed, or the distant grumbling voices of medics … this was something quite different.

Hollow voices.

Whispering, giggling.

It took some doing, but he managed to turn his head and there, in the palest of moonlight, were three dark shapes crouched over the body of a Yankee sergeant who had been riddled with rifle balls. Sam had identified him as such earlier when the sun was still up. Just a bleeding, gored mass of flesh who whimpered from time to time, snarled in his own viscera. Somehow, he still lived. His lungs still sucked air and his eyes, dear God, were still open and aware. When Sam saw the figures crouched over him, he assumed them to be Union medics or bearers.

They were neither.

"In the moonlight, Maddie, I saw their faces. They were yellow and waxy, their eyes shining and godawful black. And such was their pallor that I could see that their mouths were smeared with blood," he told her, beginning to breathe hard with the memory of it. "I craned my head a bit more even though it was agony to do so. I will tell you what I saw. In the moonlight, those pallid things were hovering over the man. Two were Yankees, one was a Confederate soldier. I recognized that one. Sergeant Stillwell. I had seen him die. I saw a Union bullet go straight through his forehead and take out the back of his head. But he was there with the others ... and they were feeding on that Yankee and he wasn't yet dead...."

"Sam, please," Maddie said. "Enough."

"You see, Maddie, all three of 'em were dead, just cold meat, and I could see their wounds quite clearly. One of the Yankees had holes in his face and the moonlight shone through them. The entire back of Stillwell's head was entirely missing. Up until then, I suppose I thought them ghouls of a sort," Sam explained to her, his face very white and pinched by that point. "But then I knew they were ghosts. They did not see me or seem to care if anyone was around. They whispered and giggled with those hollow voices and straight away, began to *feed*. They were sucking the blood from that fallen Yankee's wounds. I could hear them. They were slurping and licking like hogs at a trough and that sound was unbearable. And as I said, that poor man was still alive. I saw his eyes. They looked at me, and the horror and desperation in them was beyond anything I've ever seen before. I think ... I think I screamed then." He licked his lips with a dry tongue. "And ... one of those ghosts ... I believe it to be Stillwell ... looked right at me. There was blood all over his yellow face. He was grinning at me and his eyes ... dear God, black and soulless, but triumphant, Maddie, *triumphant*. As if ... as if death had freed some awful thing within him that he gloated over."

Maddie pressed him closer to her. "You were delirious, darling. Fevered. Perhaps overcome by the miasma of the dead."

"Yes, absolutely. Absolutely. But I saw it. I know I saw it. And later ... yes, later, when I again woke to feel something worrying my throat ... it was Stillwell. He was lapping at my wound, *licking* the blood like a cat with a saucer of milk. His tongue was cold, cold as if he had stuck it in a bucket of ice water. And it was rough-textured, again like a cat. He was lapping up my blood. I could feel him sucking my life away. I could smell the sour graveyard stink coming off him, smell the bitter odor of my own blood and … and I could hear his pleasure as he did so, a moaning that sounded quite near ecstasy."

Maddie did not want to hear more, but Sam made her listen because it had all been rotting inside of him too long now. It had to get out. So he told her in detail. How Stillwell smelled—not of putrescence; he had not been dead that long. No, it was a stink of warm decomposition that came from inside where he was black and rotten. Sam told her he cried out and Stillwell stopped sucking at his wound and looked at him with eyes that were like succulent red cherries that seeped a dark juice. Drool and stolen blood oozed from his grinning mouth. The gored cavity at the back of his skull was filled with buzzing flies. Sam heard a rustling sound and saw that the other two ghosts were wriggling over the blasted earth in his direction, not crawling but slithering like corpse worms in search of greening meat.

Sam wiped a dew of cool sweat from his brow. "I realized then that my gun was in my hand, my Remington 1858. I got off a shot and when I again opened my eyes, the ghosts were gone."

Maddie did not speak for some time, then she said, "But ghosts … ghosts that lick blood, ghosts that have odors to them."

"They were ghosts," he maintained.

"But blood … why would they want blood?"

"Because blood is the life, Maddie, as we are told. They were feeding on that which they no longer had, hoping to fill themselves with it. I don't know. No one can really know."

"They did not come back after that?"

"No. My shot brought the bearers and they took me to a field hospital."

There was no more to tell or no more that he dared tell, so he closed his eyes and Maddie did the same. No amount of talk or rationalization could explain away what he had seen and what he knew to be true. He remembered it all most vividly, and how much was truth and how much had been flavored by his reoccurring nightmares of the event, he could not say.

§

There were things that Sam told her that he had shared with no other living soul. But there were other things, terrible things, that he could not understand nor completely comprehend, and these were the ones he kept to himself. He knew something was terribly wrong and had been wrong since the island. There was a dire sickness inside him. It cast an aura around him, wrapping him up in a winding sheet and his greatest fear was that this badness would find its way into Maddie.

There were names for the sickness, he supposed, old names, but he refused to think of them. Despite his happiness, he still woke in the dead of night quite often suffering a stark fear that would not let him go. He could remember little of the nightmares, just bits and pieces—a warm tropical night, a rag doll hanging by a thread, the eyes of a snake glittering yellow in the darkness—but enough so that his entire body shook and only whiskey would unbend his nerves.

One such night, he shook and sweated so badly that he feared he would wake Maddie, so he dressed, pulled on his boots, strapped on his pistols, and went for a walk. Thirty minutes later, he found himself out on the mud flats of the big river. He stood in the muddy sand among various weedy clumps of stranded flotsam and jetsam, staring out at the wide expanse of black water. There was a sickening taste in his mouth that reminded him of bad meat. He pulled from a bottle of whiskey, trying to wash it clean, and only succeeded in making it burn that much hotter in his throat. Grimacing, he gagged and spat bile into the sand. His stomach lurched and he thought he would vomit, but he held it down. A haunted voice in his head told him that he would not only have vomited out his guts but his soul.

He suddenly felt as if he was not alone.

He looked around in a panic, but there was no one with him. Of course, there was no one. Who would have been out on those desolate flats in the wee hours of the night? He tried to shake the sensation from his mind, but it persisted. He could feel someone watching him. He swallowed down more whiskey, his free hand seeking the butt of a pistol at his hip.

There's no one, you fool. You have to stop this.

The taste of rot filled his mouth again; it was sickly-sweet and disgusting. He washed it out with whiskey and spat into the sand again. As he did so, he almost thought he saw something writhing in it. With a shaking hand, he fished out a cigarette and lit it with a match struck off his thumbnail. The flame made shadows slink about him like starving cats. The mud under his boots felt unnaturally soft and quivering, as if it was not sand he stood upon but something pulpy and rotten that he was sinking into. The idea was ridiculous, of course, but now that the thought had occurred to him—or been *made* to occur to him—the mud grew softer and his boots sank into it up to their shafts. He shook his head; he would not give into it.

You're hallucinating. Get out of here. Get out of here now. You should have known better than to come to a lonely place like this. The Hell Rider followed you here. He must have.

Yes, yes, that was it. The Hell Rider. The one who stalked him like some relentless hound. The one who sent nightmares into his head as he slept and awful hallucinations into his waking hours. The one who had laughed when he'd gunned down the boy.

Sam pulled his boots out of the muck and took a few more steps closer to the water. He pulled off his cigarette. *Gah.* The smoke smelled like burning hair. He tossed it and it hissed in the mud. He was shaking so badly by then that it took both hands to get the half-drained bottle of whiskey up to his lips. The taste was awful, sharp and acrid like urine, but he forced it down … at least until something touched his lips. Something inside the bottle that was fleshy and alive. The bottle fell from his fingers and landed in the mud. He clearly saw a snake slide from the glass mouth, coiling in the muck.

"You ain't real," he said to it, reality and unreality and maybe even *anti*-reality blending together in his head. His body was covered in cold oily sweat. His guts were knotted up in square knots and sheepshanks. It felt like his bones were shivering under his skin.

The snake watched him with flat golden eyes, its forked tongue tasting the night. He studied it with an awestruck amazement because it was much larger now. Somehow, it had fit inside the whiskey bottle and now, amazingly, it was thicker around than the bottle and easily six or seven feet in length. It continued to watch him, moving slowly, very slowly over the wet sand. The moonlight gave its scales a green metallic sheen.

He knew it was not real.

It was a hallucination.

A phantom.

Something the Hell Rider had dragged slithering from the darkest pit of his mind. On the island, he knew, there were deadly snakes—the fer-de-lance, even the bushmaster, some said, *mute fate* (as it was known)—but nothing like this. It wasn't real. It couldn't be real. *If you think it's real, it's real,* he heard a voice in his head say. *Your belief will be enough to kill you when it strikes.* It moved closer, looping over the sand. He was its prey. He shook his head from side to side. *Not real. Not real.* When it was three feet away, within striking distance, it raised its triangular head and he could sense the godless evil of the thing. It was a reptilian demon. Its golden eyes were glistening. Its entire body was quaking. He wasn't strong enough to think it away; it was real, dear God, it was real. He reached for the Colt Peacemaker on his right hip and cleared leather as the snake compressed its sinewy muscles for attack.

He fired three times.

He blinked.

He was shooting at a log deposited by the tide.

A log, a goddamn log, you idiot!

He took two or three steps to the side, nearly falling. The mud was so soft, so spongy, it was like treading on the corpses at Chickamauga. Horror and revulsion rose inside him and he thought he might scream. The Hell Rider was near, he had to be near.

Sam could feel him grinning from the shadows as a blackness crept over him, sinking him in night. The darkness was like a shroud, blowing and rustling around him. When he reached out, he could feel it brush his fingertips, flowing and dark. It was mildew-smelling. Rotten and moth-eaten, it tore under his nails. As he clawed at it, he could see the real world through its rents.

The Hell Rider was sending visions into his head.

Maybe it was even worse than that. Maybe the Hell Rider was sliding under his skin, creeping into his head and curling up in his skull like a fat kitten.

Sam wanted badly to scream, but in his hysteria, it was as if he couldn't remember how to use his mouth. His head spun and his vision blurred. He tottered on legs made of rubber. He went down to his knees. He would sink into the muck again. It would swallow him whole. He would be buried alive in it, and he was powerless to stop that from happening now. Except it wasn't muck but unburied corpses that had broiled for days in the Tennessee sunshine, blackening, swollen, crawling with grave worms. He would sink into them, into their communal drainage, which was like a sucking, fetid pit of corpse slime.

But he did not sink.

No; instead he had a dream, a vision, a nightmare. Yes, yes, he was back on the island. He could see rustling cane, the soft green jungle, and set between them, a collection of thatched huts. It was the same dream he had again and again. It filled him with immense horror and immense repugnance. The little village. He had seen it before, known it before. Outside the huts, chickens pecked in the dirt and brown-skinned children played in the mud, goats and pigs wandering freely. Women were emptying baskets of fruit and vegetables. He saw men come charging from a line of banana trees. The women screamed. The children cried. The livestock scattered. The men were armed with machetes and they began to, began to—

"No, no, no!" Sam cried out. "I don't want to see this! I don't want to look at it!"

He dropped his gun into the sand. His hands were dark with blood. He was stained with it right up to his elbows and he could taste a coppery sweetness on his tongue. He began to moan and thrash, falling to his knees again.

Then a voice said, "Samuel. Enough. You stop this right now."

He turned, a silent scream at his lips.

It was Maddie. Dear, sweet Maddie. She stood there, smiling down at him in a blue silk evening gown, her charms bursting from the chiffon bodice. A bonnet was on her head, red tresses spilling to her bare shoulders in glossy ringlets. "You can't go on like this," she told him. "You're sick. You're sick inside. You have fevers. You need to rest. You can't be out here in this damp, drinking and shooting."

Yes, yes, she was right.

She helped him up and he walked with her, with his girl, his love. Green lightning crackled in the sky, branching among the leaden clouds above. Such a thing wasn't possible, and he could not be sure if it was real or just another smoke ghost in his mind, haunting him. All he knew was Maddie's voice, which went on and on, gentle and comforting and almost motherly. It soothed him deep inside where he needed it most. "... this can't go on, my love, my dearest," she said to him and his heart ascended to a new and delicious rhythm. "I worry about you. I worry so much about you and I can't bear the idea of something happening to you. Something terrible. Something awful. We have to do whatever it takes to end this, don't you see?"

"Yes, yes."

Her hand in his own was rose petal-soft, the fingers long and smooth. Like the rest of her, he was fascinated by her hands. They were fine-boned and fragile, yet he knew their appearance belied the strength in them. When she was impassioned, those hands held him tight and her nails dug into his back.

"How long has it been going on?" she wanted to know.

"Maybe since the war ..."

"Are you sure?"

He shook his head. He had seen ghosts during the war, but that was only an intimation of things to come. "It really happened on the island. That's where it really got going and it's ... it's been bad ever since."

"I bet it has." She stopped and looked at him. She kissed him on the lips, and her mouth was joyously cool. Yes, the fever. It was burning him up.

"I watch you while you sleep and I can feel the darkness, the badness coming off of you. Sometimes ... sometimes our room smells of things dead and things reaching toward death, so I open the windows to let the river air in. That smell. I think it comes from you, Samuel. From you and what lives inside your head. It has a name, doesn't it? This thing that torments you and follows you and never leaves you alone?"

His throat was so dry he could barely speak. "Yes," he managed. "Hell Rider. That's what I call it. But it's only part of it, only part of the whole nightmare. I can't … I can't seem to put it into words."

"You don't have to. I think I know."

They were walking again, away from the strand and back into the city. He kept hearing whimpering sounds, and they came from his own mouth. He could not stay them.

"Easy, my love, easy," Maddie said. She was looking around frantically now, pulling him violently behind her along the boardwalk, breathing heavily.

"What is it?" he asked.

"Him. The Hell Rider. He's coming. He's seeking us out. We can't let him catch us or the game is over. We have to be sneaky. We have to be smart. We have to hide. He's so very, very cunning."

Sam knew that was true.

The Hell Rider had been hounding him for a long time now and every time he thought he had thrown him off the trail, he came back again. He was patient. Inhumanly patient. But he was near, very near, and Sam could feel it now, too. There was a smell of death in the air, the stench of the battlefield, not just the unburied dead rotting in their own foul secretions but a stink of suppurating wounds and gangrenous limbs yellow with infected drainage.

"*Hurry!*" Maddie said and he followed her between two buildings, into a little alleyway that branched left and right becoming a maze with no beginning and no end. She led him to a flaking green door set in a crumbling wall of brick. Rats rustled in the shadows. The moon was a diseased eye above them. When the door was closed and bolted behind them, Maddie sighed. It was pitch black in there. A match was scraped against the wall, and she lit an oil lantern which threw guttering yellow-orange light. Greasy black shadows crawled up the walls.

"Here. We're safe for now. Nobody can interfere with us now, Samuel."

"But where is this place?"

"An old pirates' den. A place to hide wanted men and ill-gotten goods. You should feel right at home here in the secret darkness."

It was a long narrow room. There was a table and chairs, a bunk with graying sheets thrown over it and a crate set upright in the corner like a mummy sarcophagus in a museum. She pulled him further into the room and he seemed to lack the power to stop her.

"I think I know how we can get rid of the Hell Rider," Maddie said. "I've been thinking on it and there's only one possible way. I think you'll agree with me. When something scares you, when something digs its claws deep inside of you … there is only one way of removing it. Do you know what that way is, Samuel Bouchard? Do you know?"

He was confused. He did not understand anything; not really. His thoughts were whirling about in his head, crowding his brain, and he could make sense of nothing. He shook his head even though a tiny voice in the back of his skull said *it's not going to be good at all and you know it.*

"Samuel … do you know? Do you?" she asked and he noticed that her beautiful crystal blue eyes were blanching, discoloring, becoming the repellent pink of pus-filled wounds, the pupils like spots of blood in bleary yolks. Her grip on his wrist was vise-like and crushing. He looked down at her hand and it was the scabrous claw of a rat, gray and scaly.

"When something scares you, you must face it, Samuel. You must meet it on its own ground and nullify its power. Things are only scary and threatening until you face them … don't you see?" she said and laughed with a dry, wizened sound like the cackling of an ancient beldame. There was a sore on her cheek, a great black ulcerous sore that seemed to be expanding as he watched … growing, consuming her face, turning it into a great shriveling black mass. *"Don't you see, Samuel? DON'T YOU?"* She licked her flaking lips with a tongue that was swollen and red like some monstrous, pregnant worm. *"DON'T YOU?"*

"Maddie," Sam heard his voice say with more control than he would have thought possible. "Stop this … you're not real … none of this is real … *please … please stop this.…*"

"Oh, have I offended you? Have I hurt you? Have I revolted you? Am I scaring my lover and sickening my sweet, sweet pet?" she asked him in a voice like crackling dry leaves. Her mouth was huge and grinning and pale in a seamed leather face, immense teeth like yellowed tusks overlapping and gnashing together.

You're not really here, he told himself. *You're still on the mud flats. You must remember that.*

And it seemed sound advice, but he forgot it quickly enough as the Maddie-thing dragged him to the crate in the corner, which he knew she would have to show him sooner or later. By that point, her dress was like a ragged potato sack, filthy and infested with hopping vermin. She was a sinewy and corded thing, blood-engorged gray ticks hanging from her throat like fat seeds. She pulled the lid off the crate and there was the maggoty body of a child within. Its eyes had sunken in, its flyspecked face bloated into a rubbery death mask. It was himself as a boy.

"You see? You see, Samuel? It is here before you! The table has been set and the offering has been made! All men must eat the thing they love the best! Now comes the time of the rending and filling, the gnawing and tearing and stuffing! Glut yourself!" she demanded, ribbons of yellow saliva hanging from the black sucking ring of her mouth. *"Do not turn away! This is WHO you are and WHAT you are, you bloodless, trembling coward! Look upon what is offered and HUNGER! LET THE GLUTTING BEGIN!"*

Without further ado, she began to claw at the corpse, digging her scabby, mold-encrusted fingers into the soft green flesh, tearing out great juicy globs of carrion and stuffing them into her mouth. Her jaws worked up and down mechanically like a letter press, maggots and clots of grave matter dribbling down her chin as she continued to feed. She exhaled great clouds of buzzing flies and fetid vapors. She gobbled and slurped with ghoulish gluttony, filling herself with loops of rancid bowel, organs gone to mush, and wormy sweetmeats.

Sam cried out, backpedaling away, his legs growing strong beneath him and carrying him to a door that would not open, trapping him in the pestiferous charnel vault as he heard the dragging footsteps of his lover coming up behind him. Her breath was like corpse gas and her lips like wriggling worms as they fastened onto his throat and—

A voice.

"Mister … mister, you okay?"

Sam blinked and he was still on the flats, the cool muddy sand beneath him, the stink of the river in his face. There was a boy standing before him with a cane pole and a bait bucket. The sun was just beginning to rise. He had come to fish river cats in the early morning.

"Yes," Sam said, picking up his gun and holstering it. "I'm quite well."

He stumbled across the flats and into the city coming to life around him, a great suffocating blackness opening up inside him where his soul had once been.

6

For many days, fever dream and loathsome nightmare became intertwined with reality, and he was not sure what was real and what was not. Maddie stayed with him through it at all, telling him he was sick, very sick, but he would be okay. She was right that he was sick; just not in the way she thought. And wrong in thinking that he would be okay. In his fever, he told her so and she just said *Yes, yes, of course, my darling. Rest now, just rest.* She did not understand and she could not understand. She merely pacified him like a frightened boy who had awoken from a terrible phantasm in the night.

On the third day, he woke in a panic, leaping from bed and hitting the floor. The Hell Rider was coming and he knew it. His guns? Where were his damn guns? He saw them on a chair across the room and grabbed them. A pistol in each hand, he stumbled shaking and disoriented from the bedroom, dressed only in a blanket fouled with his own fever sweat. In the sitting room, Maddie was drinking wine with a friend of hers, another high-dollar whore named Angeline Trombley.

"Samuel!" Maddie said. "What in God's name are you doing?"

And at that moment, he wasn't even sure. The dream was fading and he couldn't seem to remember what it was about. Maddie and Angeline looked at each other, then back at him and both burst out laughing. He realized then that his blanket had fallen away and he was standing there naked to the world with a pistol in each hand.

"Ah, my fine Mister Bouchard," Angeline said, "do you often walk about with your pistol loaded?"

To his mounting embarrassment, he realized he had an erection.

Ashamed, he turned away and dashed back into the bedroom with their laughter trailing behind him. And it was in that way that the fever broke.

§

Maddie and he lay together tighter than ever, sleeping in one skin, safe in the womb of night and the love they had made. They loved each other and enjoyed each other's company, and they did not complicate it beyond that. It was enough.

And then, like a black storm darkening the horizon and eating the sunlight, it began again. All the terrible things started anew, and Sam realized that he was a hunted man and would always be a hunted man.

It started with Maddie screaming in the gray morning light.

What he did not know and would never know was that she had woken in his arms, her nostrils overwhelmed with the smell of decayed sweetness. She rolled out of bed, sickened, and crossed to the door, opening it.

And this was when she had screamed.

Sam heard her and right away pulled his ivory-handled Colt Peacemakers, thinking trouble and smelling it, too, like something rancid boiling in a ditch. Outside the door, nailed right in the center, there was a clump of red and yellow feathers tied up in the shape of a fighting cock. Below that, Bouchard's name written in blood with a little cross painted next to it.

He knew what it meant, all right.

Just like he knew it was scrawled in chicken blood.

Maddie, being from a backwoods clan just like Sam himself, started wailing and crossing herself, asking what had he done, what had he done to have the evil hex put on him. And Sam, being who and what he was, could not tell her. Maddie told him that she loved him, but could not help him.

"Oh God, oh dear God above," she cried out with almost religious fervor. "What did you do to bring this into your life? *Christ in heaven, who have you angered? What terrible things are on your soul?*"

He wanted to tell her it was bad, but there were worse things they could have hung on the door. Much, much worse things.

He thought: *You didn't think your happiness would last, did you? Your enemies are closing in. They watch you all the time. They know how to hurt you.*

Maddie spent the remainder of the day in church. She would not see him nor talk to him. Superstition was so ingrained into her that there was no talking sense. Angeline told him that Maddie wanted him to move from her rooms, that she loved him, but he was beyond the power of mere love, and she never wanted to see him again.

And that's how it ended.

That's how what remained of his soul was burned black with pain and grief.

§

My Dearest Maddie,

By the time you read this, I shall be no more in your life. The very idea pains me deeply, but I understand your feelings on the matter and respect them completely. Perhaps it is for the best for I would not wish to put upon you what has been placed upon me by others.

So many, many times I had wished to pour my heart out to you, to empty my soul so you could understand the awfulness I have suffered through and the damnation that has become part and parcel of my existence. Alas, I lacked the courage and conviction to do so. And it was not lack of trust, but fear that what has come to pass would come all that much sooner. Now it is done.

I am riding as far away from you as I can so that the terrible stain upon my life will not soil yours as well. You thought me a brave man and told me so many times, but you were wrong. I am a coward. Fighting in a war is not an act of bravery, my dear, but an act of necessity and desperation oftentimes born of the fear of what others may think of you if you do not. And as a Southern-born man—I will not now nor ever call myself a gentleman, for such a thing is patently untrue—my honor and pride often come before good sense. So I am running. Running from the other I spoke to you of. He is but one of many that hunt me. I shall run until there is nowhere left to hide; then I shall turn and fight in a final act of defiance. The outcome, I am certain, is already fated.

Until that dark hour, you should know that my thoughts will only be of you and that my lungs breathe and my heart beats to the memory of what we shared and nothing else.

Farewell, my love.

7

Maggart was seen by many as he crossed the plains in what seemed a circuitous, convoluted path that made sense, perhaps, only to him. He was seen in Kansas, Nebraska, and Oklahoma Territory, always on the move, tracking a scent on the wind and a spoor on the muddy ground. He asked people if they'd seen Sam Bouchard, but no one could rightly remember if they had or not. No matter: there were voices in his head and he listened to them.

His buckboard passed through town after town, the box in the back, two gray horses pulling it along, the man at the reins watching, ever watching. Nobody much liked the look of him. They had all seen desperate men, dangerous men, and those driven by madness and religious mania, but there was something especially dark about this one. He had a lean, hungry look about him like a starving wolf, and when they saw him, they got out of his way and dragged their children indoors.

Maggart was aware of it, of course.

He was many things, but he did not count fool among them. It was his smell more than his look that frightened people. Not a physical odor, of course, but something much more subtle. A spiritual odor, maybe. The smell of a soul that had been roasted over hell's hottest fire, the stink of a man who was cursed. And he was surely that man. The Devil was in him, and God had turned his back on him, and the universe no longer strictly made any sense. He doubted that the world as such still spun on its axis, or that good was a powerful, stabilizing force in it.

He knew that he could have turned away from the creole witch, shut his ears to her lies and blasphemy, avoiding the wrath of God, but each time he told himself that he would, he thought of the boy. How he lay in the box like a broken doll, and how it might be when she raised him up like Lazarus.

It was too late now to stop, he knew.

He had murdered for her and completed every vile task she set before him. His soul was damned. But it was worth it if he could have but a few more hours with the boy.

By night, he would make camp in some desolate spot, rubbing down the horses, feeding and watering them. It was always far from the byways of man, rarely any closer than the outskirts of a town, and usually in a dry ravine or scrub forest where the locals did not tread. By the light of a fire, he would wait for the witch.

She always came to him.

She always found him.

He knew it was by unnatural means, some terrible witchery that frightened him to contemplate. Though her skin was dark, when she appeared it was pale, blanched by the moon, the color of ghost-flesh, her eyes often glowing red as the coals in the fire pit. He would ask why she had come and if the time of his son's rising would be soon and what more she would demand of him, but she would move past him, ignoring him the way you ignored a demanding brat.

To the box she would go, always to the box.

Standing in a nacre sea of moonlight, she would open it, muttering profane words that would make him wither inside, making motions with her hands. And her voice, her terrible voice would say things and Maggart would whimper.

"Yes, yes, I know you are cold, and I know you are hungry. But soon, oh yes, soon, what I promised you will be yours."

And Maggart would hear sounds from the box that he knew she did not make—shifting and groaning noises, the sound of fingernails scraped over wood—and he would want to run, to cry out to God, but he never did. He would sit there, staring into the flames, eviscerated on the inside, feeling something moving in the shadows beyond the firelight. He never

looked upon it. It was forbidden and he was too terrified to do so … but it came with a stench of burning hair and foul putrescence and he could hear it grunting like a swine, its cloven hoofs stomping and circling.

Then it would be gone and the woman would stand behind him, sometimes placing a cold hand upon his shoulder and she would say, "There will come a time when those of true faith will be chosen to serve."

And the time was growing near, he knew. What that service would entail, he did not dare contemplate.

8

A week after he left Baton Rouge, Sam was back in the piney woods, and he was not honestly sure why. His intention had been to ride west, but like a metal filing drawn to a magnet, he had ridden north to the Sulphur River country, a place he certainly did not want to go. By the middle of the day, he was lost in an ashen woodland with not so much as an old pig trail to guide him. The woods were gray and dead, the tall pines desiccated and crumbling, looking much like a forest of graveyard monuments.

How? he wondered. *How could this have happened?*

All had been green and living not ten minutes before. Now everything was dead. Even the undergrowth was lifeless. After riding in what he was certain were circles for well over an hour, locked in the depths of the dead forest, the trees lined up around him like the bars of a prison cell, he brought his roan to a halt and dismounted. The horse nickered nervously.

"Easy," he said, stroking her neck to calm her. "Easy now. Let us see what this is about."

Something was terribly wrong, but he refused to show fear; he refused to panic. He had done both before many times, and he would not follow that path again. At least not until he made sense of this place.

Doubting the physical reality of his surroundings, he stepped over the sandy loam and around a post oak, seeking a tall longleaf pine. It was gray as fireplace soot. He reached out and touched its furrowed bark. It went to fragments under his fingertips, a cloud of sooty dust blowing

over his coat. A few stray branches fell from overhead. They broke apart like cigarette ash upon hitting the ground.

Sam walked from tree to tree, anxiety growing in him.

Every single one he touched broke apart into a powdery residue. The grasses underfoot crunched; the loam was split open by great jagged cracks like desert earth. He came upon the skeleton of a snake curled at the base of a withered bush. There was not a single strand of flesh on it. It looked as though it had been meticulously picked clean, like a mounted specimen you might see in a classroom or a museum.

Everything seemed real.

He could touch things, feel things. It did not seem possible in his mind for this to be a hallucination sent to him by the Hell Rider or one of his minions … yet such a gray swath of death seemed incomprehensible. If a fire had raced through here, things would have been blackened, not turned gray and dry. Trees would not be standing. The skeleton of the snake would not be so perfectly gleaming white, as if it had been dunked in an acid bath.

No, this was no natural phenomenon.

This was something else.

It was then that he thought he heard something like a crackling footstep out in that gray desolation. He knew he had heard it. Someone was out there, and he knew who that someone was. Just because he could not see him, did not mean he wasn't there.

Breathing deep, practicing calm, he fished the whiskey flask from his coat and pulled off it. *That's it,* he thought. *That's how you do it. You show no fear. You do not panic and you do not lose your nerve.* He fished out a home-rolled cigarette and lit it with a match. He blew smoke out in rolling clouds. The Hell Rider was out there, watching him. *All right then, watch.* Sam stepped cautiously about, circling his horse, examining the graveyard forest while he surreptitiously peered out of the corner of his eye for movement. More than once, he thought he saw a shifting shadow or a blur of silent motion among the trees. Every time he took a step, so did the Hell Rider.

"I know you're there," Sam said, blowing smoke out of his nostrils. "Come out and show yourself. I'm ready. Do you hear me? I'm ready."

The silence was unbroken save for the breeze rattling a few bone-dry limbs together. He took a few steps back toward his horse and the Hell Rider took a few more steps closer to him.

These games, these damn games. He felt his anger rising and that's exactly what his adversary wanted: to increase his unease, amplify the tension, make him do something foolish which, in this case, would be charging out deeper into the forest with guns in his hands.

Sam shook his head. *I won't do that. You can't make me do that. You will come to me on my terms, not the other way around.*

He waited.

He listened.

After about fifteen minutes, he heard footsteps coming in his direction. No attempt at stealth. Underbrush was crackling, grasses and loam crunching. The Hell Rider was coming. He could already smell the stench of open graves. Closer, closer still. Sam could hear his footsteps but not see him. Was that how it would be? Doing battle with something he could not see?

He gasped as he saw two luminous red eyes watching him from the shadows thrown by a deadfall.

There he was.

Waiting.

Sam took a few steps in his direction. He edged in a bit closer, but not too close. The eyes were gone, winking out like shooting stars. This did not stay him. He was tired of the game and he wanted it to end. He walked toward the deadfall, cautiously, slowly, but determined. Sticks cracked in its depths. Leaves crunched. Things shifted, moved, rustled. The deadfall was created by fifteen or twenty immense pines that had collapsed into one another, their branches fanning to the ground, sheets of gray moss and creepers hanging down in blankets. Beyond, there was a cave-like darkness from which blew a warm, noisome odor, the stench of not one dead thing but many. He peered into that darkness, thinking, wondering.

It's in there, waiting for you. Question is: have you got the steel to go in after it?

He heard a hissing sound from the dark hollow beneath the deadfall.

It echoed strangely. Snakes? Maybe. But chances were it would be nothing that prosaic. Behind him, more crackling footsteps. He whirled about quickly, his hands filled with pistols. A black form moved among the trees. Terrified and somehow exhilarated, Sam gave chase. He darted between trees and jumped over fallen logs and crashed to a halt.

There was a dark figure suspended between two trees. It looked like a scarecrow in a gray, ragged shift, sticks and hay and yellow knotted straw grass sprouting where its hands should be, its head like a black, furrowed gourd that was so rotten it was collapsing into itself. Its body was made of thick serpentine roots that grew out of it and coiled over the ground. It did not move. It did nothing but dangle there by the vines that held it. A half dozen huge crows with shiny black feathers perched on its head and shoulders. Cawing noisily, they picked at it greedily, plucking out pink strings of tissue and gulping them down.

Just a dead thing.

That's all it was. Just a dead thing, shriveled and soft and invaded by parasitic creepers. But it was more than that, much more, and the terror threading through him confirmed this.

Sam had a mad, nearly overwhelming need to cry out.

The gourd-face was splitting open, cracking like an egg, melting away in black viscid strands that oozed and dripped. Beneath it, he saw a shaggy, inhuman face with blazing red lamps for eyes and a crooked mouth. It was a tenebrous, malevolent thing that could have ripped the soul out of him by the bleeding roots anytime it chose. But it did not choose. Not yet. And that was the true, shocking evil of the thing—it did not want to destroy him quickly but *slowly,* it wanted to take its time with him like a cat disemboweling a mouse. Its true joy, its true satisfaction, was watching him become a mindless ruin of a man, a terrified, yellow-livered, trembling shell that could be stepped upon with ease like a scuttling brown spider.

It would destroy him inch by terrible inch.

One piece at a time.

One nibble followed by another, until there was nothing left inside him but the black running bile of mindless horror.

Sam shouted things he could not later remember, emptying his pistols into the gruesome husk. The crows scattered, wheeling about him, laying open his face and hands with their claws, leaving him there, prostrate in the dry loam at the feet of his dark pagan god of suffering and expiation. The Colts were still in his hands, his fingers still jerking the triggers, the clicking of empty chambers echoing through the depths of the dead forest.

When he came out of it, the blasted husk still hung there, blown into fragments that dangled in the breeze. Somewhere, far away but possibly quite close, he heard a low bestial growling followed by a high peal of cackling.

Beaten, glassy-eyed, laid open outside and within, Sam stumbled back toward his horse. By the time he got there, a black rain began to fall. It left streaks like India ink down his face. It went on for ten or fifteen minutes, until the ground was an ebon slough of bubbling mud that stank like a dozen battlefields giving up their festering dead.

Twenty minutes later, the forest was green again.

§

In one ratty hotel room after another, he never stopped thinking about Maddie and what they had and would never have again. And the more he thought about it, the more he pulled into himself until his life closed around him like the shell of a clam.

In a squalid railroad hotel in Texarkana, feeling the pull of Louisiana and Baton Rouge in particular and the terror of the piney woods, he spent days in his room, drinking and shaking with fevers that seeped from him in stinking rivers. He hallucinated and vomited blood and sobbed in his sleep. The stench of decay grew stronger day by day, until his room was a sweet/hot envelope of rancid carrion that brought buzzing flies and crawling beetles.

And in his head, that same squeezed-out, used-up voice, rang out: *Run, you pathetic sonofabitch. Run now, or the smell will get worse until it's your smell, and they find you. Because they will. They most certainly will, and you know it. They'll sniff you out and come in the night with teeth and claws and guns and make you die like no death you can envision. They'll feed you your own flesh until your throat is clogged with meat or strangle you slow and easy with your own entrails. The Hell Rider will have nothing less than his pound of quivering flesh that is named Samuel Bouchard.*

Sweating fevers and nauseated by the vile stench of rot, the cheap trade whiskey burning in his stomach like acid and coming back out again as warm foam, Sam would not listen. Stubborn, sick, feeding full on the diseased teat of his own dementia, he could not move. The smell lay over him green and thick and it flowered inside him like corpse blossoms.

He could run. But where? Where would they not find him?

There was no place. No hole deep enough and no shovel big enough to dig it. Not now. Not after what he had seen and what he had done.

Guadeloupe, he thought. *Goddamn Guadeloupe.*

Sobbing in his throat, he tried to sleep, and maybe he even did for a time, until the lids peeled back from his eyes to show him the secret womb of night birthing things around him. He could hear a hissing sound out in the corridor like water poured on a hot stove lid. Something out there passed by like a dark wind through a country churchyard, and the tumbledown hotel felt it right into its bones. It felt the invasion and the stirring of nameless things inside it. Its skeleton of old joists and older timbers creaked and groaned, its whitewashed skin of planks shivered.

Sam knew he could wait no longer, because what was out there was casting for his scent.

So carefully, so very quiet a spider spinning a web was like an industrial loom in comparison, he gathered his things as that horror from out of the night sniffed for him, grunting like a pig. Then he unholstered one of his Peacemakers and put three rounds through the door.

Then he and his meager belongings went out the window, dropping to the rooftop below and the dirt street beneath. The livery. His horse. Sick with revulsion, he rode out of Texarkana, knowing he would never, ever come back. Like Baton Rouge, he did not dare return.

And behind him, in the crooked dark alleys of night, something roared its displeasure that he had again slipped from its grasp.

§

Death edging in closer day by day.

Sam got good at hiding. Silver camps in Utah Territory. Cow and garrison towns in West Texas. Tent cities and dusty bunkhouses in the Nevada gold fields. Lonely sod houses on the high plains. Anywhere he could either blend into the mulling crowds or be alone, really alone, so he could hear the dead footfalls of his enemies coming through the switchgrass.

And when he didn't hear them, which was rare, he always smelled them, because they came with a dirty animal stink on the warm wind, the stench of rotting hides and black earth and the things that crawled in them. It seemed to get worse on the hottest days or on around sunset when the night things came out to prowl. He was always ready. Maybe his hands weren't so steady, and his brain boiled with fevers and livid nightmares, but he stood ready when they came out of the shadows and the shimmering waves of desert furnace heat.

He crossed Indian Territory, cutting through weed-choked river breaks and following dusty cow trails into oceans of pale grassland. All the while he listened, cocking an ear to the whispering wind, listening to the bluestem hiss and rustle as if things unseen crept through it. The wind was ever-present in those empty lands, howling and moaning in its dismal solitude and sometimes at night he heard the canebrake rattling as things moved through its dark, congested recesses. He told himself it was deer or rabbits, maybe a black bear off its feed. He would sit by his meager fire as darkness locked in, scraping boiled beans and biscuits from a tin plate, his guns near to hand and his heart galloping in his chest.

It was on these nights that he thought of Maddie. Her memory made his heart sing, then weep because he was alone, so terribly alone and there was no cure for that.

Sleep did not come easy out in the desolation of the Territories. His mind produced ghosts, and his nerves were steel wires humming far into the dark watches of night. He would lie there in his bedroll, guns at the ready, listening to the leaves rustling in tall willows along river cuts or the distant baying of a lonely coyote. Those were the good nights. On the bad ones, the silence would be limestone-heavy, the darkness woven from black webs. These were the nights when the ground was too hard and the air too chill and he would lie there, eyes peeled like grapes, breath rasping in his lungs, certain he could hear reedy, evil laughter from the shadows and furtive scratching just beneath the blanket of stillness. He knew there was no one out there, at least no one human, and his mind would conjure up the wraiths of things long dead that stalked the ebon silences.

He was terrified by what he could see and what might be watching him. Even if he forced his eyes closed, his mind would drift in the oblivion between this world and the next, and he would see Guadeloupe and a graying, pitted face pierced by needles. The yellow mouth would open with a croaking sound and say, *You are never alone, Samuel Bouchard. You who have courted death and made iniquity your concubine, you are forever joined to the evil you sought and made your own.* That hideous face would haunt his mind for hours, grinning at him with a simian smirk like a starving monkey carved from the black wood of death.

And on those rare nights that he did sleep, he would dream of glistening, coiling things rising from the split cadaver of Maddie Borcheaux, things like yellow-eyed carcinomas that grew fat in her silken depths as she withered to sticks.

He did not believe the dreams were his own, but something sent to him like a seed upon the wind to take root in his weary mind. The dreams were knife blades that slit his arteries and made him bleed, and when they started, he knew it was time to move on.

He was hunted and his enemies were many. Grinning things with big white teeth and scarlet eyes that simmered with a flat evil. He was good at hiding and escaping, but he could never stay anywhere for long. He might confuse them for a while, but in the end they always picked up his scent and followed it to its source.

Guadeloupe, he thought as always. *Goddamn Guadeloupe. It never ends.*

They came with the smell of death and that's when he would run, never certain if that stink of decay was coming from them or from himself. For there was no doubting one thing: ever since it began, something necessary and important in him, something that made a man a man, had wilted and gone to rot.

After the island and what he had seen there and what he had done, he was closer to the grave than to God. And his life, such as it was, became a desperate and hunted affair. He lived with pistols in his hands and fear in his heart, an eye always cast behind him. He lay in his bed at night, sweating and shaking, listening for footsteps on the stairs or the dank smell of corruption. And waiting, always waiting for the soft and dire rustle of the Angel of Death spreading his wings.

That's what it was like for Sam Bouchard.

That was his life.

9

The situation was this: though Sam was gone, Maddie could not stop thinking about him. There was guilt, of course, because she had driven him away out of her own superstition and elemental fear (though she would never have called what she felt deep into her bones by these names), denying herself the passions of her heart and in the process, weakening not just her soul but her mind. For many weeks, she barely ate or slept. She conducted no business. She entertained no guests, not even her dearest friend Angeline, who had become like a sister to her through the years. She wanted nothing better than to seek Sam out, yet she was terrified by the very idea.

So for uncounted days that became weeks, she isolated herself in her rooms, shut away, staring nervously at rows of candles she had lit, clutching good luck charms and praying until her head whirled and her body became wobbly from the lack of food.

Then there was an epiphany.

Though he was gone, he came to her in her dreams. Not just once or twice, but all night, every night. By then, she was physically and mentally exhausted, worn thin by her private terrors and those unseen things she was certain were moving around her, watching her with baleful eyes. Sam would tell her how much she meant to him and that he wanted to take her away to a place where they would be safe, just the two of them. The idea both intrigued and terrified her because, by that point, she was certain that the two of them together was evil chemistry.

In her fatigue and with the help of sleeping powders, she began to sleep ten and twelve hours every night. And always Sam came to her, kissing her, stroking her hair, touching her in all those wonderful places she liked to be touched with his strong, firm hands. And always she listened to what he had to say. Once or twice, she woke from these dreams, sweating and gasping for breath as if cold hands had been strangling her, certain that it was not Sam at all that visited her but some horrible demon that wore his form.

Still, she slept and he came and they talked. He began to tell her that their souls were joined and there was no fighting it, no escaping the inevitability of fate. That their love was much stronger than any dark forces or black magic. He told her that they were one, and as such, the ultimate culmination of their love would be for them to have a child together. The very idea frightened her, but night after night he explained how it was, again, inevitable and it was what God wished of them.

One day, she invited Angeline in and they shared wine and bowls of spicy shrimp gumbo that Maddie found she could no longer stomach. She told her dearest friend—who was, understandably, worried about not only Maddie's physical health but the state of her mind as well—all about the dreams and how they were much more than that. How Sam really did come to her. Or, at the very least, his soul did. Then she told her how they were planning to have a child.

"But they're only dreams, my darling," Angeline tried to explain to her. "Surely, you can see that?"

But Maddie saw no such thing. This was different. This was real. It was concrete. At night, their dream selves met on a special plane and their spirits intersected.

"Oh, Maddie, don't talk of such things! That's witchcraft and sorcery and devilment! Two spirits cannot conceive a child. That is God's work and you're blaspheming the union of man and woman … don't you see that?"

Maddie laughed. She hadn't meant to, but there it came: dry, dark laughter. The sound of a disturbed mind. She laughed because Angeline, at this late date, was preaching religion, something she had never had much use for. And, because Angeline, poor, sweet, confused Angeline, did not understand that there were beautiful forces of creation at work here that she could not comprehend of.

After Angeline had left, Maddie was relieved because it was tiring work trying to enlighten the ignorant. Regardless, the entire experience made her certain that Sam was right—they should have a child, a symbol of their love that would be brought into this world to celebrate the union of their souls. The child would grant them God's favor and no longer would they be tormented or hexed by the terrors of the night.

Sam came to her again that night and asked her if she was ready to consecrate their love to a higher power. And Maddie said, *yes, yes, oh dear God in heaven, yes.* It would be so, he promised her. He grinned at the very idea sardonically like a stuffed monkey. And when she woke, she was shivering and shaking, remembering the darkness of his eyes and how cold he had been when he pressed his lips to her throat, nipping her playfully, and sucking her blood. She could still feel her hands on him and how shaggy he had been, like some wild beast.

10

One evening, huddling in a cold camp beneath a storm-bent cottonwood tree, Sam watched the sun going down over Black Bear Creek, the waters like blood from the red clay banks. There was a sound of distant thunder, flickering heat lightning at the horizon. His grub sack was nearly empty. He supped on tinned peaches and jerky that had the texture of pine bark. But it was something to put in his belly. Sometimes he forgot to eat, and at other times his belly was twisted like a screw and he couldn't bear the idea of food. The simplest things—sowbelly or canned tomatoes—became unpleasantly grisly fare that tasted like blood and raw meat. He had to be careful. He always had to be careful, even with what he ate. Once, not three days before, he had been chewing a mouthful of salt pork when he had felt something slide over his tongue with a cold looping. Gagging, he spat it out and found that it was riddled with long green worms.

Whether they were real or not, he did not know, but it took his appetite away for some time.

So as he ate the peaches and jerky, he examined every bit before he put it in his mouth.

"Just another game," he said to himself in a low, guarded voice. "That's all."

But knowing that the Hell Rider was creating nightmares and dreadful hallucinations and channeling them into his head did not make him feel any better. His sleep was tormented. His waking hours were suspect. Now even food. They would starve him. It was just another way of weakening his resolve. Another way of destroying him.

Sighing, Sam finished the last of the peaches. They were sweet and cool on his tongue. As he made to swallow them, he felt them move in his mouth. *Shit.* He gagged out a mouthful of squirming bugs. He washed his mouth out with his canteen. When he looked again, there was only a glob of half-chewed peaches on the ground.

See? You can trust nothing. The Hell Rider and his kin will make it harder day by day and you, you stubborn cocksure fool, will keep fighting and fighting them. Soon enough you won't be able to distinguish between fantasy and reality. They'll send a dozen rattlesnakes, and one by one, you'll realize they're nothing but phantasms. When the thirteenth shows, you'll pick it up, laughing, shouting out at them that they don't scare you ... only the snake will be real and it'll sink its fangs in your throat.

He swore under his breath, staring out over the river with red-rimmed eyes. He rolled a cigarette as night came on, smoking in the gathering darkness and feeling the anxiety night always brought begin to work itself through his bones. It filled his belly and began to crawl up into his chest. He'd known fear like that in the war, of course, wondering if he'd live to see another day—but this was different. This was more than terror for his physical being, but a terror of losing something much more valuable. He was not a spiritual man and he had little use for religion or imaginary deities that ignored you when you begged for their help and turned a blind eye to suffering and pain, to children starving and men dying awful dirty deaths in horrible wars of attrition. Yet he was convinced he had a soul, that there was something more to a man than his flesh and bones, a spark, a spirit, a life force, a ghost that drove him forward day by day when there was no hope of deliverance. There was something and it had nothing to do with bibles and hymns or preachers spouting hypocritical vomit in pulpits. Whatever it was, the enemies he had made were intent on taking it from him. It was not enough to kill him. They wanted him to defile himself. They wanted to reduce him to a sickly, crawling cur so that he would beg for death and offer his soul to them with his own weary, bloodied hands.

Won't happen. Not now, not ever. I'll fight because I don't know any other way.

He had not planned on lighting a fire that night. He could never be sure if fire frightened them off or drew them in. He decided he would wait in the dark for them.

But as the blackness of that moonless night became complete and impenetrable, he began to lose control of his nerves. Whiskey did not help. Robbed of his sight by the darkness, he listened to the night until his ears hurt. Leaves rustled. Branches creaked. The current lapped at the banks of the Black Bear. He tried to distinguish these things from other nefarious sounds that hid beneath them, cloaking themselves.

Finally, he could take it no more.

Luckily, he had assembled a collection of twigs, kindling, and pine boughs in case he needed them. Now he lit them, fumbling with his matches, getting the blaze going, sweat running down his face as he felt unseen things creeping in the night, reaching out for him. The fire caught and held. Weak yellow flames rose into orange and red spikes, pine needles crackling, the dark pushed back and a circle of safe illumination stealing away some of his terror.

Not all of it, of course.

Ten minutes later, he drew one of his Colts and fired at a shape that flew overhead only to realize it was nothing but a night bird passing by.

But even with the fire blazing and his guns at hand, his heart thudded dully in his chest. His skin was clammy, his hands trembling. A nameless sense of unease stole over him, and the night world beyond his ring of firelight became an alien place haunted by grim specters and distorted shadows that seemed to grin and leer at him, daring him to seek them out. He thought of Guadeloupe and the warm tropical nights, the dark folk and their dark beliefs, the strange smells and noises of the jungle, the alien tongues spoken in the streets.

He was lonely and afraid and near destitute. What he would have given for some company, another body to share the fire with. Indian Territory was full of bandits of every stripe, and tonight he would have welcomed them to his fireside.

As he sat there, drinking and smoking and worrying, fear sucking into his pores and sweating back out in a sour effluvium, he began to think of who he was, where he was, and, most importantly, *what* he was. He was not really certain. The things that drove him had made him into something he had never been before. It was as if his identity was being stolen from him piecemeal. When he thought of a man named Samuel Bouchard and the life he had lived, it seemed a strange event. Something maybe he had read about in a yellowback novel or had heard yarned around a fire. Yes, he was losing his identity, and as he lost it, he lost his soul in bits and pieces.

The very idea of that scared him more than anything he had ever known. To lose a limb or even a life was one thing, but when your spirit, your mind, was taken away it was a dark matter indeed. Although he could not remember crying in many years, his trail of self-pitying thoughts were interrupted by the sound of his own broken sobbing.

As he heard this, he also detected the sound of things moving beyond the firelight.

"I WILL NOT!" he shouted into the night, drawing his pistols and firing into the darkness. "I WILL NOT BE BROKEN!"

He fired three or four more rounds, listening to them echo across the empty lands around him. The very idea of a madman named Sam Bouchard talking to ghosts and firing at will-of-the-wisps made him begin to bray with cold, ugly laughter. It was a desperate, deplorable situation but suddenly he realized he was not afraid. He felt like he had in the war when he was certain his life was nearly over and he would be toes-up in a matter of moments—he fought harder, wanting to die with steel in his heart and smoking pistols in his hands.

He shouted.

He laughed.

He cried out in his lunacy how he feared no man, no spook, no night-hag or grave-crawler, no entity on this side of the grave or beyond it, daring any of them to come for him, because he would give them a fight they would not soon forget. Within minutes, his ire had died away, and he slumped back before the fire, more certain than ever that they were winning because his mind was beginning to splinter.

Back up against the cottonwood, he drifted off to sleep sometime before dawn. He dreamed of Maddie Borcheaux, his sweet wickedness. She came for him, a pale bride writhing with worms, legs like fleshless broomsticks, her lovely red hair crawling with grave vermin, black soil streaked over her gaunt, sunken face. Her dress hung in gray tatters, one bloodless breast poking out and showing him a nipple that was gray and flyblown. There were rustling sounds inside her and he knew they were the feeding sounds of graveyard rats that had nested in her.

He woke crying out.

It was light.

The day was overcast and gray, the surrounding meadows and scrub forest rendered colorless. The sky was the color of boiled potatoes. He brewed coffee and gave his mare some oats and watched the day come to life. It was, he decided, time to either lay down and die or truly make a fight of it.

With that in mind, he knew it was time to see Shorty Brice.

§

Two days later, his heart clogged with the filth of his own existence, Sam was on his blue roan, the noose ever tightening. He rode fast and rode hard, making for Shorty Brice's cabin in Texas, staying mostly to back roads and lonely spots where his enemies would have a hell of a time getting to him. Even now they were on his trail, closing in.

But I won't make it easy for you; you can be sure of that.

After days of hard riding, he made the upper reaches of the Sulphur River, and all the way, he was certain he was being followed. Maybe it was nerves and maybe not. He led his horse by foot over the sandy loam of the moist bottomlands, through thick stands of cypress and Texas pine, magnolia and sweetgum. He knew the general location of Brice's cabin. Back in Guadeloupe, Shorty had talked of little else. And then, after two days following the river, he saw it: a simple log affair nestled in a grove of cottonwoods.

Although Sam was dirty and his boots were caked with mud, his flesh peppered by insect bites, and an awful fatigue lay heavy upon him, he smiled. Smiled and felt a warmth overtake him. Shorty Brice. *Goddamn.*

He prodded his mount into a walk and moved through the high Indian grass and Virginia wild rye, admiring the beauty of Shorty's fine little spread. He picketed his horse in the shade near a splintered gray sap house. What he didn't like was the silence. From all Shorty had told him of this place, it was a working farm, but there was no sign nor sound of industry. The fields looked overgrown, and there were no livestock about. Shorty had a wife and two children. Such a silence was unnatural. In fact, it was eerie. All he could hear was the breeze sighing up in the boughs of the high pines. It almost sounded like breathing.

Sam waited there, an uneasiness tickling in his belly. "Anyone about?" he called out, his voice dying in the stillness.

The silence was undisturbed.

Feeling the weight of the pistols at his hips, he moved slowly—and cautiously—up the hill to the cabin. With his background, a situation like this spoke of an ambush. But that was crazy. Shorty and he were like brothers.

But he ain't here, Sam thought. *Ain't nobody here.*

§

Yet that wasn't exactly true. Maybe Shorty and his kin weren't about, but Sam was nearly positive he was not alone. He stopped, licking his wind-burned lips. He studied the cabin and outbuildings. The hay bales. The tree line. The feeling of being watched not only persisted, it came to term inside him like a living thing.

"Shorty?" he called out again, his hands seeking the Colts in their scabbards.

His voice came back at him, something harsh and biting like tenpenny nails speared into his belly. He unleathered the pistols.

The door of the cabin was hanging by one leather hinge.

It was badly used, splintered and scathed, several pine boards staved right in as if something of immense weight and strength had struck it dead-on. Sam froze there in indecision, his throat gone dry. Locusts buzzed in the trees and a distant hawk cried out in the sky. A ribbon snake slid off lazily through the grass.

He crept nearer, his hands moist and sweaty on the butts of his pistols.

A high, hot stink of putrefaction was wafting out of the shattered door. As he got closer, he saw that not only was the door smashed and scathed, but set with deep ruts that looked much like claw marks.

Sucking in a wheezing breath, something blowing hot and cold inside him, Sam kicked the door in the rest of the way and charged inside. The smell of death was thick and suffocating and the reason for that became quickly apparent: there was a mangled body on the floor, a body that had been shattered and mutilated, abandoned in a sticky pool of its own blood that had long since dried.

Sam knew it was Shorty. There could be no doubt.

His guts coming up the back of his throat, Sam went down on one knee. The stink was unbelievable. Clouds of bluebottle flies rose and descended on the body in a buzzing swarm. Shorty looked like about two hundred pounds of raw meat going to rot. There were red spikes poking out of him that Sam quickly realized were shards of bone. His face was nearly peeled from the skull beneath and he had been split open like a sausage from throat to crotch, his bowels pulled out and tossed around in crusty pink loops. One hand still clutched an Army .44 in a death-grip.

It was horrible.

But what was worse was that he looked ... *eaten.* Like some beast had been devouring him, chewing on his viscera and tearing globs out of his throat. There was more than a stink of decay to him, but something almost worse: a sour, acidic odor that burned Sam's nostrils.

But then he knew.

Urea. Ammonia.

Whatever had killed Shorty, had *pissed* on him. Whether it was marking its territory or doing something much more revolting, there was no way to know. Only that once it was done eating, it had perhaps lifted a leg and voided its bladder on him and Sam hoped to God he was dead when that happened.

Pig-pee, that's the goddamn stink of pig-pee. And you know what that means.

He could look no more.

He turned away, stepping outside where he could smell the pines and feel the sun on him. He pulled a home-rolled cigarette from the tin case in the pocket of his duster and scraped a match off his boot. The smoke tasted good, if not a little stale. It helped drive the stink of the cabin out of his head. He walked over the sandy loam to the smokehouse, leaning up against it, everything inside him feeling loose and runny. He wanted to cry for Shorty (and for himself), but he was plain out of tears. The well had run dry.

Don't matter what I do, he thought then with an uncharacteristic bitterness, tasting defeat in every word. *Don't matter what I do or where I go. My fate has already been settled and I'm nothing but a wind-up toy turning in circles.*

He ran, he tried to outdistance those that came for him, but somehow they always doubled back on him or crept around in front and lay in ambush. They always seemed to know where he was going and what he was going to do, as if maybe in the greater scheme of things, he was not in control of his own destiny. Didn't matter how he went to ground or in what direction he broke new trail, they knew, they always knew. He was like a doll being pulled along on a string.

He stared out at the high stands of shortleaf pine and bluejack, the Indian grass and wild rye that sloped down toward the muddy bottomlands of the Sulphur. There was a beauty to it all, he supposed, but there was also a threat. And he sensed more of the latter than the former.

He strolled around Shorty's spread, trying to figure what came next.

He found mud-walled pens, barren corrals, and sad-looking chicken coops thrown together out of sticks and clay, but he found no stock. Not so much as a feather or a heap of petrified dung. Everything was poorly tended, run-down, and ill-cared-for. The only true sign of habitation were the broken whiskey bottles in the barn. Of those, there were many.

It looked as if Shorty had sold off his animals many, many months before and then pickled himself on tanglefoot and coffin varnish, popping corks and draining bottles and doing little else.

He was waiting. Just like you, he was waiting for something, and that something finally came.

Yes, Sam felt that to be true. But where was his family? Where was his wife—*Jenny,* he thought her name was—and the two boys? Shorty had been so proud of his land and his kin. Though he was a hard-charging Yankee out of Pennsylvania, he had fallen in love with Texas after the war. He had married a Texas woman from Tyler and raised his boys to be Texans.

But where the hell were they?

A sound from the direction of the cabin.

The blue roan nickered down at the sap house.

Swallowing down a lake of fear, Sam approached the cabin, pistols in hand. The closer he got, the faster his heart beat and the more sweat ran down his face. This was it. This was what he had been waiting for. The smell of black decay thickened in the air and he could nearly taste its sweet, high foulness on his tongue.

Wait.

Mere feet from the broken door, a cloud of flies buzzed past him. His throat was filled with sand, the flesh at his spine inching in cold waves. Inside, he could hear grunting, pawing sounds … then something much worse: the sound of feeding. A slavering mouth tearing into something soft and mucid, chewing noises that made his stomach rise into his chest. He brought up his Colts with trembling hands and heard a wild, shrill squealing from inside, the sound of a swine in great pain or filled with great rage.

He waited for it, his entire body shaking, then something shriveled yellow inside him and he ran.

He had never run from a fight in his life … but the condition of Shorty's body and the fear that lived and breathed full-blooded inside him pushed him away. Instantly ashamed that the heart of a squaw beat inside him, he dashed to the smokehouse and slammed the door shut behind him, throwing the catch. The walls were set with cracks and knotholes so sunlight spilled in, showing him the blackened roughhewn beams above and the brick pit in the center of the dirt floor. The ashes in there looked many months old, and there was no sign, other than the pervasive odor of salting and smoke-curing, that it had been used in a long time.

Or maybe it had been.

There were brackets to either side of the door and a stout section of post oak that fit into them quite nicely, barring it. Shorty had done this. There was no doubt in his mind. Shorty had rigged the door so he could use the smokehouse as a sort of a bunker if things got bad. And they sure as hell had.

Sam waited there, everything jangling inside him.

It's gonna come for you next, and you know it, he thought. *It was probably waiting in the woods, waiting for you to arrive as it knew you must. Now it's finishing up with Shorty and then it'll be your turn.*

His hands were sweaty on his pistols. He peered through one of the knotholes, but he couldn't see the doorway of the cabin, not from his position. He was trapped in a box. Cowering like a rat in a hole. Well, dammit, he wouldn't have it. He'd lived by his wits and guts and instinct too long to back down now. He was going to go out there and die like a man.

Then an awful stench of black mud and filth filled the shack and he knew it had come for him. The beast was waiting out there, waiting for his bravado to get the best of him. When that happened, he would charge out of the shack right into its arms.

He waited.

It waited.

The only sound out there was a buzzing of flies as they lit from the horror itself. A few of them found the cracks, crevices, and knotholes, flying into the shack. Sam didn't bother swatting at them.

Now ... yes, a sound.

The sound of hoarse, rasping breathing. He could imagine the thing out there, muscles bunched, patience worn thin, voracious appetite far from slaked.

"All right!" he called out to his adversary. "Make your damn play!"

At first there was nothing. The breathing out there deepened and he thought he heard a sound like teeth grinding, but that was it.

Then—

Something brushed against the shack.

Something clawed at the door, making it shake in its frame. Whatever it was, it was circling the shack now, dragging its claws over the gray weathered boards. It pressed its bulk up against them, making them creak, but they were still strong and it would take more than that.

Sam let out a little cry as he saw an eye just as ripe and plump and red as a juneberry peering through one of the knotholes. It withdrew before he could get a real good look at it, but what he saw was filled with a lunatic, almost malevolent sort of hatred.

He heard the thing pull back into the grass.

Now was his chance.

He brought his eye cautiously to a knothole and looked out there. He saw a shaggy, loathsome shape that moved away quickly in a blur. Had he seen it? Had he really seen it?

It was quiet out there now. The seconds ticked by with infinite, uncomfortable silence. But the creature was still out there. He could hear it rooting around—pawing at the dirt around the smokehouse, brushing against the walls, and breathing with a bestial stertorous noise. It shook the shack. It growled. It squealed with rage.

Sam waited for it.

When he heard it pad off, he again stuck his eye to a knothole and gasped at what he saw. The creature was three feet away, snorting. It looked like some monstrous razorback hog, an upright wild boar with a dirty gray hide and stiff black bristles that looked sharp as needles. Gore and slime dripped from its tusked jaws. Its eyes were a brilliant translucent shade of red set in menacing upturned sockets.

He saw—for maybe three seconds before it charged, launching itself at the shack—a massive and well-muscled beast. The shack shook with the impact, splinters of wood and grit raining down from above.

Sam thought the shack would come apart, but it didn't. He fired three .45 caliber slugs right through the wall in the direction of the beast. It shrieked with a piercing, porcine sound and rammed the shack again and again. The boards were cracking, splitting open as the creature kept bashing into it with incredible force. It seemed to come from all directions at once, riled beyond anger, fueled into an unearthly wrath of destruction. Now it turned its rage against the door, hammering into it and tearing at it with black talons that looked to be attached to humanlike fingers. It tore boards free and Sam brought up both pistols and fired straight at it, hitting it with four rounds.

It cried out and he heard it pad away, squealing and shrilling. The roan made a screeching noise that ended soon enough and Sam knew it had gotten her. He kicked his way through the remains of the door and stumbled out into the light. There was no sign of the boar. In the distance, he could see blood glistening on the sap house. It looked as if it had been painted red.

Panting and shaking with a combination of terror and fury, Sam loaded his pistols quickly with deft fingers well-practiced in the art.

There.

Something wet in the grass.

Blood and a great deal of it. He'd cored that sonofabitch. Now it was wounded. Now it was even more dangerous. What he needed was his rifle, but the .44 Winchester was in the saddle scabbard. The Colts would have to do. He didn't know what that thing was, some feral pig out of hell perhaps, but if he could put a few slugs in its head, he knew he could kill it.

Steeling himself, pumping himself full of killing hate, he followed the blood trail through the grasses that came up above his knees. The beast had created a path through them like a bull elephant, stomping them down and leaving glistening red drops on broken stems in its flight.

Sam followed hesitantly, very hesitantly.

The indian grass was high and wild, the bunched blue-green blades rising up nearly to eye-level in places, the golden plume-like seed heads above his shoulders. The beast was hoping to draw him in, maybe get him turned around or confused in the Texas tallgrass.

It's setting a trap and you're waltzing right into it.

Maybe. Maybe not. If the beast was setting up an ambush, it was doing a sloppy job of it. He could hear it grunting just ahead, snorting and squealing. It was making no attempt at stealth. And the further he went, the more blood he saw. If that was a trick, then it was a damn good one.

The beast let out a shrill cry in the distance and he caught sight of it peering through the grasses at him with beady red eyes filled with malice.

What Sam discovered to his relief was that it was nearly impossible for it to hide in the grasses. Unless you were a full-blooded Pawnee, you couldn't travel through their depths without leaving a trail that was easy to follow. He could see a weathered, leaning structure just ahead, a low-roofed affair that looked like a hog barn. The beast was making for it, probably hoping to get the jump on him. He followed the trail toward it, then stopped.

Hell is this?

The path through the grass diverged into three separate trails. The beast was definitely no dumb animal. This *was* a trap. Even bleeding out, the creature was extremely cunning. Sam had no choice but to move forward. He chose the center trail and maybe that was a mistake because the beast charged from the left on all fours. He fired a couple wild shots that missed completely, just managing to throw himself to the side as its tusks sought to disembowel him. They caught his duster and ripped it open, but he got free, rolling across the ground and losing one of his Colts, but coming up smooth and easy with the other and drilling the beast's retreating form not once but twice. He saw the second slug rip a shank of meat from its spine.

It howled and screeched, but it was not dead.

As Sam climbed to his feet, he thought: *Headshot. I gotta get that sumbitch right in the head. Ain't no other way.*

He found his other Colt and, pistols in both hands, he ran toward the barn. It was a rickety structure, planks missing from the roof and boards rotted from its walls so the light got in there, but it was still shadowy. It had been a pig barn, all right. The stink of pig piss and pig shit nearly reamed out his nose. His eyes watered and his belly jumped. Clouds of flies lit from the filthy straw.

"Here I am," Sam announced. "You wanted me and here I am."

The boar charged from the shadows. It was a hulking powerful creature, but it was wounded and had lost a lot of blood. Its charge was drunken and wobbling and Sam sidestepped it easy enough, getting off another shot that blasted one of the ears from its skull. In the process, he slipped and fell into the mud and manure and filthy straw.

The boar stood there, upright like a man, and he saw that it had a row of teats down its underside. They were pink and swollen, in great contrast to the puffy, lumpy white flesh beneath.

A sow then, he thought with horror. *A sow.* Sometimes it was a sow and sometimes a boar.

It stood there on short muscular legs; cloven hoofs planted securely in the manure. Its arms were too much like those of a man, the fingers long with black claws that looked extremely sharp. Its body was scarred and rutted, a shaggy beard-like growth of greasy hair hanging down to the teats like a mane.

Sam saw that its bristles stood on end, humped shoulders bunched and roped with thick arteries, massive head set forward. Slime and bile hung from its snout in ribbons, tusks gleaming and sharp though yellowed and splintered as if by great age. Making a low slobbering sound in its throat, it looked down at him, eyes like raw meat crying pink tears.

He could see the bullet holes in its hide. Blood had run from them in scarlet webs. It was watching him, breathing hard, trembling, the flattened nose at the end of its snout quivering.

But it wasn't attacking.

That's what he didn't understand. It was just standing there, bleeding out, waiting for him to make the next move. Flies swarmed over it, investigating its wounds, crawling swollen from creases and ridges in its flesh.

"When you get to hell," Sam said, "you tell your maker I won't go down without a fight."

The swine laughed with a hoarse, ancient cackling. *"And there I shall wait for you,"* it said.

Then it squealed with a guttural shrieking, its jaws opening and revealing a set of blunt, thick teeth that looked like they were made for grinding bones. Sam felt the pistols in his hands and fired point-blank, blasting its skull into red suet, raw wet matter splattering into the heaps of fly-specked dung. It folded up and fell into the mud, actually sinking five or six inches.

Sam fled.

Something was happening to its carcass. It was bloating and hissing, rivers of worms leaking from it. Enough. Out in the sunshine, he fell to his knees, breathing in and breathing out.

After a time, he stumbled back along the path to the cabin and the sap house below. The roan mare had been split like a stick of green wood, pools of red flooding the earth. Her innards had exploded from her in a greasy stew of yellowed bowel, purpled stomach, and blued lung sac. That she was dead was the only small mercy he knew that day.

A weight settling over him like a cement slab, he went back up to the cabin so he could retrieve Shorty's remains and bury them properly. And in his head, the evil voice of the swine echoed interminably: *And there I shall wait for you....*

11

When Sam finally came for her, Maddie was not sure if she was awake or dreaming and part of her was certain that it no longer even mattered. Images had been flooding her brain. Fields of clover. Haystacks. Men and women fornicating with nameless animals. Piglets feeding at the teats of swollen pink sows. Then human babies joining them. Finally, things that could not possibly have been human—squirming, fetal horrors with clawing fingers and suckering mouths thirsty for milk. Then even this vision was replaced by a setting sun the color of blood that cast its sanguine light over crumbling, above-ground tombs and gray sepulchers with hordes of hissing buzzards on their roofs.

There was meaning to it all. She was certain of this. Some sort of symbolism, but the more she thought of what it might be, the harder it got to think at all. So she stopped trying and just lay there on the bed, staring at the patterns of moonlight on the ceiling, and they became sort of a reflecting pool, and she saw herself. Still young, still pretty, still very desirable ... though something had changed, and she was not sure what it was. But a darkness had crept into her, and she looked withered, unhealthy, skin pale and eyes like pools of poison.

Sam was with her. His voice was speaking, saying terrible things. "Here we have the foulness that is woman," he said and his voice sounded old as death. "Here is the temple of Eve that you have profaned with your whoring and blasphemy. What was to be used for the begetting of children, you have misused for the illicit, sacrilegious means of profit. Dirty hands have touched you, and dirty minds have lusted after you, and you turned coin by spreading your legs."

She told him no, that it was not that way, it had never been that way, but it was a lie and he knew it and she knew it, and as he dragged himself over the bed like a cat in estrus, she could feel an unpleasant, sickening heat coming off him. He repulsed her. Her heart told her it wasn't so, but her stomach rolled over even as a gnawing, rapacious hunger opened up between her legs.

"Do you deny the iniquity of woman? That you are a seething pestilence? A slut? The contaminated seed of Belial?" he asked her.

Shaking with lust, she shook her head. "No! I don't deny it! I am those things!" His insults made her burn ever hotter, made what was between her legs absolutely boil. She needed him inside her and she would have crawled through shit if that's what he wanted. If only, dear God above and Satan below, if he would only mount her and they could rut like animals.

Then—sweet Christ—he was on top of her and she had never wanted him so badly, despite (and possibly *because* of) the awful things he said and his eyes which were like blood-filled scabs that looked not only at her, but in her, making her writhe with disgust even as she trembled with need. He stank of pig wallows and animal dens. Then he was in her and it was horrible—he was freezing cold as if he had slid an icicle into her and she screamed, she fought, she cried out the names of saints but that only excited him more and he drove his lance like ice-cold pig iron into her faster and harder. Her lust was extinguished like a sizzling wick. The pain was unbelievable. It was not love. It was hate. Pure, ugly hate driving into her and her hands clawed at him.

His body was a crust that broke away revealing a shaggy, swollen, greasy form. She could feel the bristles of his flesh and it was not Sam, oh dear Christ, it was not Sam. She had been fooled. She had been seduced by evil, an ancient spawn of hell that was violating her. A grunting, squealing swine demon that thrust its cold, filthy member into her, breathing its hot breath of tombs into her face and leering at her with luminous red eyes that burned her soul black.

She felt the demon plant its foulness in her, filling her with its seed which was cold, gushing into her, spilling out of her, drowning her in primal ooze, a congealing, nauseous pool of animal-fat tallow. And in it, the demon's offspring coiled inside her like a worm. It was an imp. A devil. And it wriggled in her womb like a maggot in soft pink meat, its eyes already opening, black scabs in a twisted, elfin face.

She could feel the horror moving in her, clawing at her insides, nibbling at her entrails.

And then the demon was gone.

But what it had left inside her would not leave. Not until it had sucked every last drop of blood from her.

12

The haunting.

It came in many forms and wore many faces. It came out of fissures and dark spaces and shadowy graves of nonexistence, descending upon him, picking away at his reason and sanity.

In Kansas, Sam took a job as a stock detective for the Sumner-Stockton outfit. They had thirty thousand head of cattle they were fattening up on the sweetgrass of Smoky Hill Valley after the drive from Texas. Next stop was the stockyards of Abilene. But until that happened, there were rustlers to be dealt with. Most of them were poor homesteaders and hard-luck cowpunchers who wanted to start their own spreads, but lacked the income to do so. They were real handy with a running iron, altering the original brands and driving Texas beef into their hidden pens. Sam's job was to track them and kill them. And it was always killing, for cattle rustling was a hanging offense, and those boys were not only wily but determined that their necks would not be stretched.

After his tenth man, Sam lost track of how many he put down.

Somewhere during the process, he began to wonder why he was doing it at all. But he knew. God help him, he knew. Maddie. It was

Maddie. His soul had been ripped open in Guadeloupe and made to fester at Shorty Brice's farm, but Maddie's ultimate rejection of him was the salt that was poured into that gaping wound. He was suffering and something inside him planned to make damn sure that others suffered as well.

A few days before he was thinking of riding off, he smelled the stink of carrion on the wind. It was in Junction City this time, just before sunset. Casting a wary eye in all directions, he tied his sorrel mare off at the hitch rail and made his way into a saloon called the Short Horn. There was sawdust on the floor and the bar was nothing but a plank suspended atop whiskey barrels. A haze of smoke and seared beef and body odor hung in the air. In such a place, the smell of death was indistinguishable from the rotting buffalo hides stacked in the corners and the hide hunters themselves, whose buckskins were stiff with dried blood, marrowfat, and the juice of buffalo entrails. There was a particularly revolting smell to these men. One of rotten meat, decaying teeth, rancid fat, and dirty asses.

Sam found an empty table, rolled himself a cigarette, and avoided the eyes of the buff hunters. When they came into town, they were always looking for something: drinking, fucking, or fighting. All of them had Army revolvers and Green River skinning knives at their belts. They were best left alone.

The barkeep's name was Corey. He put a glass of beer and a shot of forty-rod on the table and said, "Howdy, Mr. Bouchard. Was wondering when you'd show."

"Were you?"

"Yes, sir." He looked around warily. "Was a fellow here looking for you earlier. Big fellow in a buffalo coat. Didn't give no name."

Sam felt a singular weakness in his belly because he knew what it meant. And even if he hadn't, the look in the barkeep's eyes spoke volumes. This was a man used to buffalo hunters and desperados and violent Texas cowhands. He did not shake easily, but there was something close to terror in his eyes. "He was …" Corey swallowed. "He was …"

"Yes?"

"He was right peculiar, Mr. Bouchard." Corey swallowed again, wiped a dew of sweat from his brow. "Real pale, you know? Scars all over his face. Kept smiling all the time, just grinning like a cat. He smelled just plain awful, like he'd been sleeping in a grave. And … and those eyes … they were real cold, real black. Said … said he'd be waiting for you. Didn't say where."

"Thank you."

It meant, of course, that the Hell Rider and his lot had caught up with him yet again. They always did in the end. They would destroy him here, too, with nightmares, hallucinations, and horrors that stalked in the night. He needed to get away. As far away as he could. That would shake them off his trail for a time. But it was probably already too late. He would have to stand and fight. There was nothing else. The question remaining was: would his adversaries be real or mere delirium?

Sam sat there for a long time, nursing his whiskey and smoking. Then he went out into the street.

Night had come down, sweeping across the prairie and it brought a silence and a stillness that was chill and forever. The moon had risen full and white, deepening the shadows and limning Junction City with a surreal glow that was nearly phosphorescent.

Sam saw no one in the street.

A cool wind was blowing and making rain gutters rattle and loose planks creak. His hands were shaking as he made to untie his mare. And it was then, something cold and white twisting up inside him, that he smelled an awful stench like spoiled pork and moldered bones smoked over a fire. There was the sound of cloven hoofs plodding through the dirt. He turned fast, his hands on the butts of his Colt Peacemakers. He cleared leather in the blink of an eye, but there was nothing, nothing at all. Just that icy wind that stank of open graves.

"Show yourself, goddammit," he said, his nerves beginning to fray.

From a pocket of shadow between a livery barn and a boarded-up dance hall there came something like a white and churning mist that stank of sulfur. A dark, grotesque shape began to rise up out of it. He saw eyes the color of blood and heard the chattering of teeth. Then a ghastly, crooked form stepped out and it carried a Colt Dragoon pistol in one gnarled claw.

"Samuel Bouchard," said a voice that was raw and scraping, "I have come for you."

Dappled by moonlight, Sam saw it was a man in a filthy buffalo coat and a flat-crowned hat seamed with mold. His face was deathly pale, jagged and cracked open like the surface of a shattered mirror. He was smiling with huge yellow teeth. The fist that held the Colt Dragoon had moss growing over its back that threaded the fingers together.

Sam recognized who it was right off … or who it *had* been.

Frank Wiecek.

Wiecek was Missouri trash who'd made a name for himself during the war as a guerrilla, robbing and looting and shooting men in the back. He'd been pardoned at the end of the war, made his living by hunting men and animals and collecting bounties. He was known for his hotheadedness, cruel demeanor, and a gun that never missed. Something which had failed him in the end, for none other than Wild Bill Hickok had gunned him down dead in the streets of Newton, Kansas, three months before, when Wiecek dared call the master shootist out. He was not the first man to make such a deadly mistake.

Dead three months.

And now, apparently, he had returned.

But Sam knew this was not really Wiecek. This was nothing but foul walking meat driven by a diabolic mind. What had come to kill him was no man but a wicked thing that emptied cribs and sucked breath and crawled in graves.

This is a zumbee, he thought. *Not dead, not alive, just like in Guadeloupe.*

"I have come for you," Wiecek said again in that clotted voice and as he spoke, steam blew from his mouth in misting clouds. "I have come for you, Samuel Bouchard."

If it had really been Frank Wiecek, there would have been no announcement of his intentions. He would have waited for Sam outside the saloon and pumped three rounds into his back from the shadows. But then this was not really Wiecek anymore than it was really a man. It was a thing, a walking corpse.

Sam stood there, pistol in his hand, a heaviness in him that made him feel almost lethargic. A rancid stink blew off his assassin that reminded him of dead minks heaped in maggoty piles.

Wiecek stepped forward with a lumbering, almost painful gait. He brought the Dragoon up, his knuckles having burst through the skin in white knobs of bone. His grinning mouth was huge, his red-litten eyes like pathways to hell. Clots of dirt dropped from his coat.

"Why?" Sam finally said and was surprised that he had said it at all. But he really wanted to know. "Why? *Why?*"

Wiecek stood there, his black grin widening like a chasm until it met all the cracks and fissures in his stretched gray-white flesh and his face literally began to split open, something diseased and anti-human pushing through, straining to be born in a disgorged soup of festering blood and worms and graveyard slime. His entire face began to move. It became charnel wax that oozed and flowed, bone shattering, eyeballs popping like bloody oysters, muscle and tissue macerating, meat torn out by the black roots as something like a vulture-gargoyle strained to be free.

Sam let out a tortured cry because he knew what it would become next.

And before it burst free in rivers of puckered and pink tumorous flesh, he dove to the ground just as the Dragoon went off, a .44 slug passing harmlessly over the top of his head but close enough to part his hair. Before he hit the dry, parched earth of the dirt road, the Colt pistol in his hand had been discharged. The .45 caliber slugs drilled into Wiecek's belly and chest, the exit wounds spraying tissue that squirmed with crawling things as they hit the wall of the livery.

Wiecek made a weird mewling sound like a flayed cat and fired the Dragoon again and again with a resounding, hollow booming that echoed off the faces of the buildings.

Both shots were wild.

And by the time the second one was off, Sam had put two rounds in his head, into his molten face. His skull came apart like a jelly jar in an explosion of filth. He dropped the Dragoon, took two more steps and fell face-first in the street. He shuddered for a moment or two and then was dead again.

By then, of course, people were filing out of the saloon and the sporting house across the way, crowding and pressing in for a look and none of them seemed to like what they saw—a heap of sepulchral waste that had once been a man named Frank Wiecek. Green coiling worms and red eyeless beetles boiled up out of him in a rancid froth and then died with him, creeks and eddies of corpse drainage pooling in the dirt.

One of the buff hunters spit a gob of tobacco juice at the corpse. "Dead," he said. "Goddamned dead."

Standing there with a smoking pistol in his hand, Sam said, "Yes. And he's been dead a long time."

§

Whether it was plain stubbornness, stupidity, or a death wish on his part, Sam did not run. He did not pack up his traps and ride out of town. He was tired of life on the dodge. Something inside him—maybe it was pride—had decided it had had enough. It wanted things to end. Whatever it was, it could not be reasoned with. It wanted to fight. It demanded the right to make a last stand and die like a man and not a cowering, hunted thing.

So be it.

The day after he had gunned down Wiecek, he withdrew his money from the bank, provisioned up for a long ride, made certain his horse was ready, then in the late afternoon he went up to his room and he waited. If he needed to run, he was prepared; if he died, all his affairs were in order. His room was simple: bed, chiffonier, washstand, a table with one chair. He sat there, laying out cards for a game of Patience, sipping whiskey and waiting for it to begin. Because it would. Make no mistake of that.

He thought: *And you'll be here, waiting for it.*

He smoked a cigarette and pretended he could not feel the walls closing in on him. Now and again, he dabbed the gathering perspiration at his temples with a clean handkerchief. He swallowed a slug of whiskey. It burned all the way to his stomach. His hand shook and the shot glass rattled on the table as he set it down. The shadows were growing thick in the room. He lit the oil lamp and tried not to look around. He checked his watch. It would be full dark in thirty minutes. The idea of that made his heart pound.

This is what you wanted.

Yes … at least earlier it was what he wanted. When the sun was bright and the day was warm, it was easy to be fearless. After all, who was afraid of the dark at high noon? He breathed in and out, calming himself. *You've faced death before,* he told himself. *Now you face it again.* Certainly, but what they would send was what worried him: the idea that he would lose his mind before he even had a chance to fight.

He flipped over a few more cards.

His fingertips were sweaty, the breath catching in his throat. He sat there, a very conservative-looking man in comparison to the shaggy, dirty, steel-eyed rough rider he had been when he had originally ridden into Geary County. He was dressed in a boiled white shirt and string tie, a black Prince Albert coat and striped trousers. Well-polished gray lizard boots were on his feet. His bowler hat was on the table. As an agent for the Sumner-Stockton outfit, he was expected to look and act like a gentlemen, even if his job was murder. He carried only one Peacemaker. Strapping on two of them made him look like a gunman looking for a fight. That was the last impression he wanted to give.

He heard a sound in the room, then another. A chill settled over the back of his neck. He unholstered his Colt and set it on the table. He looked around and saw nothing. The gun in his hand, he stood up and stretched.

There was a sound behind him.

A noise like something with many legs was scrambling up the wall. There was nothing there. He heard it again. He looked, but there was nothing, of course. This was how it often started, with subtle phenomena meant to unnerve him. It was working, but he acted as if he was unfazed.

He thought: *They better work a little harder than that.*

He paced back and forth until it was full dark out. By then, he found it nearly impossible to sit still and that was why he knew he had to. He sat down. He thumbed cards. He reached for the whiskey bottle again, then decided against it. No, no, it wouldn't do to dull his senses now. It wouldn't do at all. For the next hour, he made himself stay there. He ignored the noises of things crawling over the walls, what sounded like breathing from inside the closet. Even when he heard the springs creak as a weight settled onto the bed, he paid it no mind. It was not easy.

Finally, he could take it no more.

His heart was pounding.

His skin was crawling.

His hands were shaking like those of an old man.

He went to the window. He saw a few gigs pass in the street below. Groups of soldiers from Fort Riley out helling around laughed and called out to one another. Behind him, there was the sound of claws being dragged over the door. Sweat trickled down his spine. He pulled out his watch. The face of it blurred. It became a grinning countenance. He slid it back in his pocket. Swallowing, he looked down into the street. He saw no one. It was empty, it was—

Jesus.

There. Across the street, down near the corner. The painted ladies of the hog ranch were gone. Beneath the overhang, he could see a dark shape nestled in the shadows. He blinked several times, but it was still there—a tall man in a black duster with a campaign hat on. Beneath the broad brim, he could see two feral red eyes looking up at him.

It was the Hell Rider.

The goddamned Hell Rider.

Finally, Sam could see him. Maybe not completely but as clearly as he had thus far. If only he had his Winchester, he could have drilled a .44 slug right into him. Something thumped inside the closet. He heard the snorting of a wild hog. It squealed, it pawed at the inside of the door. His nerves tightening, Sam looked back out into the street.

The Hell Rider was gone.

He saw a shadow play along the boardwalk, then it, too, was gone. He sighed. Even if he had had his Winchester, he couldn't go shooting through his window down into the street. He had killed many men in the line of duty when he was a soldier and as part of his job with the Sumner-Stockton outfit. He had killed them to survive in the years in between. But ever since he rode out of Baton Rouge, he had killed men for no reason other than he thought they were someone else or some*thing* else. It pained him greatly and only added to his overall degrading mental state. Besides the obvious, that was the reason he couldn't go shooting into the street. The Hell Rider was toying with him, making him see things that weren't there so he would gun down another innocent.

What was in the closet was getting enraged.

He went over to the table and gathered his things, putting the bowler atop his head. All the rest of his gear was at the stable. There was nothing in the chiffonier and certainly nothing in the closet. He did not like closets and never used them.

With one last look, he left, shutting the door behind him.

13

The creole witch always seemed to find him just before sundown. She was like a ghost that came and went at will. It didn't matter if he was outside a town or lost in the depths of the grassland, moving along a deep-hewn river cut or in a swale, she would be there. And the frightening thing was that Maggart could feel her coming, maybe with his mind and maybe with his soul. His hands would shake and his teeth would chatter and it would feel like something necessary and fine inside him had gone black with rot. Then she would be there.

Sometimes she spoke to him and sometimes she just stood in the fringe of shadows and stared at him with smoldering dark eyes as he sat before the fire, trying to swallow some jerked buffalo meat to keep up his strength which was beginning to wane.

Often, she would lie in the back of the buckboard with the box and whisper things he did not dare try to hear. Other times, she raised her hands to the moon above and sang profane melodies that made his heart catch in his chest, or she would wander out into the darkness again and again, returning with bones that she scattered and formed into pagan circles, which was some sort of heathen magic.

One night, she stood behind him and her breath was hot against the back of his neck and she said in her smooth Caribbean accent, "Once upon a time there was a dead man who ran from his destiny and Death followed him. A lone rider that would hound him to his waiting grave. The dead man thought he could hide, but he couldn't. He thought he

could run far enough, but he was always found. He left his love behind and Death found her. It seeded iniquity in her womb that sucked the life from her. The dead man did not give in and in his wake, there was dying and suffering."

"That is the man we seek?" he asked.

"Yes. We know where he is. But he must present himself to us."

Maggart did not understand any of it. Only that the tone of her voice, her words, or something malefic just beneath them, made a sickness take root inside him. His heart would pound and his eyesight blur, awful thoughts racing through his head, and all he would be able to hear was the blood rushing in his head. The darkness would become that much darker, and he could feel it reaching out for him, consuming him, making him one with it in some blasphemous consummation.

Then came the night when terror lived inside him because he knew something awful would happen, something even worse than anything thus far. She made him pull the wagon up the trail until they came to a crossroads of sorts where two men, desperados or thieves perhaps, had been hanged from the limbs of a lightning-blasted oak. Buzzards were at them, sitting on their shoulders, spreading their dark wings and pecking away at their dead faces. The sound of their beaks drilling into carrion was one of the most horrible things he had ever heard.

"Here," she said. "This is the place."

He made camp there, the night wind pushing the smell of death into his face. He started a fire and as he squatted before it, she undressed and stood before him, the firelight painting her brown skin with licking tongues of orange. From the hide bag she always carried with her, she took a tin of some oily unguent that smelled of tallow and animal fat. With careful, precise motions, she greased herself with it. Then she danced widdershins around the fire and there was something about her movements and her glistening nakedness that aroused him, made him feel like he was lost in a dream of fevers and madness.

Once again, he heard the grunting of swine out in the darkness and the pounding of hooves as something circled them. He saw black eyes out there in the firelight, just as dark as the twin bores of a shotgun and heard a low, inhuman laughter.

"Tonight," she told him when her dancing stopped. "You will lie with me so that we might seal our bargain."

Beneath the hanged men, she pushed him down into the dry grass and mounted him, riding him fiercely, filling him with great pleasure and carnal delight, but also making him feel repulsed deep inside. As he neared climax, she withered into an ancient, twisted wraith of jutting bones covered in leathery skin, her graying face that of a corpse—eyes sunk into dark hollows, lips shriveled away from gnarled yellow teeth. Something like spines or stiff horsehair erupted from her body and her puckering mouth sucked at his throat with terrible leeching sounds.

Despite it all, he emptied himself into her, which made her giddy with rapture. She danced again around the fire, cackling madly. If he had doubted it before, he knew then that he had most certainly sold his soul to the Devil.

Later, washed down in moonlight, she wrapped herself around him and said, "Now things are needed so we can be ready."

"What things?" he asked.

She grinned, the moon making the palings of her teeth seem to glow. "I need the blood of a child...."

14

The town marshal of Junction City was an exotic character named Albert Gutierrez, though his original name was Alberto del Jesus de Castillo y Gutierrez. He was a full-blooded Spaniard with a haughty, almost regal sort of bearing, intense dark eyes, and broad muscular shoulders. Any time of the day he could be seen about town dressed in spotless white cotton pants and matching shirt, a red silken sash shoulder to opposing hip, a .44 Hopkins at his waist in a custom-made holster, a Southwestern sombrero atop his head and fancy-tooled black leather boots that he kept so shiny that if they caught the sun, the glare would blind you. He was, they said, a good man.

Though the town was named because of the nearby junction of the Republican and Smoky Hill Rivers, it was the junction of three railroads—the Union Pacific, the southbound Missouri, Kansas, and Texas line, and the northbound Junction City/Fort Kearney branch— that was its lifeblood. Every week, Texas beef was shipped out and wide-eyed easterners were shipped in. The latter were looking for adventure, for glory, a fortune for the taking. In general, they left a month later, broken and destitute. But in between, it was Gutierrez they sought out, and he was more than happy to tell them about the railroads and cattle drives, the fine restaurants and hotels, the stockyards and stables, the churches and schools, gambling houses and whorehouses and dance halls. It was all there, as far as he was concerned.

Strangers coming in often asked him if he was Mexican, but he congenially explained that he was indeed a Spaniard out of Madrid. He never took offense to the question, because he had lived in Mexico some years and loved the country. He was gracious in all things, and his manners were courtly. He always opened doors for ladies, bowed his head and clutched his hat to his chest in their presence. He addressed all men as *sir*. He had an amazing memory and he never forgot a face or a name. He rarely passed anyone in the street without a word or two. It was not his way. He knew very well that the power structure in any frontier town was not the men, but the women who stood *behind* the men, so he played up to this. *Ah, buenos dias, Mrs. McClure. Is that a new bonnet you are wearing? Might I say with all due respect how well it goes with your eyes?* He also knew that the rich must be given their due. *Mr. Gannon, how nice to see you. Is this your son? My, what a handsome strapping fellow he is!* And when he came upon newlyweds, he often held his hands out to stop them, then casually stepped back. *This is a scene I long will remember. Such a handsome couple! How happy and joyous your lives will be!* To the good people of Junction City, Kansas, Albert Gutierrez was a friend and admirer, he was a favorite uncle and new-found brother, he was commonplace and exotic, a character that had stepped from a book and the fellow who lived next door, he was all and everything, poet and rascal, lawgiver and saint, a dream of a friend and a sonofabitch if you broke his laws.

And it was Gutierrez that Sam Bouchard sought out after he left his hotel that night. He knew the marshal would be in his office, so he went over there, the streets rowdy with cowhands and soldiers, whores and pickpockets and gamblers. The sound of shouting and laughter were underscored by the music of pianos and scraped bull fiddles. It was a wild night, all things considered.

"Ah, Mister Bouchard," said Gutierrez when his visitor came through the door. "How nice of you to drop by, sir."

Sam liked Gutierrez, as did most people, but he was pretty certain that the marshal did not approve of him. A stock detective was basically a hired gun, and there was a truth to that, and both men knew it. Sam sat down, thinking he should have been doing other things. He had not eaten in two days and he had slept little more than an hour or two. The idea of eating and sleeping was something of an alien concept. He could not remember the last time he had done either and truly enjoyed them.

"Word has reached me," Sam said, "that you have been asking questions about me."

Gutierrez dismissed this with a wave of his hand. "Ah, but people do like to talk in places like this. Questions? Yes, but then I ask questions about everyone. It is my job. I keep a file of everything and everyone in my head."

"And that's all it is?"

"What else could it be?"

Gutierrez poured them both coffee. Sam sipped his. It was surprisingly good for jailhouse brew. He waited because he knew that the marshal wanted to talk to him about something, but there was no way he would until he was ready. He was a cordial man, his mannerisms old world; he could not be rushed.

Gutierrez sat down. He jabbed a thumb toward the door. "Listen to them out there, everyone anxious to drink and gamble and love themselves to oblivion. They come into town with a mad desire to spend every cent of their hard-earned pay."

"You never interfere with any of that, do you?"

Gutierrez shook his head. "My deputies are out there. As long as there is no shooting or stabbing or beatings or rapes or robberies, I do not concern myself. My job is to keep the peace, but it is also to encourage our friends out there to empty their wallets. And the good people of this town would not care for it if I got in the way of that, now would they?"

"No, I don't suppose so."

"It reminds me of the fiesta in Mexico City when I first came to this part of the world."

Sam nodded. "A lot of armed men out there. Sooner or later, somebody will get hurt."

"Maybe. If so, I will intervene. If a man shoots another, then I will come for him. I will ask for his gun. If he will not give it to me and come with me peacefully, then I will kill him. And when I kill him, his friends will try to kill me. And if they do that, then my deputies will try to kill them. Before long, I will have a federal marshal and troops from Fort Riley patrolling the streets ... ah, you can see where such a thing will lead?"

Sam smiled thinly. That was the beauty of the thing, because he knew for a fact that Gutierrez had only killed one man in the five years he had been town marshal. The legend that grew up out of that was enough to keep folks peaceful. And when he walked into a saloon, even the meanest, orneriest men respected his law because in the back of their minds they were thinking that here was a man who did not just hide behind a badge, but a man who had killed before and would kill again.

"All of which," Sam said, "has very little to do with why you wanted to see me."

"I wanted to see you, my friend?"

"Yes, indirectly. By asking questions about me, you pretty much invited me here. So now I'm here and I'm ready to answer your questions."

Gutierrez nodded. "Your logic is ... unassailable." He steepled his fingers and stared over them at his visitor. Finally, he lit a cigar, but only after offering one to Sam, who refused. "I suppose there comes a time when men must be blunt with one another. Not rude, surely, but blunt. I shall now be blunt with you."

Sam waited. Gutierrez didn't really interest him. He was more concerned about other things out in the darkness that were stalking him.

"You are a very nervous man, Mister Bouchard. Of course, I mean no offense by that, sir. I have watched you here in my town for many weeks.

And each time I see you, I am struck by the fact that you act like a man who is ... *pursued.*" Gutierrez considered that, then nodded. "I think that would be the correct word. You are fidgety, restless. You look behind you a great deal. You peer into crowds as if you are expecting to see an enemy. You appear—yes, even now—as a very troubled man."

Well, no one could say he wasn't perceptive. "In my business, you make enemies. Men get sent to the gallows and to prison. Sometimes their friends seek vengeance for them. And sometimes men get out of prison, and they want their pound of flesh. A man like me has to be careful."

"A man who lives by the gun."

"Yes."

Gutierrez sighed. "That always worries me: men who live by the gun."

"You live by it."

He shook his head. "No, you are wrong, Mister Bouchard. Carrying one as part of your duty and living by one are two different things. I have shot four men in my life. One died, the other three survived, I am happy to report. I pulled the trigger on them because they gave me no choice. I did not enjoy doing it."

"And you think I enjoy it?"

"Do you?"

Sam knew better than to get angry. Gutierrez could cause a great deal of trouble for him. The last thing he needed was to be spending the night in one of his jail cells. He had to play this cool. "No," he finally said, "I don't. I make my living as a stock detective. It's my job to stop rustlers. I hunt them down and I'm only too happy to deliver them to the law peacefully. But if they pull a gun on me, and most do, I have no choice."

Gutierrez shrugged. "You are employed by the Sumner-Stockton combine. A very powerful group. I would not, of course, interfere with their business. But as marshal, certain things reach my ears and I have to look into them, much as I wish otherwise. You have killed many men, Mister Bouchard. Even these weeks you have been in my town, you have taken a number of lives. Some say you have killed far too many and some that did not need killing at all."

Ah, well, there it was.

Sam had suspected this from the start. He should have known where this was going. Two days before, there had been an altercation. Sam was hot on the trail of three brothers—Race, George, and Denver Spenning—who were (it was well known) rustling cattle from the larger combines, altering their brands, and selling them to the highest bidder. In Kansas, beef meant money, and the Spenning Brothers were making a great deal of it. The Sumner-Stockton herds grazed on the open range, which was public land, so it was not so difficult for a trio of well-experienced ranch hands to collect up strays and sell them off. They did it discreetly and covertly.

Sam ran across George Spenning in the street one day and George said, "I hear you're gonna kill me."

Sam told him that he wanted to kill no one, but that he and his brothers had better stop rustling Sumner-Stockton head.

George told him, "If you don't kill me, they will."

What he meant was that if he turned against his brothers' schemes, they would kill him, and if he kept rustling with them, Sam was sure to kill him. It was a very clever ruse and it nearly worked. Unfortunately, Sam was a little savvier than that. He knew who called the shots for the Spennings. George could act as if he was being bullied into things, but he was the kingpin of the trio, and he was a hard customer by all accounts. George told Sam that his brothers and a few of their confederates were lying in wait for him. That it was only a matter of time before they killed him, if he wasn't careful. But if he wanted to find them, that most afternoons they could be found lounging about at the Briscoe House shooting a few hands of poker and drinking themselves silly.

It was a trap, of course, and Sam knew it just as he knew he had a mustache on his face and eyes in his head. But George was wily. There was no doubt about that. The trap wasn't that they'd be laying for him over at the Briscoe, but that they were gunning for him. It was a hoary bluff and no more, but it was intended to make Sam jump on his horse or high-step it down to the Union Pacific yards and grab the express for points unknown (before he was stretched out on a mortuary slab and ventilated like a sprinkling can courtesy of the Spenning brothers).

So Sam played along.

Acting more than a little concerned, he packed up his traps and kit bag and rode away from the Momson Arms—already missing the smell of sweet pine and sap in the two-story log house, not to mention the hotcakes and maple syrup every morning—making damn sure that George Spenning saw him. Which, of course, he did because he was lounging across the street with the old-timers outside the bootmaker's hut, listening to high, randy tales of holding off seven hundred Comanche warriors at Adobe Walls (Sam knew this because the old white-bearded buffalo hunters had told him the same stories). Across town, he took a room at a boarding house, then promptly at one o'clock, he rode over to the Briscoe, which was your typical grimy shebang hog farm, a long wooden shack splintered and gray by the weather. Once it had been a cow barn, but now it had been converted to hold another sort of livestock.

Sam went in there, pistol at his hip. He was playing a lone hand, but that was something he'd always been good at. The dirt floor was sprinkled with sawdust to absorb spilled beer, blood, urine, and gobs of tobacco juice. Along one wall, there were no less than twenty alcoves with blankets tacked up to give the whores and their patrons a little privacy while they squirmed in the dark for two bits. The stench in there was enough to ream out the nostrils of a pig used to slopping in its own shit. It was a commingled, heady brew of unwashed bodies, piss, vomit and greasy sex all mixed up into a steamy miasma of filth. A couple of bedraggled cowhands leaned against a plank bar, one of them scratching at his dirty backside with an investigative thumb. The bartender, a sloe-eyed chili with two fingers on his left hand, set up shots of whiskey that was nothing but raw alcohol flavored with molasses, pitch, and burnt sugar, given a bite with hot peppers and whatever was handy. It wasn't called snakehead and tarantula juice for no reason.

Sam saw the Spenning brothers before they saw him. He was on them before they could get the draw on him. George went for his gun, but by then Sam had a pistol in his hand and he drilled George through the left eye socket, scattering what brains he had against the wall. Race and Denver didn't even make the attempt.

"I catch you boys rustling Sumner-Stockton head again, I'll plant you in the same hole," he told them. Afterward, doing his civic duty as any law-abiding man, he went and got the marshal. And the undertaker.

Gutierrez said, "I like to keep this town clean. I like people, *my* people, to know they can walk these streets safely."

Sam chuckled. "You got two, three hundred Texas hands out there now raising hell. You want to make this town safe, you need to get out there and start doing it."

Gutierrez sighed long and low. "As an employee of the Sumner-Stockton combine—"

"Former employee."

Gutierrez raised an eyebrow. "As such, you must know that this town exists because of the cattle and the men who drive them. They pour thousands and thousands of dollars into our coffers. Would you have me shut down the saloons and dance halls, gambling houses and brothels? I would be lynched within hours."

"And besides," Sam pointed out, "you get a percentage of the take."

"Your tone begins to trouble me," Gutierrez said, his face darkening with anger.

Sam turned around quickly, his eyes wide and steely.

"What is it?" Gutierrez asked.

"Thought … thought I heard something outside."

"You probably did. It is a busy place out there tonight."

Yes, it certainly was, but Sam was sensing something else that did the slow-crawl right up his backbone. He had been feeling it too long now not to recognize it when it came. He cocked his head, listening.

For a moment, there was nothing but the noise in the street … then there was something else. He could hear someone moving up the boardwalk outside with a measured, almost painful sort of tread—the jingle of spurs and the creaking of something like saddle leather, only it had nothing to do with a horse and everything to do with the man with the spurs. *He's tracked you again. He's sniffed you out as he always does.* The boots came up the walk, paused outside the door, then continued on.

"You don't look so well, Mister Bouchard," Gutierrez said with real concern.

He was right. Sam's face was pinched and yellow, eyes like glass balls, his mouth pulled into a line tight as a healed scar. His body jerked with fear-induced convulsions. A vein throbbed at his temple. Now the old terror was on him again, working its way right down into his marrow. There was no spit in his mouth. Terror, real terror, burned through him like a wild grassfire as he heard the clomping of the boots outside and the jingle of spurs. A wind blew up against the front of the marshal's office, something like grains of sand brushing against the window panes. There was a hollow, fleshy thumping like a living heart beating inside of a skeleton.

Something fell onto the desk.

Just a common bluebottle fly. It lay on its back. Its legs bicycled and its wings gave one ineffective last buzz and went quiet. It was dead. Gutierrez flicked it away. A rank, hot odor filled the office. It stank of fusty animal dens where pelts and bones rotted in warm, seething darkness.

"That smell," Gutierrez said.

Another fly fell to the desk followed by a third and fourth, then they were dropping like rain, seemingly born out of the air, filling it in black, buzzing seams and droning clouds. They covered the windows and darkened the walls. Both Sam and Gutierrez were enveloped. The flies were in their hair and down the backs of their necks, speckling their faces and trying to fill their mouths. The office was a veritable cyclone of winging blowflies that brought with them the hot, offensive stench of a week-old corpse.

Sam, backpedaling away from the desk, driven to sheer mania by the feel of tiny legs on his face and countless wings brushing his eyelids, shrieked and shouted. The office was moving with sluggish, heaving waves. It was like a carpet someone was shaking out.

Through it all, he saw Gutierrez change.

He was up against the wall, enveloped by thousands of hungry, nipping meatflies. He looked like a writhing, fuzzy sock. His body was horribly contorted, twisting and shuddering. And through it all, Sam saw him begin to change. His gaping black mouth hissing and squealing, he began to split open. Monstrous, wormlike forms poured out of him, bulging out of him like entrails from a slit open belly. Pink, convulsive ropes pushed out of his mouth, nostrils, and eye sockets until it looked like he was licked by dozens of glistening, swollen tongues.

Not human, not human, not even human, were the words that played at manic levels in Sam's head. Being who he was and what he had been through, he reacted in kind: he pulled his Peacemaker and put two rounds into Gutierrez … or the coiling, slithering, fly-specked nightmare he had now become.

Then he ran.

His mind baked by madness into hot desert sand that filled his skull, he half-ran, and half-stumbled out the door. And the flies came with him. As he dragged himself up the boardwalk, he saw them coalesce into the tall, grim shape of the Hell Rider.

15

Sam woke sometime later to find himself in an alley, pressed between a stack of empty wooden kegs and a pile of scrap lumber. Lightning seemed to flash inside his head. His mouth tasted like it was full of dust. The Peacemaker was still in his fist. It took a moment or two for him to remember how he had gotten there, and even then, he could not be sure. He could not be sure of anything. He remembered the flies and Gutierrez. He remembered shooting him and then fleeing for his life from the stark, relentless form of the Hell Rider.

I killed the marshal, he thought then with rising panic. *I killed him and I'll hang for it.*

Did it happen?

Did it really happen?

He couldn't be sure. Had it been an hour ago? Two? Three? His gear was over at the stable. If he could get there and ride out, fade into the countryside and go to ground, he just might have a chance.

He stood up slowly, uneasily, weak from the lack of food and rest, his thoughts tumbling over the top of one another. He found a barrel of rainwater down the alley and splashed some into his face. Then he stood there, uncertain now what was real and what was dark fantasy. He pulled out his tin case of cigarettes, lighting one with a struck match. The shadows jumped around him. His hand trembled so badly, he could barely get the cigarette to his lips.

Think now, you must think now. You must clear your head of rubbish so that you can think, reason.

Yes, yes, that was the thing. He breathed in and out, drawing slowly off his cigarette. Calmer, he leathered his Colt. Better to have it in its holster. He could do no more damage with it that way.

He left the alley and made his way up the plank sidewalk past brick-fronted buildings and saloons, dance halls and mercantiles with grain sacks piled out front. The dirt streets were filled with people, ranch hands and soldiers, tenderfoots and gamblers, painted ladies and hide hunters. Sam lost himself in their midst, moving steadily southward, always on the lookout for men with tin stars but, to his relief, not seeing any.

Loud, God, it was all so loud.

Voices shouting. Screaming. Laughing. Swearing. A constant murmuring, a reverberation that made his skull vibrate in his head. He winced at the strident, tinny sounds of poorly-tuned pianos that were far too happy and the ancient Celtic dirges of wheel fiddles that were far too sad.

As the volume of it reached what seemed an excruciating pitch, he pressed his hands over his ears and ran until he found an empty street. Or it found him. Alone, finally alone. But was that better or worse?

He stood there, the night pressing in. He wore a black scowl on his face, breathing in and out to calm himself. In the distance, he could hear the noise of thrumming humanity. It throbbed ceaselessly like a beating heart.

Then suddenly, it was gone.

There was silence. A dead, impossible silence.

Tricks, tricks, tricks. Your mind. Do not trust your mind.

Now there was the smell of death—old death. The dusty, nitrous stink of cadavers mummified and blood gone to dry red sand. It blew down the streets on a hot wind of pestilence with a shallow, moaning sound of emptiness and age.

Sam froze there outside a tailor shop, moonlight showing him bolts of fabric in the window that glimmered scarlet like fresh blood.

He began to shake, then he began to sweat. It broke from every pore in his body. It ran down his face like tears, pooling beneath his eyes and making his scalp feel hot and greasy. His shirt clung to him like a wet rag. The perspiration was chill and foul-smelling. It carried the sour, yellow stench of a dying man's breath. He shivered uncontrollably.

It comes now, he thought. *It comes now.*

Barely able to stand upright, doubled over by weakness, he waited. His hand shook so badly he could not get the Colt from its holster. His entire body was palsied with fear. The fever raged, his brain boiling in his skull. Now the sweat running from him didn't just smell of sour foulness; it took on the acrid stink of pig piss and urine-drenched straw. It was nauseating and his stomach bucked in his abdomen.

Then, a sound … the sound he so dreaded.

"No," he said, his voice airless and cracking.

He heard the awful, encroaching *clump-clump-clump* of heavy boots on the board sidewalk and the discordant jangling of spurs. They rang out sharp and lethal. They reminded him of carving knives drawn against one another in preparation for the slicing of a fat goose.

He tried (ineffectually) to tell himself that it existed only in the narrow corridors of his brain. He wanted to believe it. But even as he tried to dismiss the approaching boots, they grew louder and louder, pounding like sacrificial drums.

The Hell Rider was coming and there could be no denying it.

He came on with a grave-deep chill and a smell of moldering oblong boxes. Sam could hear the approach of his boots … yet there was no one on the walk.

Not there, not really there.

But the boots were closer now, their stride faster and more confident as if their owner had found what it had been looking for and was stalking eagerly in its direction.

Still, there was no one.

The Hell Rider was a phantom, a non-entity, an incorporeal thing. Now he or *it* was but twenty feet away and Sam, knowing he had to move, to flee, saw shadows crawling over the planks. They were looping and slithery as if several dozen blacksnakes were sliding over the splintered boards. An ethereal shape was rising from them like smoke from a charcoal burner. It became a stark, manlike shape that was dark as coffin wood. It had form. It had intent. Its serous red eyes flickered like candle flames.

"Samuel Bouchard," it said in a voice like dull blades scraping over bones. *"I have come for you."*

He stumbled along through rutted dirt streets and over creaking boardwalks, hiding, listening. He was a mouse and a cat was sniffing him out. He ducked behind a heap of buffalo skins outside a tannery, breathing hard. *Clump-clump-clump,* came the boots. They and their jangling spurs passed by.

Sam started to breathe again.

The boots paused at the end of the boardwalk where two roads intersected. In the moonlight, there was no one there, but Sam could sense his adversary just fine—the fetor of the unburied dead was indicative, as was the almost metallic rasping of his respiration. The Hell Rider waited, casting for scent, then moved off into the night.

People, thought Sam. *That was it! He won't be able to pick up my trail if I'm surrounded by people.*

There was probably truth in that. His scent would be masked by hundreds of others. It made him feel hopeful … at least until he remembered that he had also shot a town marshal this night. If he was seen, the law would be after him and the first place they would look would be saloons and dance halls.

But it was a chance he would have to take.

At least for a time. He massaged his temples. There was booming thunder and forking lightning in his brain, a horrendous storm that made his brain throb. He stood up, carefully coming out of hiding.

Footsteps.

Across the street.

Cold sweat poured from him. The Hell Rider was still casting for his scent, an indefatigable bloodhound. But Sam had an idea now, a little something to tip the odds in his favor. He had to lose himself in a crowd. That would be the first step. He moved quickly. Down the boardwalk, then around a corner. Groups of hell-raisers clustered in an alley, and he sought them, ignoring their jibes and challenges. They were meaningless; less than meaningless. They had no voices that he could hear. He threaded his way through them, out of the alley, then across the street. People everywhere— whores and cowhands, drunken miners and soldiers looking for a fight. *Good, good. Bring them on, more and more.* He immersed himself in crowds, was bumped into, shoved, jostled. He got trapped in a group of men. Like a stick pulled along by a rushing river, they carried him into a saloon called the Buffalo Head.

Standing room only. A wild, heady night in Junction City. Singing and laughing. An out of tune piano. Drunken voices. Mostly good cheer. A few minor arguments and fistfights that were broken up quickly enough. An easterner in a brushed fedora fell off his stool, vomiting on the floor. He was quickly ejected out the batwings and Sam took his seat. He ordered a whiskey, swallowed it, ordered another.

The Hell Rider would not pick up his scent here.

He was safe here.

He *had* to be safe here.

He ordered a sandwich and chewed it slowly, washing it down with a warm beer. Ham. Roast beef. He couldn't be sure. It had no flavor. Whatever it was, it felt good in his belly after not eating for so long. His head cleared a bit.

Next to him, some craggy-faced sodbuster was talking about snakes. How the Indians used them for curses and for cures, just like back home in Taney County, Missouri. White River country, the man said. Snakes were the Devil's children, but they were all God's creatures nonetheless. The Lord God could strike you down with snakebite, he claimed, but he could rise you up all the same.

"Do you hear what I'm saying to you, stranger?" the sodbuster said. "That which brings harm, also brings strength. Do you understand that?"

Sam understood, all right. It made all the sense to his disordered mind and yet made no sense at all. He grumbled something, and the sodbuster kept right on talking, most of what he said drowned out by the noise coming from every possible direction.

Despite being lost in the sea of humanity, Sam began to feel uneasy. Something was going to happen. A man across the bar was staring at him. Sam did not know him. As he watched, the man's face began to swell as if it was snake bitten—it became a purple-blue agony, eyes bulging, mouth shriveled to a black pinhole. The flesh began to split open with a rubbery, shearing sound and Sam could plainly see something moving in there, an undulant and mucous form that he knew could not be real.

Look away, he told himself. *It's another hallucination, look away.*

But, as always, there was a fascination to it that was bone-deep, self-destructive, and inescapable: he looked because he *had* to look. Now the most preposterous and unpleasant thing occurred. As the sodbuster went on with his lecture on snake lore, the tongue of the man across the bar fell out of his mouth. It plopped to the bar top with a moist, splatting sound. Sam could not have heard it with all the noise, yet he did. It sounded like a wet fish dropped to the deck of a boat. Now it began to twist and writhe, knocking aside a shot glass. Like some huge, fleshy leech, it inched its way along the bar, leaving a trail of glistening slime in its wake.

No one noticed, of course, because it was not for them. Once again, it was for Sam alone. It was coming for him and he knew it. The closer it got, the more he began to shake. It was more than a severed tongue. Now it had the golden, speckled eyes of a toad and a yawning mouth of needle-like teeth. If it reached him, he knew, it would sink those teeth into him.

Sweat beading his face, he cautioned himself not to go for the gun at his hip. That's exactly what his enemies wanted him to do—open up in this crowd and take out a few innocents.

The sodbuster began to laugh. He was pointing at the tongue now and its creeping progress down the bar. He laughed so hard that tears rolled from his eyes and his entire body shook as if he were undergoing some sort of seizure.

Nobody, save Sam, seemed to notice.

The sodbuster continued to laugh, and as he did so, trembling with spasms, blood ran from the corners of his mouth in tiny red creeks. His laughter began to sound more like screams of agony.

Sam knew it was all in his head because it had to be in his head. You couldn't really laugh yourself to death, and there was certainly nothing funny about the tongue.

The sodbuster's eyes bulged from his head and then popped like bubbles, each one disgorging a yolky emulsion of slime and transparent goo. He still laughed and screamed (perhaps both at the same time), and as he did so, his face quite literally fell apart, sucking into a central chasm. Several of his teeth hit the bar top. One of them made a tinkling sound as it landed in an empty shot glass.

The tongue was still slithering along.

What it might have done, Sam never learned because there was a sudden concussive noise that made the entire saloon shake. And the perfectly amazing thing was, it wasn't in his mind. Mugs and glasses on the bar rattled. Several people fell off stools. There was swearing and shouting. A branching crack appeared in the mirror behind the bar and several bottles of liquor hit the floor and shattered.

The batwings blew open with a storm of howling wind and dust. A shape stood there—huge, shaggy, a grotesque monstrosity with leering red eyes—that seemed to fragment in the wind. Except ... it wasn't fragmenting, not really. Dozens, then literally *hundreds* of tiny wriggling things were blowing off of it, funneling in a wild, whipping storm.

Maggots.

Sam saw them on the bar. In glasses. On hats, in hair, wriggling on faces. People were fighting and screaming to escape, knocking each other out of the way, trampling those who had fallen down. The bar room was literally being buried in maggots.

Sam did not wait; he shoved people, elbowing and punching, running out the back way into the alley. Five minutes later, he was on his horse, riding out of Junction City, and hell followed in his wake.

PART TWO: THE HAUNTED

16

For Maddie, the days were long and the nights longer. Her blue eyes had darkened to a steel-gray and her beautiful (and much-admired) red hair had gone a sickly shade of orange like rust. Shuttered in her rooms, windows shaded, sometimes only a long candle burned to chase away the shadows, which were much darker and much livelier than they were anywhere else. She sat in her chair near a window, watching the sunlight play along the edges of the curtain by day and praising the moonlight by night. Whoever she had once been, she was no more.

Now and again, her only one true friend, Angeline Trombley, would stop by, bringing her food that she would rarely touch and trying to speak with her, trying to talk sense to her.

And although Maddie could hear her voice, her words were lost on her. She could only think of the parasite in her, the Devil's love that had swollen her belly these past many weeks. Angeline recognized, of course, the state she was in, telling her that there were doctors who could get it out of her. Something which women in their line of work had to do from time to time. There were countless abortifacients available. But Maddie would simply shake her head, listening to the sweet voice singing inside her, the terrible lullabies that put her not to sleep, but edged her further into madness.

"You can't just sit here in the dark and pretend that this is not happening," Angeline told her. "Something has to be done. Plans have to be made."

And Maddie would cackle with cold laughter that disturbed her friend to no end because it sounded like the laughter of a child ... shrill, scraping, even deranged.

But it's not me! Maddie wanted to tell her. *Can't you see? Can't you know? I'm not laughing! It's making me laugh, oh dear sweet Jesus, it laughs with my mouth and speaks with my voice but it isn't me!*

But she could not impart that to her friend, because what was inside her did not wish it.

And Angeline, poor kind big-hearted Angeline, would look upon her in the guttering candlelight with terror in her eyes. For hearing that voice coming out of Maddie was like hearing a stone gargoyle speak.

Maddie was always grateful when she left because she feared the evil would seep out of her womb and contaminate Angeline, turn her into a night-thing, a grave-crawler like the horrible incubus inside her.

Oh, please never come back, darling. Get away from me. Don't risk your soul....

Maddie waited in the darkness, her life a nightmare, her mind a pudding suet of madness. All her life, her beauty was all that she really had. She had used it, exploited it, and cared for it lovingly, but now when she dared look in a mirror what she saw was a horror. Her back was bent, her body twisted like a root, her hair lusterless and streaked with white. Her smooth, porcelain face was cadaverous, set with ruts and wrinkles, cheeks hollow and lips like cracked leather. And the eyes looking back at her were not her own, but bleeding purple-red blood clots set in puffy sockets the color of raw meat.

Her mouth would smile, white teeth gone gray and crooked, and the voice of the incubus would say, *"Aren't we so very delicious?"*

Sometimes she would pace the floors, back and forth, back and forth, in her lace-up boots, her skirts rustling about her like the shroud of a ghost. She would force her misshapen body to move, despite the fact that she was weary and emaciated with barely enough strength to keep her eyes open. Once, during such an exhausting bout of pacing, she caught sight of herself in the mirror and screamed. She had become a giant, haggard puppet with claws for hands and a bright red painted-on mouth that was licked by a swollen black tongue.

"How pretty we are," her voice said. *"How pretty, ripe, and delicious."*

It was the unclean, awful, rasping voice of the imp that dwelled inside her, sucking her blood drop by drop. And as if proof of its dominance and perhaps bored by her petulant defiance, it would make her crawl on the floor on her belly like a snake, pissing and fouling herself. Often, it would force her to masturbate for its amusement, making her buck with orgasm after orgasm as her voice screamed inside the drum of her skull and tears rolled down her face.

Even though she tried—mostly ineffectually—to starve herself, the imp would not have it. On her hands and knees, she would be forced to eat any meat that was brought to her. She ate it on the floor like a dog, naked and cringing, gnawing on the scraps and cracking bones with her teeth so she could suck out the marrow. The grease and fat she rubbed over her breasts and body like a balm until she was glistening and rank-smelling. The imp only let her eat once the food was several days old and abundantly flyspecked.

And that was her existence: a slinking, filthy ghoul wasting away day by day as that which incubated inside her grew fat and strong like a well-fed leech.

17

In the Texas panhandle, Sam heard tell of a breed who went by the handle of Katherine Trueblood. Folks said she could do things others couldn't and see things beyond the pale. According to the tale told by ranch hands, drifters, and a besotted Arapaho named Billy No-Nose, her mother was a shanty Irish whore and her father was a Kiowa war chief named Sleeping Wolf who'd been with Big Tree at the Salt Creek Massacre. She lived in a tumbledown shack at the edge of a rail town called Epsipalia and was generally shunned and feared. Some called her sighted and others said she was nothing but a foul, cauldron-stirring *bruja*.

Though he considered himself a modern, reasonable man, Sam was from swamp people and there was a dark core of superstition inside him that he could not think his way around. In the Bayou, his people had traditionally turned to wise women, conjurors, root doctors, and even witches in times of trouble when they needed divination beyond the five senses.

And this was what brought him to Epsipalia.

He rode in on a hot, dusty afternoon on his sorrel mare, coming in slow and eyeballing the lay of things as was his way. He had to be careful. He always had to be careful. Buckboards and gigs and ranch wagons passed by him, their drivers sullen and narrow-eyed. They looked at him but he did not look back. Regardless, he was watching all the time, sniffing out trouble the way a lone rider will.

Epsipalia was a typical rail town that stank of horseshit and grime. There were lumberyards and ice houses on its perimeter, parlor houses and saloons and false-fronted buildings lining its well-rutted main road. There was a Stockman's Club, tent bunkhouses, and liveries. Rows upon rows of simple houses with church steeples rising above them. He passed a lone brick jailhouse. Out front were hard-looking men in frock coats with Colt pistols at their hips. Stock detectives probably. They watched him the way a bird will watch a snake. He walked his sorrel over to the livery, paid to have her stabled for the night, and struck out on foot.

Despite the heat, the streets were busy with wagon traffic and pedestrians. High-yellow girls called out to him from sporting houses, and brush poppers in horse-thief hats skulked about the smithy's shop. Laborers, drunk on mescal, stumbled up the boardwalks in hobnailed boots, and drifters drank beer from wooden buckets. A group of desperados helling around gave him the snake-eye, but he refused to play that game. There were six of them with Whitney Navy pistols, all anxious to test his grit, but he was fresh out.

A couple boys were playing mumblety-peg with a frog-sticker and he asked them if they knew of a breed named Katherine Trueblood. They shook their heads. He pushed through the batwings of a saloon and started asking around, but few of the grubby men would even speak. The bartender was a different story. He looked Sam up and down with a practiced and critical eye, seeing a tall and rawboned man in scuffed cavalry boots and a worn canvas duster, a felt bowler cocked on his head, trail-weary and unshaven and possibly desperate.

"Sure, I know the one you want," he said. "Got herself a shack out yonder. But I warn you, friend, one man to another: leave her alone. At best, she'll poison you with her cure-alls and at worst, she'll slit your throat."

As he sipped his bourbon, Sam said he'd keep it in mind.

The bartender said she was known locally as "Katy Three-Hands" because she robbed with the right, murdered with the left, and stole away souls with the third. Her father was no Kiowa, but a full-blooded Tonkawa cannibal put to the knife by Quahadi warriors on the order of Quanah Parker himself after his band were found roasting a Comanche brave over a fire.

"She's trouble, but that's your business."

"It is," Sam said.

With the bartender's directions, it didn't take Sam long to track her down. She lived in a hut out in a yellow, parched field surrounded by the claim shacks of squatters. Bottles and gourds, bone-and-bird-feather talismans dangled from the roof overhang and he was reminded of lonely hovels favored by stump witches out in the bayou. The door was a weathered hide tacked to the frame.

He pulled it aside and smelled something like tallow and hog innards. "Katy Three-Hands," he called into the hot darkness. "I would have business with you."

There was something like a peel of dry laughter from inside and it chilled him. Then a voice, scraping and raw: "Wouldst thou? Then drink, pale rider; sip from yon gourd that hangs above my threshold."

Sam saw the gourd and considered it. The idea of drinking whatever sort of hog piss Katy Three-Hands had brewed-up left him cold, but he knew there was no way around it.

"Proceed, stranger," she called to him. "If thou wishest my help, then give unto me thy trust."

Her archaic speech disturbed him in ways he could not adequately fathom, but he snatched up the gourd and popped the cork. The smell coming out was vile, like rotten berries and dank swamp mud. Breathing hard, he brought the gourd to his lips and took a swallow. The taste was acidic and bitter; it burned like the juice of chilies on his tongue.

"There," said Katy Three-Hands. "Now, thou and I are on common ground."

Sam winced and replaced the cork, hanging the gourd back up. "What in the hell is that?"

"Why, son, it's naught but rattler venom, hemlock, baneberry, snakeroot, and dead man's piss." She giggled at that. "That is what those fools down to the saloon would tell thee, eh? But I assure thee, it's naught but a draft to open yon third eye."

Her humor—if that's what it was—was lost on him because immediately he wasn't so sure it *was* a joke. A burning started first in his throat and then in his belly. His knees went weak and he slumped there in the doorway, his head spinning and his guts crawling up the back of his throat like snakes. He cried out as fear that felt cold as ice and hotter than fire gripped him, consumed him, made him shiver and sweat.

In his head, he was seized and dragged screaming through corridors of dread by childhood terrors—the fear of his old man's leather strap, the huge rats that haunted the wharves of the Tickfaw by night, the alligator gars that prowled the river bottoms, Renny LaToure's tales of the big hairy man in the Bayou Cyprès—that became fog and then flesh and then a screeching hyper-reality that made him cry out as formless, ancient nightmares reached out of the darkness to claim him.

What happened to him then or where he was taken to, inside or outside his head, he just didn't know. Drums were beating and bells were ringing and bodies that were greased and undulant seemed to squirm around him like eels in a breeding pond. He sensed darkness and felt silence and heard alien tongues from alien mouths seem to lick the air around him, making it wet with their roping webs of saliva. Physically and psychologically, he was panicking, quivering and sobbing, his muscles made of rubber and his belly filled with soft warm butter. He was nothing. He was alone … yet he was in a crowded room and he could not scream himself free.

And then, as his heart threatened to gallop to a halt, there was some immense and rising weal-pink, oily monstrosity towering thirty or forty feet above him, glaring down at him with an almost organic malevolence of hatred and pain. It was a misshapen hog-thing with pointed ears laid back against a bristled skull, its eyes like burning wicks floating in red oil. Its mouth grinned at him, a black-furred wound festering with necrosis, pulsating with gaping ulcers that had eaten great holes in its tusked jaws so that he could see the gnashing yellow palings of underlying teeth. Pink bile dripped forth, hanging in foul ribbons, and it stank of pus-saturated battlefield dressings, the stink of death, of infection, of morbid sepsis.

As it reached for him with great clawed fingers, it called his name with a rushing hiss: *Bouchard … Bouchard … Bouchard. You wear the ragged skin of a corpse, you are made into death, and grave dirt is your bed.*

Sam shook and writhed as if he was trying to shed his hide, but there was no escape and sanctuary from that which had claimed him as a worm claims carrion. His skin was dirty and slimy, the winding sheet peeled from a cadaver, and his willpower was crumbling papier-mâché that disintegrated in his head.

He could feel a vast, seeking evil of limitless awfulness closing in on him, calling his name and making him its own.

When he opened his eyes, the monstrosity was still there, its teats full like swollen, hot-veined balloons and he saw that figures danced about it, begging to be crushed and mashed beneath its split-hooves. He ran from it, but whenever he looked back, he saw that hideous hog-thing filling the sky, gliding from a womb of fire and smoke, dropping maimed handfuls of its worshippers from gnarled pink-gray fingers as it filled the earth and popped it like a soap bubble, its mass increasing exponentially to lay open the underbelly of the cosmos itself.

When he came out of it and saw that he still leaned in the crude-framed doorway of the hut, it took a few moments to remember who he was and where he was and what it could all possibly mean.

He waited there, gasping for breath, hearing sounds gathering around him. *Hallucination,* he told himself. *Nothing but hallucination from that snakewater the old hag had you drink.* But the sounds persisted—the *clump-clump* of cloven hooves, the grunting of swine. A sharp blade of fear cut through him but he knew it was only in his mind and he had to fight it. He tried to laugh at the absurdity of it all, but all that came out was a cackling that was too loud, too ugly, and too close in tone to a scream.

I'm not afraid. I am not afraid.

He told himself that even down in Guadeloupe or in the war, he had not truly been afraid. He had not known terror, true terror, since he waited for his old man to come home, drunk and angry, strap in hand. But the truth was, ever since he had been a boy he had been afraid of just about everything and the only way to defeat that fear or at least come to terms with it was with bluster and blow and acts of suicidal bravado. If he pushed his chest out far enough nobody would see the scared little boy hiding in his skin.

"I am not afraid," he said out loud this time. "I am not afraid."

"But thou shouldst be, for demons scream in thy head," said a voice that was wise with age.

Then he got dizzy and he felt his knees strike the dirt floor of the hut and the next thing he knew he was lying there, feeling weak as a newborn colt. His limbs wouldn't move. The only thing that seemed to work were his eyes and what they showed him was that he was at the feet of Katy Three-Hands. A low fire was burning in the hearth and there was a greasy smell in the air as if meat were being smoked. In the dimness, he saw that there were shelves crowded with what looked like patent medicine bottles and baked clay jars. A wolfskin was tacked to the wall. There was a table heaped with what must have been dried lizards and locusts, the shriveled remains of birds.

He expected her to be old, but like many Indians she wasn't so much old as weathered. In the shadows, her face gleamed like polished mahogany. She reached out a hand to make a sign over him and it was wiry and corded like cane straw, the fingers twisted like twigs. She wore some sort of black shawl over her head that draped down to her shoulders and beyond. Her eyes were dark and shiny, ablaze with life, the rest of her tired and slumped.

He didn't know how long he had been there or how long she had been looking down at him like some pitiful whipped cur. The fear was still sweating out of him, draining the darkness from his soul.

"Thou art coming out of it, eh, boy?" she said and her voice was like a knife scraped along the inside of his skull.

He could not look at her, he could not gaze on her terrible eyes that knew things no man or woman should know. If he acknowledged her, she would begin to tell him things, secrets from beyond the veil of death, evil sorceries from the dark dawn of the race. His spine felt rigid with his terror of her.

"Thou canst only cower and curl up for so long, Samuel Bouchard. Awake and face thy ghosts."

The sound of her voice now made him angry. She had played tricks on him, she had clouded his mind with her hexing. "What … what did you do to me?"

"Not what I have done, Samuel Bouchard, but what thou hast done to thyself."

With that, she laughed at him. Her mouth peeled open to reveal toothless gums and a wagging tongue. Deep-cut wrinkles edged through cheeks. Her entire face laughed at him.

He sat up with some effort, still wobbly and unwell, his vision blurring then sharpening. He felt naked and degraded before her, helpless with atavistic fear. She was a witch. Yes, a witch like one of those old, withered swamp-water hags in the bayou, an unclean thing that tapped the root of primeval fear and practiced a baneful sorcery, calling up the dead and summoning ancient shadows to sit by her hearthside.

He could smell the garlic on her breath, the black graveyard earth under her fingernails, the tombs she had defiled, and the infants she had strangled in their cribs. Her eyes were obscene; her soul was an open grave.

Sam watched her, feeling the need to put her down like the rabid dog she was.

"Thou art compelled by evil. Thou hast drunk full at the trough of suffering. Thou hast filled thy belly with the meat of human bile," the hag said to him, shaking a sticklike finger at him. "Beware, Samuel Bouchard, for what you have sown shall soon be reaped, and what hath been called up in thy name cannot be put down. Listen! Cast an eye behind thee, for even now it approaches to sharpen its teeth on thy bones—"

"Shut up, shut up, shut up!" he cried out, delirious with hate, with the need to seal her goddamn mouth and end her wicked life before she transfixed, tormented, and hexed other unwary souls. She was a spider astride her web, swollen fat on stolen blood, and he was the boot that would stomp her.

He grabbed iron and stuck a pistol in her face. "I kill you, you old witch, and nobody cares. They'll just be glad to be rid of you."

"Aye, how true it is," she said.

He stared down the barrel of the Colt at her, fearing her, feeling the chill she inspired and hating himself for it. She was a broken, miserable, used-up old thing. A human rat. He had killed dozens, and she should have shaken with terror but she did not.

"I came for advice, you old bitch. I came seeking your help, and you made it worse."

She shook her head. "There's no help for thee, Samuel Bouchard. There's only the grave reaching out. Thou hast offended a powerful black medicine, and thy sins come home to roost."

She did not cackle or grin nor even gloat; she merely told him the truth that he feared in his heart. There was no escape from that which trailed him. It was getting not only closer by the day, but by the hour.

"Please," he said. "You have to help me."

She shook her head, throwing a pinch of powder into the fire that turned the flames a brilliant green. "KNOW THIS, SAMUEL BOUCHARD," she cried out in a terrible wailing voice. "KNOW THIS AND KEEP IT IN THY HEART: THEY SACRIFICED THEIR SONS AND THEIR DAUGHTERS TO THE DEVILS UNNUMBERED! THEY POURED OUT INNOCENT BLOOD, THE BLOOD OF FIRSTBORN CHILDREN WHOM THEY SACRIFICED TO THE IDOLS OF CANAAN, AND THE LAND WAS POLLUTED WITH BLOOD!"

"Shut up!" he told her. "I don't need some crazy pagan witch quoting scripture at me!"

To this she laughed and her laughter boomed in his ears and made the thoughts in his mind tremble. He could not think. His brain was pierced by arrows.

"I am closer to the spirit in my dark and old ways than thou shalt ever be, or all the hypocrites and charlatans and multitudes of sinners and liars that fill every church in the land. Never doubt that, or that thou shalt go down to worms and dust for the iniquity thou hast sown."

Trembling inside and out, he staggered out of the hut, sick with it all, knowing he had built his own gallows and tied his own noose, and no hell-witch possessed by holy scripture and devil's brew was going to set him free.

18

Although Samuel Bouchard had put two bullets into him, Albert Gutierrez had not died. One bullet went through his left shoulder, the other grazed his left bicep. Both still pained him some six weeks after the fact. But it was not this that made him take to the trail after Sam, even though as a Spaniard he considered what Sam had done a blood offense that must be answered in kind. No, he took to the trail after Sam because the surviving Spenning brothers—Race and Denver—were riding hard after him, planning on making him pay for the death of their brother George, that Sam had shot down in Junction City. Gutierrez, being a man of some honor, believed it was his duty to get to Sam before they did.

And what then?

Then Gutierrez would place him under arrest and he would stand trial for shooting him. But he had to find him first and after some ten days on his trail, he realized that would be no easy thing. Perhaps it was impossible, but he would attempt it. Race and Denver Spenning were cattle rustlers, horse thieves, deviants, and a general nuisance in Junction City. And they were also cold-blooded killers. If they got to Sam first, well then, Gutierrez would see to it that they both hanged.

He considered this a reasonable course of action.

But stopping the Spenning brothers from killing Sam was only part of the reason he took to the trail. There was another, darker reason, one that troubled him deeply. The evening that Sam shot him, he remembered the swarming flies. It had been absolutely unnatural. There had literally been thousands of them. He could still feel them covering him, biting and nipping. But minutes later, after he'd been shot, they were gone. And how did one explain that? That episode combined with crazy tales that came out of the Buffalo Head saloon concerning a veritable storm of maggots, made him wonder about Sam Bouchard.

Who he was.

What he was.

And what sort of terrible things were haunting him.

The longer he was on the trail, seeing things, hearing things, Gutierrez began to wonder if this was a business he wanted any part of. His next intimation that there was something very unnatural in the wind came at a little town called Apaxis on a fork of the Verdigris River. There was very little left of it. It had once been a rail town, but the railroad had bypassed it several years before when the local gypsum mine all but played out. A freak lightning strike had set the town to burning a few years after that.

These were the facts that Gutierrez knew, mainly by hearsay. When he rode in that day, there was very little to see but debris and timbers overgrown by wild grasses, the remnants of a road, a scattering of black and craggy trees. The only thing that still stood was a ruined church and that creaked and groaned in the wind. He would have ridden right through, save that he saw six or seven bodies heaped before the church steps. They had been well-picked by buzzards. Such was their condition, it was really hard to know how they had died.

As he stood there, wondering and thinking, he heard a voice whispering inside the church. He went in there and found a dying man with his head resting on a flower-pattered carpet bag that was filthy and ragged. The man was dressed in a sheepskin coat and his blood, much of it dried, had pooled out all around him.

"What happened here, my friend?" Gutierrez asked.

The man tried to focus his glassy eyes, pausing in his prayers to a god that had apparently forsaken him. The man said that he had been living in the church with a group of squatters for many months, minding his own business (something Gutierrez doubted, figuring he knew a rustler when he saw one). One day a man passed through, a lone man with dark eyes.

"Did you speak with him?"

The dying man hadn't, but from his description—a tall, gaunt man with a mustache and twin ivory-handled Colt pistols—Gutierrez had no doubt that it was Sam Bouchard.

"And he killed your friends?"

The dying man giggled with madness, then coughed out some more blood. "No ... not him, but the one that came after him."

And this was where his story became not only unbelievable, but disturbing in its implications. Gutierrez thought, of course, that it was not one man that followed Sam, but two. Namely, the Spenning brothers. But it wasn't so, according to the dying man.

"Just ... one, son," he managed. "And it weren't a man."

He told his story, proceeding slowly and carefully despite his grievous injuries and pain, as if he was giving his last confession. Gutierrez listened and did not dare interrupt, though, obviously, it was more fever dream than reality. He died moments later and Gutierrez buried him behind the church.

As he rode out of the graveyard wreckage of Apaxis, the dying man's words played through his mind again and again.

The one that came around sundown weren't no man, mister. It was the Devil. Eyes red as blood and the face of a cadaver. It wore a flapping coat of animal skins and human hide and furs spiky with dried blood, all strung together and stitched up with thews. It carried big-bore revolvers and skinning knives long as your arm, and had necklaces of human ears black as figs and all manner of dead things around its throat. And when you shot it, it did not die. It just kept coming and coming, oh sweet Jesus, it just kept coming.

There was something terrible, shocking, and possibly even inhuman in the wind. Of course, as a modern man, relatively well-read, experienced in the ways of frontier men and their penchant for yarning, he tried to dismiss it. But he could not dismiss what happened in Junction City.

Somehow, someway, it was all tied to Samuel Bouchard.

Something inside Gutierrez was awakened, some impending sense of horror perhaps inspired by his Bible-learning and the superstitions he

had heard at his mother's knee. Whatever it was, it would not lie quiet. As much as he told himself that such things as devils and demons and what not were the product of primitive minds, he could not stop the disquiet that began to take hold of him.

19

What kept them going at first was hate. Pure, blind, unreasoning hate. It kept them on the trail of Sam Bouchard, united in that single purpose, even though they could not stand one another.

Race Spenning was a hulking, dusty figure on horseback, a mountain of a man in filthy buckskins with a Parker shotgun laid over his lap and a butcher knife sheathed at his hip. He was a cold-blooded killer with glossy black eyes and a greasy beard that hung to his chest. Very often, the remains of his last meal could be found in it. He was in direct contrast to his brother, Denver, who was small and furtive, like a rodent trying to pass itself off as a man. He wore steel-rimmed glasses, a brushed Stetson, and a fine wool suit. He was immaculate in his appearance, if somewhat reptilian in manner. While Race wantonly murdered for profit, Denver did it because he enjoyed it. He was a dead shot with a Navy six who enjoyed watching the death throes of his victims.

Both were desperate, both were deadly, and neither were gifted with working brains.

They had relied on their older brother, George, for that. He was wily and devious by nature, with a gift for subterfuge that simply eluded the other two. He never came on strong, always appearing weak and indecisive to his enemies, lulling them into a false of security before striking. Under George's leadership, the Spenning brothers stole horses and ran cattle, selling trade whiskey and rifles to the Osage and Cheyenne. But that had all come to an end, of course, when Sam Bouchard killed George at the Briscoe House in Junction City. Without George's mind and connections, they were left in the cold. And they planned on making the man that had taken away their livelihood (not to mention their brother) pay for it.

They trailed Sam for many weeks, and even to their somewhat strained minds, his movements made no sense. He moved west, then east, south, then north. He followed a river for days, then cut across the plains or through a forest. He skirted towns for weeks, then lost himself in them. He seemed to be going in circles with no set destination.

"Like he knows we's after him and he's trying to cover his tracks," Race said.

"If he knew that, then why wouldn't he lay in wait for us? Ye saw him take down George," Denver argued. "He's fast and he's fearless. But he's afraid of something and I wonder what that might be."

These were the sort of conversations the brothers had and never did they reach a common consensus concerning Sam Bouchard. They had dealt, in their time, with all stripes of hustlers, gunmen, thieves, and crooked lawmen. These were their people. Regardless of how dirty and corrupt they were, their actions always made a certain amount of sense when taken as a whole. But not this Bouchard fellow. He was a quandary. He was a special case and without George to do the hard, deep thinking for them, both Race and Denver were simply out of their depth.

Yet, as confused and befuddled as they were, they kept after him. And the longer they were on the trail, the angrier and more frustrated they became. It seemed, they were always one step behind him. Every town and village and desolate trading post they stopped at, it seemed Sam had just left the day before. He passed, people saw him, and that was it.

"But we's gonna get lucky," Race said again and again.

"Ah, just shut up," his brother told him.

When they rode into a little hamlet called Thibedeau on the Texas/Arkansas border, they weren't in much of a mood. Their money was running low and they hadn't had a good meal or a taste of whiskey in days.

Thibedeau was an ugly little place that looked like it had been thrown together out of the discarded scraps of more respectable towns, a collection of shacks and huts and tent-roofed lean-tos crowded together as if they were afraid. It had rained and the streets were rivers of mud, children running about in the slew, chasing livestock—chickens and scrawny pigs—with sticks, either to corral them or beat them senseless.

Dogs were barking and hard-looking men and slatternly women lounged about on stoops. Two men dragged the corpse of a third from a saloon where an out-of-tune fiddle sounded like it was not played with a bow but a saw-toothed file.

While Race took the horses over to a livery, Denver got down to the business of asking questions of the locals. Some said they had not seen anyone answering Sam Bouchard's description, others said so many, many people passed it was hard to say, one hard-bitten trail rider looking much like another in their eyes. Still others would not even answer. One woman spit tobacco juice at him.

Tired of it all, feeling low and ornery, he went into the saloon, pushing through a knot of stumbling drunks. The air in there was close and rank, stinking of body odor, cheap perfume (what his mother had always referred to as *toilet water*), and burnt powder. There was blood on the floor soaking into the sawdust and dirt, which explained the powder smell of a freshly-discharged cap-and-ball pistol and the corpse being dragged down the street. In the corner, sitting atop a pickle barrel, was a one-eyed man playing the fiddle. When Denver looked at him, he grinned with a toothless maw and scraped his fiddle faster, making a fumbling, ear-bleeding attempt at "Buffalo Gals" that had all the finesse of a hacksaw cutting through bone.

Denver grabbed a stool at the bar (which was basically made of planks nailed together) and ordered a whiskey. The keep was a hard man in a leather vest. He had mutton chop whiskers and eyes like a snake.

"If ye would, sir," Denver put to him after paying for his drink. "I'm on the lookout for a fellow name of Sam Bouchard. That name mean anything to ye?"

"It does not," he said. "What you want with him?"

"Why, we're old friends. We was in the war together. I want to hook back up with him."

"In the war, eh?"

"Sure."

"If you say."

"You the law?" another fellow asked him.

Denver chuckled and sipped his whiskey. "No, sir, not me. Fellow

I'm looking for ... oh, ye'd remember him ... sort of hard-looking, I guess ye'd say. Wears a brown duster and bowler hat, fancy lizard boots and ivory-handled pistols. Has a mustache."

A big fellow in wool pants and clumping miner's boots passed by, bumping into Denver and nearly knocking him from his stool.

"Watch where you're sitting, maggot," he said.

Denver found his hand automatically going for the Navy six at his hip. Then, thinking better of it, he smiled his rodent's smile of narrow yellow teeth, and apologized for being in the way in his typically condescending manner.

"I ought to kill you," the big man said and from the look of him—long greasy hair, face etched with knife scars and ancient wounds, the corner of his lips pulled up in a crooked grimace—he appeared to be the sort that did not make idle jests.

People were watching now. Here on this long, dull day which was like so very many in their despairing, throwaway lives, they were maybe going to see another killing. It would be something that would be yarned about for years. The fiddle player let loose with a flurry of shrill, out-of-key notes that were supposed to be "Aura Lee".

"Now, Burt, settle down. The fellow apologized. Be on your way."

"I already killed one man today," he boasted. "A second won't much matter."

The reedy fiddle playing rose in volume.

Denver did not know if Burt was talking to him or the barkeep or both. He was decidedly an evil sort. He carried a nickel-plated .45 Colt on one hip and a skinning knife on the other. He offered Denver a most ugly grin like that of a mad dog considering biting into a leg, then turned away ... then just as fast, he swung around and punched Denver in the face, launching him from his stool. Before he could even get to his gun, Burt was on him, hitting him with a flurry of fists. Then they were tangled together, punching and scratching and screaming at one another while the regulars watched with rapt attention and the fiddler scratched his instrument in harsh, biting accompaniment.

The barkeep figured it was no longer his business. Elbow on the bar top, he sipped a flat beer.

Now Burt and Denver, both bloodied, bruised, and raging, circled one another with knives in their hands.

"Kill you," Burt promised. "Gonna kill you."

Denver spit blood. "Then ye best get to it, cockspur, because I'm going to carve yer balls off."

The locals pressed in closer. Why, this was really going to be one to remember. Nothing like a good knife fight to get the blood pumping. Everyone was so enrapt in the proceedings that they did not notice the hulking man in buckskins step through the door. Swearing under his breath, he knocked them aside and stepped behind Burt and cracked him in the head with the butt of his Parker. Burt folded up, dropped the knife, and Denver did not hesitate—he jabbed him deep in the belly three times with his doubled-edged fighting knife.

"Figured you'd get yourself in trouble," Race said, swinging his shotgun around to see if anyone wanted to dance. There were no takers. Even the fiddle player had stopped piercing eardrums. He watched as did the others as Burt slowly bled out, moaning as he flopped about in a spreading pool of blood.

"Gonna bleed out," someone said.

"Maybe you oughta stick him again, so he don't get away," said another.

"He ain't going anywhere," Denver said. He was crouched next to Burt, studying his death throes in detail, smiling with bloodstained teeth, a droplet of pink drool rolling down his chin. "He's dying slow and in terrible pain. Ain't that so, Burt? Ain't ye hurting something terrible? Bet ye wish it'd just be over with, don't ye? That ye'd just die and be done with." Denver giggled, adjusting his spectacles. "But it ain't gonna be so. Ye gonna be squirming here in yer own blood for many long hours."

Race ordered bacon and beans from the barkeep and scooped them from a tin plate with a wooden spoon, slurping and sucking them up, oblivious to the amount which lodged in his beard. "We riding out when I'm finished," he announced. "We don't have no time for no slow dying."

But Denver shook his head. "Gotta wait to the end, brother of mine. Sometimes ... sometimes they says real interesting things right afore their candle's blown out."

The regulars drank their beers, intrigued by Denver. He was one cold-blooded sonofabitch and he fascinated them.

"Seen a fellah one time, Burt, that was gut-shot, and it took him near on twelve hours to extinguish. Never seen a man with so much damn blood in him." Denver licked drool from his mouth. "How much ye figure ye lost so far, Burt? A pint or two? Gotta be all that." He took Burt's gun and gathered up his knife, looking at the knot of anxious faces. He dug into his coat and slapped two silver coins on the floor. "Got me two dollars here that says he's dead in two hours. Anyone want to take that?"

"Ain't gonna be no betting," Race said. "We get places to get to."

"Ye hear that, Burt? My brother don't have time for this nonsense." He scooped up his money and put it back in his coat. "A shame, a real shame. We got ourselves some real gaming to be done and my brother wants to hurry on out the door. What ye say about that, Burt? What's that? Didn't quite catch it, son."

Burt was soaked red, blood gurgling from his mouth.

"Yep. Terrible waste, Burt. I agree." Denver sighed, took Burt's knife and slit his throat with it. Standing up, he sighed and tipped his hat to all present. "Well, barkeep, ye can have his gun and his knife to pay for burial and what not."

As they walked out the door, the regulars studied Burt's final seconds with barely restrained glee, and the old man started scratching on his fiddle again, knocking out a dissonant version of "Devil's Dream," which seemed more than fitting to the occasion.

20

It came to pass that Angeline could take it no more. The terror she felt for Maddie became a living, breathing contagion inside her that tormented her constantly. Though Maddie had warned her to stay away, sometimes pleading in a broken voice, Angeline decided that enough was enough. She either got her friend to see reason or she would go to the proper authorities and have her committed. It was all that was left to do.

She still had a key to Maddie's rooms, so she used it one morning, stepping into the hot, fetid darkness that smelled of human filth and rotten food scraps. This was Maddie's lair and she saw a thin, hunched shape scurry from the light that came in through the open door, seeking the coveting darkness.

"Maddie?" she said, her voice thin and weak.

There was no answer, but she could hear her in the sitting room, breathing with a phlegmy tubercular rattle. There was a shape in the darkness near the window, a nodding form wrapped in what might have been a blanket.

Swallowing her fear, Angeline closed the door behind her, stepping into the short corridor that led to the sitting room. She paused at the doorway, feeling the beat of her heart in her chest. *Maddie's quite possibly insane now,* she thought with dismay. *You must accept the fact that she might not even recognize you and if she does, she might be become violent at any moment.*

Breathing fast, she took a single step into the room.

"Maddie?" she called again, this time with slightly more volume.

"I asked you not to come back," said a low, dry voice from the darkness. "I begged you not to."

"But I'm worried."

That got a wizened tittering from her friend. She could just make out her blanketed form situated there between the cold fireplace and the window with the heavy velour curtain pulled over it. A scant wedge of light came around its edge and she could see that Maddie had degenerated into a broken old woman. The light illuminated a tress of scraggly hair and a hand like the shrunken, mummified claw of an eagle that clutched the blanket.

Maddie's lips parted with a crackling sound. "Say … say what it is you want," she said in the voice of a beldame withered by the years.

"I want you to let me bring a doctor here," Angeline told her, coming right out with it. "You need … care."

Maddie uttered a low cackling. Angeline felt fear like a cold brick drop into her chest. *That's not her … it can't be her. Oh, good God, it can't be her.* The terror she knew at that moment was primitive and instinctual. It lingered inside her, the fear of the unknown and alien things beyond comprehension, the sense that her friend had been taken over by a sentient, living malignancy.

"You must leave," Maddie said in her wheezing voice. "If you make it angry, it'll never let you leave these rooms alive."

Angeline shook her head from side to side, telling herself that Maddie was not possessed by evil, but completely insane, but she did not believe it for a moment. The shadowy form before her was not simply mad in the head, it was physically and spiritually deranged. And, then, Maddie let the blanket fall away and in that feeble shaft of light she could see enormous breasts like cow udders fat with milk and a hugely swollen, bloated belly whose skin was scaly like the underside of a reptile. It was a grotesquely exaggerated pregnancy that could not be real and as she watched with escalating atavistic horror, she saw that the belly moved ... shuddering, contracting, pulsating like a beating heart.

The ragged hole of Maddie's mouth said, "Go ... you must go now ... it's ... it's becoming unmanageable."

But something in Angeline refused to leave, even though common sense told her to get out of there as fast as she possibly could. She stepped closer, the hot fermenting stink of what grew inside Maddie making her head swoon and her guts roil with bile. Maddie made a hissing sound like a cat and Angeline cringed, but only momentarily. Overwhelmed by love for her friend, by curiosity and anger at the entire situation, she moved quickly, grabbing the curtain and yanking it open.

Maddie screamed as if boiling water had been thrown in her face. She had become a lolling, throbbing carcass of flesh yellow as chicken bones. Her skin rippled with terrible soft pulsations, leathery hands quickly covering her eyes which were like the gray meat of oysters bulging from their shells. But the very worst thing was her belly and what pressed up against the thin, rubbery membrane of flesh from the inside like a mask: the grinning, simian face of the imp.

What happened then was forever blotted from Angeline's memory. She screamed. She backed away. She tripped over a chair, scrambling drunkenly to her feet as a terror that was white-hot burned through her like carbolic acid. And in her head, she heard the voice of the imp squeaking like a gate on rusty hinges, *Run, Angeline, run you little whore, because one of these nights I'll crawl into your bed and press my hot, lice-hopping nappy body up to you and slide my cock into you and it'll be cold as a corpse when I fill you with my seed and plant my garden in the well-fertilized soil of your womb.* These words were like an icy needle sliding into her brain.

It took many, many days for her to come out of the shrieking madness that owned her after that morning. But one thing was certain—she never, ever returned to Maddie's rooms.

21

Fort Smith, Arkansas.

It was as good of a place as any to lay low. After a time, he started wondering if he was losing his mind, holed up with his guns, crucifix, and gris-gris, praying to any that might listen. That made him get out of his North Street hotel and wander the city. It was important for him to act like a man, regardless of what might come. He wouldn't let them take that away from him.

But they already have, he often thought. *They already have.*

In those days, the greatest tourist attraction in Fort Smith was the Federal Courthouse for the Western District of Arkansas. It was here that Judge Issac Parker operated. His U.S. Marshals had jurisdiction over Indian Territory, a vicious no-man's land of marauding gangs, bootleggers, and killers. People would line up to watch the prison wagons coming in, then fill the courthouse to see Judge Parker dispense justice.

Sam was there one warm afternoon, marshals with Winchester rifles leading in a group of Choctaw and white-trash thieves in leg irons. That's when he saw the black man in the courthouse. He was young and well-dressed, his eyes shining like oiled ball bearings.

And those eyes were on Sam.

Sam got out of there quick, but the black fellow caught up with him soon enough. He threw something at Sam—a little black ball.

It was made of wax rolled up with flakes of corpse flesh and hair. In Voudoun circles, it was known as a witch ball or conjure ball. It was a curse gris-gris, meant to bring about death and misfortune.

Sam ran and the black fellow followed, as Sam knew he would. He led him into an alley that cut alongside a big, gothic-looking brewery. When he came around the corner, Sam was waiting there with Colt pistols in hand.

The man looked at the guns, seemed unimpressed. His face was black and shiny, the whites of his eyes shot through with pink blood vessels. "A place has been prepared for you, Samuel Bouchard," he said. "A cold place."

"I got business elsewhere," Sam said, beyond angry, beyond frustrated, a hatred that was white-hot and smoldering filling him up now.

The black fellow was watching the guns in Sam's hands as a mouse might watch a rattlesnake, knowing that death was near.

"It's always been my practice never to shoot an unarmed man," Sam said. "But you're no man. You worship the serpent and call the dead from their rest. You're vile. You're a pestilence."

The black fellow did not try to deny it and that only made Sam that much angrier because the score was never settled and they never stopped hounding him. He jerked the triggers of his pistols, making the black fellow dance and shudder and finally go down, spilling his life from smoking holes punched in his belly.

Then Sam went back to his room, knowing it was never going to end.

But also knowing it would not be easy for them, that he would take as many of them with him as humanly possible.

This was his vow to himself.

§

That night, he could smell it on the wind: a high, hot putrescence.

In the corridor outside his hotel room, there was a bone lying in the middle of the floor. Sam went cold at the sight of it. He figured it was a dog's bone. He saw plainly that his name was scratched into it. He did not step over it. He stepped *around* it, got into his room and waited for what came next, loading his weapons and making sure his knife was sharp. He had planned on taking the usual precautions to ensure that no one jumped him whilst he slept: tin cans hanging from the window sash and bottles before the door, but that wouldn't be necessary now.

He thought: *You can't go on week after week like this. You can't subsist on a few nightmare-ridden, sweat-soaked hours of sleep.*

He knew it was true. He'd lived like that during the war, in a perpetual state of exhaustion and confusion, marching from one battlefield to the next with rarely anything more than coffee or a few beans in his belly. After a time, the physical and mental fatigue got the better of you and everything became lost in a gray fog. You were not sure of the day or month. One blood-soaked battleground was much like another. One soldier with a gun looked like any other and it seemed that you killed the same men again and again, their ghosts rising to torment you in a charnel mist and a smoke of vengeance.

When you drove yourself like that for any length of time, your nerves went and your guts filled with butterflies, your hands shook and you made mistakes, awful mistakes.

And that's what they want: they want you tired and worn and half out of your mind with terror. That way, your own memories haunt you, your guilt torments you, and you bleed yourself dry one cut at a time.

"Dammit," he said under his breath. "Concentrate."

Yes, that was important because the haunting was coming again. They were throwing another nightmare at him and he had to be ready. He didn't give a good goddamn what Crazy Horse had said, it was *never* a good day to die.

He waited there, feeling the guns in his hands … only their weight seemed wrong. Familiar, yet wrong. And he soon saw why. In his hands were not his Colt Peacemakers but the Remington Army .44s that he carried in the war. But that was not possible; they had been taken from him when he was captured at Hatcher's Run. No, no, he was hallucinating again or being *made* to hallucinate.

He blinked his eyes and shook the ghosts from his head. There. Better. The Colts were in his hands. He swallowed dry fear. He listened.

Outside the door, he heard something. A light step ... a scratching. Then feet padding away.

Hell was this?

Curiosity trumped fear and anger trumped anxiety. He went to the door and unlocked it. *Okay, then. Let it come.* He heard nothing but the thump of his own heart as he threw the door open. There was nothing in the corridor but shadows bunching in the corners, sculpted into phantoms by the flickering gaslight. He knew better than to look too hard into them. When he did that, they trapped his mind and showed him the grinning faces of those long dead.

Trying to draw you out. That's what this is about.

Right then, for the first time in what seemed many days, he felt his old confidence seep back into him. There was steel in his eye and iron in his guts and fear was no longer part of his natural rhythms. Good, good. Fear was their tool. It was one of their primary weapons that made their victims defeat themselves. It no longer possessed him. Feeling oddly invincible, he moved down the corridor to what waited there.

It would come.

And it did.

About twenty feet from him where the corridor dead-ended at the turn of the stairwell, he saw the air began to shiver, to roil. It was like a door opening and he saw something waiting there, something huge and bristled. Another hell-swine, this one a boar. Although he knew deep inside himself what the significance of that was, he refused to weaken himself by admitting to it. The monstrous hog waited there, its nares puffing out white steam, its malevolent eyes like smoldering red coals. Its flesh was humped and ropy, white as whalebone, its tusks gleaming and anxious to rip him open.

It stepped out of the roiling shadows that shimmered like desert heat waves, snorting and squealing, its hooves thumping on the floor. Sam could feel a sickening sort of warmth rolling off of it that reminded him of fevers and stank of sick wards. As he waited for it, everything inside him shaking, he realized just what a massive beast it was. He bet there was an easy ton of meat on it. It was larger than any swine had a right to be.

"Come on then," he said, waiting for it with pistols in his hands and knowing that they would never stop a thing like this.

The beast stomped and pawed at the floor, blowing steam and exhaling fetid breath that was cold as the grave. It was a ghost and he knew it was a ghost, but that made it no less deadly in his mind. Maybe it really wasn't there and maybe it was. If it was indeed a phantom, only his belief in its reality would kill him, but if it was real …

It charged.

Pushing a rolling wave of frigid air before it, it bore down on him, seeming to grow larger and larger until it was like an immense steam locomotive coming at him.

Then it wasn't there at all.

There was only a man named Samuel Bouchard with pistols in his hands, sweating and gasping, shriveling yellow with absolute fear. His face was beaded with sweat, his heart banging away in his chest.

"Mister … you all right?" a voice said.

Like a slap across the face, Sam came out of it. Maybe it was real and maybe it was fantasy and maybe it was a little of both and neither. He blinked a few times and saw a portly man standing there in a doorway. There was a gun under his coat.

Sighing, Sam leathered his Colts. "Thought I saw something … it's nothing. Pay no mind to me."

"You should be careful with those guns so no innocent pays the price."

Sam wanted to tell him to mind his own damn business, but he didn't. He had the strangest feeling that even if he said such a thing, it would be beyond this man to comply.

"Name's Jeb Altoon," he said, offering his hand.

Sam refused to shake it and part of the reason was that he didn't want Altoon seeing how bad his hand shook and another reason was because this Mr. Altoon was a little too familiar for his own good. Sam was sure he knew him from somewhere … but where was that?

"I'll bid you goodnight," Sam said, backing away toward his own door.

Altoon watched him, a greasy smile on his face, his eyes filled with secrets that were dirty and low.

"Got a bottle in my room if you want to talk about it," he said.

"I don't," Sam said.

He stood in his doorway until Altoon disappeared into his own. He lit a cigarette and leaned there, thinking, trying to remember. His brain wasn't working so well these days. Altoon's face meant something and he should have been able to remember what. *Think, think.* By the time he finished his smoke it came to him. That cocky smile. That piggish face. Yes, he had seen it before. Once in a saloon in Junction City, then again outside a whorehouse in Epsipalia. And hadn't he been in the crowd outside the courthouse in Fort Smith? Sam was almost certain he had seen those eyes watching him there, too.

Your path is willy-nilly, he told himself. *The chances that Altoon is following the same one is pretty remote, don't you think?*

Finishing his cigarette, he stepped back into his room. He stared over at the rumpled bed. There had been a time when a bed meant sleep, it meant rest, it meant shutting his eyes and awaking refreshed. But that time was gone. Now he looked at the bed as a nest of nightmares. He wouldn't sleep again this night and if he did, God help him. Sighing, he pushed the door closed with the heel of his boot and heard something thump against it.

He whirled around, the pistols in his hands.

Oh ... oh Christ ... not that ... not that ...

He saw a leathery brown sac hanging from the coat hook on the door. It looked large enough to hold something maybe the size of a melon, but he knew what was in there was nothing like that. This was bad. He shouldn't have been surprised because the haunting was getting worse week by week, yet he *was* surprised because he knew this sort of thing was black medicine that took a lot of power and knowledge to create. This was more than haunts and nightmare visions and hell-boars.

Sweat running down his face, he could almost smell the hot Caribbean jungle again. He tried to think about what he must do now, but his head was not clear.

He stared at the sac, knowing it—and what was inside it—was for him and no one else.

You could run, he told himself, *before it has time to finish. You could run hell for leather.*

Yes, but this was heavy conjuring and if they had gone to the trouble to bring it down upon him, they would not give up and maybe some night, as he thrashed in the throes of a nightmare, they would bring this thing to him again … only he would not be able to defend himself.

He leathered one of his pistols and slid his Green River knife from its sheath. Carefully, he moved in closer to the sac. It was pulsing slowly, expanding and deflating like a breathing lung. He could feel the waves of sickly heat emanating from it. His hands were shaking and his stomach had rolled over in his belly like a pill bug. The sac was breathing harder now with a low hissing respiration. He could hear something moving in there, shifting like a fetus in a womb. And now a sort of scratching noise. *Scritch, scritch, scritch.* A bead of perspiration rolled down his forehead. His eyes were bulging from their sockets. The terror inside him was huge and white and he could not get it under control.

Trying to control his own breathing, he jabbed the sac with his knife and it swung back and forth from the coat hook. Something scratched in there again like a rat pawing inside a wall.

Go ahead, the sac seemed to be saying to him. *Slice me open, because the sooner you do, the sooner you're going to see what I am.*

Sick with fear, sweating inside his own skin, Sam jabbed it with the knife again, and then he slashed it. The knife was sharp, a three-inch slit opening in the sac like a mouth. Black juice dripped free, and its stink was like rotting fish, unclean and horridly fetid. Through the slit, he could see three or four gleaming yellow teeth set in gray, puckered gums. He could hear the teeth grinding, blubbery lips smacking, a pink tongue licking over them.

Remember? Remember how it looked the last time you saw one of these? How the flesh seemed to move over the tiny bones beneath? How it seemed to … wriggle?

Sam was overwhelmed with terror now and as he backed away, he did not even try to stifle the scream that came from his mouth as the birth sac continue to shear open, what was inside ready to be born. Only no scream came out, just a dry exhalation of air that quickly became a high, mad moaning in his throat.

He saw two little hands that were gray and wrinkly emerge. They were tipped with tiny black claws. They gripped the torn edges of the sac and pulled it apart like a man opening a curtain. The sac tore completely, more of that reeking black filth gushing out and hitting the floor like wet vomit. The pool of drainage rippled on the floor, things moving in it, worming things and crawling things. The hot stench of it filled the room with a toxic, miasmic gas that was hot and nauseating.

By then, Sam had backed away to the bed.

Whether it was the stink or the fouled air itself, he did not know, but he could barely stay on his feet. The room tilted this way and that with vertigo. His head spun, his knees rubbery. He saw tiny purple dots before his eyes.

The thing, that hideous diminutive thing, had emerged completely now, pushing itself free like a freak birth from a placenta. It was greased with amniotic fluids and pink chunks of tissue, hanging there from the sac by one hand, dangling back and forth like a swollen spider on a thread. It was about the size of a Raggedy Ann doll, maybe a bit bigger, a bloated and fleshy thing with sticklike limbs and skin that was the gleaming pink of a skinned rabbit streaked with gray, tiny black bristles poking out like the thorns of a rose stem. Sam could see a networking of black veins pulsing beneath its flesh. Its face was wizened and shriveled, looking like that of a hairless grotesque ape, its black doll's eyes glistening, its mouth huge and filled with gnashing teeth like a wind-up monkey. It had no nose, just a triangular depression where one might sit, matted oily black hair sprouting from the crown of the skull.

It watched him.

It grinned at him.

Slime and black jelly dripped from it.

It made no hostile moves, and that was because it was biding its time, as things like it always did. It knew his head wasn't right. It knew the air was bad. It knew the lack of oxygen to his brain was making him light-headed and giddy. It was waiting for him to drop. It was waiting for him to go out cold. Then it would come for him, and he knew very well what it would do. It would bite him, and it would keep biting him until the agony drove him insane, and then, and only then, would it tear out his throat.

He tried to aim his short-barreled Peacemaker at it, but his vision was blurring and he saw two of them dangling there with pendulum strokes. The gun in his hand had become a Remington Army .44 from the war again.

Focus, you have to focus.

He squeezed the trigger and a slug punched a hole in the door, a good six inches from its target. He fired again and this time his aim was so far off he put a hole a good foot away from the little creature. He thought he heard it laugh with a rasping sort of sound, but maybe that was his imagination. His knees finally gave way and he sat roughly on the bed. He could hear voices from down the corridor. *That crazy man in Twelve was shooting his irons off!* The voices stayed distant. Nobody was about to come to the door when a drunken lunatic had pistols in his hands. No, they would wait for the law or for him to pass out or run out of ammunition.

But then someone did.

There was a rapping of knuckles on the door.

"GET AWAY!" he shouted. "GET THE FUCK AWAY FROM HERE IF YOU KNOW WHAT'S GOOD FOR YOU!"

But whoever it was kept rapping their knuckles. The creature dangled there, licking its thick lips and grinding its teeth. It was amused, terribly amused.

"Mr. Bouchard!" a voice said. "Please, Mr. Sam Bouchard! It is I, Jeb Altoon! We met earlier! Please let me help you!"

"GO AWAY!"

And Sam realized at that moment, despite his head being filled with drifting goose down, that he had never told Altoon his name. He had not even shaken his hand. Which only proved that seeing him around had been no accident.

"I'm coming in," Altoon said.

In his near-delirium, Sam almost laughed.

The door was not locked and he indeed came right in, standing there with a scowl on his face, a .31 Cooper pistol in his hand. Just by the way he held it with ease and confidence told Sam that he knew how to use it and he had used it many times. He wrinkled his nose at the awful stench in the room.

"Why don't you set that Colt down, Mr. Bouchard?" he said. "There's gonna be no trouble now."

"You should leave before it's too late."

"I think we could talk better without that jewelry in your hand."

Sam looked at the gun. No, he wasn't about to put it down. He couldn't afford to.

Altoon sighed and flashed a Pinkerton badge at him. "I trailed you across Indian Territory, up into Kansas and down into Texas and now back to Arkansas. I don't know who you're hiding from or what you're running from, but I can offer you protection."

Sam lowered his pistol, knowing full well he was in no shape to use it. "Who hired you?"

"Don't know. I get wires. You've led me on a merry chase. Before you get riled up … understand that I'm not here to arrest you on anything, I'm merely reporting your movements to my superiors."

"Report them to who exactly?"

"Don't know."

Sam grinned, his eyes stark and mad as they darted to what waited behind the door and back to Altoon. "Well, I'll tell you. It's a woman. A creole bitch out of Guadeloupe, well-spoken like an educated white, a French-Carib accent just as smooth as cream. Her eyes are yellow and full of hate and when she takes a strong disliking of you, she'll call demons out of hell to settle you."

"You're out of your mind," Altoon said and Sam could see he was thinking about shooting.

"Am I? Then maybe you ought to see what's behind the door."

Altoon's breathing had increased now. He looked uncomfortable in his skin. Never taking his eye off of Sam and his Colt, he reached an arm out, stepped aside and slammed the door shut. He had time to see the rent leathery bag hanging there and the little manikin dangling by one wrinkled hand from it. His mouth opened and he said, "What the hell is that?" And then the creature launched itself at him with a shrieking *SKREEEEEEEEE!* and its teeth clamped down on his gun hand. Altoon cried out and fired a single shot as his hand jerked and Sam felt the bullet pass over his head and punch into the wall.

Altoon fell back and hit the door, sliding down its length as he squirmed and fought, trying to tear the little horror from his hand. The thing would not let go. Its jaws clamped all that much tighter and Sam clearly heard Altoon's knuckles break with a wet snapping. The creature ripped at them, pulling out red strings of mangled gristle, biting and biting again.

The Pinkerton detective screamed his mind away as the little creature darted about in a blur, biting and biting and biting. It tore a shank of bloody meat from his throat. It nipped off the end of his nose. It divorced him of three fingers. It ripped his lower lip free. Then it jumped down his legs as he flailed at it, his mutilated hand spraying blood against the wall. It clamped its teeth between his legs and Altoon screamed with a piercing, girlish sort of sound as something beneath the teeth—two things, in fact—went with a rubbery popping noise like walnuts.

"EYAHHH! YAHHH! YAHHHHHHHH!"

Sam felt immense pity for him as any man would have, but there was nothing he could do for him. Already the room was spinning and his vision was blurring. He tried once, vainly, to find his feet but his knees were filled with pudding and he fell back on the bed. The most he could do was scoot up into the corner, wedge himself between the headboard and the wall, fighting to stay conscious as the fumes in the room overwhelmed him like poison gas.

The voices in the corridor got louder, but no closer. Nobody dared come to the door and peer inside. Not with what they were hearing. Sam made to call out to them but his voice was barely above the mew of a kitten.

Altoon was not dead.

Broken by fear and insane with agony, but not dead. He crawled over the floor like a living carcass, webbed with blood, mouth frozen in a scream. He inched forward slug-like, leaving a greasy trail of fluids in his wake. The manikin rode him like a conjoined twin, still nipping and biting, squealing with delight at its victim's degradation and madness.

Sam tried to get it in his sights, but its image kept blurring. His mind was filled with black fuzz that was thickening and closing off his thoughts. Everything was narrowing to a pinhole.

He needed air, good breathable air, to clear his head.

Since he couldn't draw a bead on the doll-like form tormenting Altoon, he fired twice in the general direction of the window and heard the glass shatter with both rounds.

But that was all he heard because he blacked out.

He wasn't out long.

A few minutes at most. The fresh air revived him. He could feel it blowing in through the window. His eyes opened and his vision was clear. The Colt was still in his hand. He made a quick assessment of his body and he was in one piece. From where he was sitting, he could see Altoon sprawled, one hand reaching toward the door.

He was not moving.

He was a corpse.

And under the circumstances, that was the most he could aspire to. Sam licked his lips, scanning back and forth for the manikin. His head was clear now. Terror was crouching in his belly, but he trusted in his abilities as a shootist. If the thing showed itself, he could hit it.

But where was it?

It's here. You know it's here. It's trying to make you crack.

He wondered if he was giving the little monster too much credit, but he didn't think so. There was an incarnate evil directing that thing and it liked very much to toy with its victims. It was here. And it would show itself at a time of its own choosing. It could have been anywhere. Under the bed was his guess. Just waiting for him to step down so it could seize his ankle in its teeth.

Listen.

Yes, he was almost sure he could hear it breathing with that same low hissing that had come from the leathery birth sac. But it was subtle, barely there, and he could not place it. The thing was, he had to make this happen because any minute now the sheriff and his boys were going to show with a whole lot of questions that Sam did not want to answer.

The breathing, thin and reedy.

It seemed louder as if the creature was getting excited and maybe it was. He could hear it gnashing its teeth. It was either under the bed or on the floor near the bed, biding its time.

He did not move.

Let it think he had passed out again. Sam nudged his pillow and let it fall to the floor. He immediately heard the telltale *click-click-click* of its tiny feet. It *had* been under the bed and now it rushed out to attack. It stopped somewhere near the end of the bed.

Its breathing was faster.

It was grinding its teeth harder.

It couldn't wait much longer. Sam instinctively sensed this. He did not know much about what brought such a monstrosity into being, but he was willing to bet that it was of limited duration. The creature's life cycle was winding down even now. It had to attack before its life force ran out.

He did not move.

The manikin made a wheezing sort of sound as it breathed. It was weakening and he knew it. It couldn't play the game much longer, nor could the woman who was directing it, energizing it with her soul and mind, both of which must have been stretched quite near the breaking point.

Now.

He heard a rustling at the foot of the bed. The manikin was climbing up the blankets, breathing heavily, a sweet and gassy stink coming off of it as if it were rotting from the inside out. He saw its little clawed hands grip the coverlet as it pulled itself up into view, a twisted moppet whose bones were bursting through its skin in yellow rungs. A sharp septic stench blew off it. Its flesh was a glaucous gray, a pulsating jelly that could barely hold shape. One of its eyes was missing, the other was a blanched white, and he knew it could barely see … if at all.

It opened its lethal jaws, a steam of putrescence rising from it. He could hear its tiny heart thumping madly in its chest. It gathered itself for attack, its puckered face torn open now in five or six places, lips fragmenting away from shriveled gums and jutting teeth.

"Not this time," Sam said.

He jerked the trigger and ended its miserable existence.

The .45 caliber slug was like a cannon ball striking it. It blew apart, exploding like a bag stuffed with blood and meat. Gore splattered up the walls and over the door where it ran in clotted red streaks. Its tiny bones rattled on the floor and then went still. And somewhere, some distance away, Sam could hear its mistress screaming in pain.

I'm not running anymore. Now I'm the hunter and I'm coming for you, you bitch.

Sam jumped out of bed, threw his few belongings into his bag and went through the shattered window. He dropped his bag into the alleyway below and shimmied down a drainpipe. By the time the sheriff and his men arrived, he was already riding hard toward the outskirts of the city.

22

Maggart crossed the muddy road, his guts tied into reef knots, pushing through a cluster of cowhands. One of them, feeling randy and offended as fools often do, took hold of him, intent, perhaps, on teaching him some respect. But when Maggart put his eyes on him and the cowhand saw what smoldered in them, he backed away. Which was probably the first wise move he'd made all day.

Maggart's hand loosened on the butt of the .36 Colt at his hip. He cast one last burning look at the cowhand and continued up the road to the medicine show. Inside him, there was something black and rotten where, he knew, there had once been a soul. It throbbed weakly inside him like a diseased heart.

A tangle of people were watching a snake-oil salesman hawk his wares, bottles of a patent medicine curative that he promised would relieve joint pain and arthritis, headaches and gout, female complaints and kidney troubles, infertility and hair loss. The tonic was selling well because the gathered sodbusters, dirt farmers, and drifters were desperate people who lived desperate lives. They were always on the lookout for anything that would relieve their suffering. Many of them prayed daily for deliverance, but since God ignored them, they were in the market for anything to alleviate their anguish.

Maggart had no interest in the swill that was being sold, knowing full well its active ingredient was either alcohol or laudanum. He watched the crowd—the grubby, hardscrabble farmers and their families—with a mercenary eye, noticing all the loose children running about.

Several times, as the wheels of his mind turned in dark directions, he tried to walk away, but he knew he couldn't. Not until he had what he had come for.

You dare not disappoint her, he thought. *The bargain has been made and you signed your soul away in blood.*

No, maybe not literally, he figured, but symbolically, yes. The creole witch owned him. He was a puppet on a string and if she wanted him to dance, he would dance. And if she wanted him to do less pleasant things, then he would have no choice but to do them.

But what she asks.

Yes, this was the ultimate damnation. It had been bad enough killing that preacher, even if he was nothing but a parasite that sucked the blood of the unwary and the naïve. He could justify that in a way, but surely not this. God, never this. Not what he had come to do.

Suddenly, standing there, watching the children playing and running about, their miserable lives already plotted out for them, he began to shake. Sweat ran down his face and his teeth chattered. He remembered his mother and how she had tried to beat the black sin out of him, certain that all children were playthings of the Devil. He felt the fear of her now and, more so, the fear of what stood behind her: the church. It was a nameless, formless, ancient sort of terror that seized him. The fear of eternal damnation. Of hell and death and iniquity.

"No," he said under his breath. "I will not do this. I will not make an offering to that hell-spawn."

But the boy, he thought then. *She has the boy. He is dead, but she still has him. She has imprisoned his essence. And though he is dead, he is not dead enough.*

Maggart went to the first saloon he found. He placed a coin on the bar and the whiskey was brought. He swallowed shot after shot of it, telling himself that liquor was an agent of the Devil, too, but that it would give him strength. The strength to live righteously.

But she knew.

Somehow, she always knew when he disobeyed. When he turned against her, disregarded her wishes. *If you do what I ask, in the manner I prescribe, I can give you what you want. I can make your boy alive again. But only if you do what I ask.* He could feel her there, just behind his thoughts. Her anger, the venom that seeped from her.

The whiskey burned as he swallowed it. And as he drank, though he knew it was wrong in so many ways, he prayed in his mind with the voice of the frightened child he had once been. He prayed for deliverance, for piety, for the divine intervention of the Lord and His mighty hand that would swat that heathen, evil, fornicating witch into the blackest pits of hell where she belonged.

Then … something indeed happened. He was filled like an empty cup, but it was not with sanctity or blessed purity but a foulness black as ink. He giggled. He grinned.

"Lots of lovely families in this town," he said to the barkeep. "Lots of beautiful little children."

The barkeep said it was indeed so. That despite the darker elements that were attracted to locales like this, it was a place of families. They were the bones the town was built upon.

"Yes, the children—meek and mild and filled with the love of God," Maggart said, drool trickling down his chin.

No, no, no! he raged inside. *It's her! That witch! She has control of me! Can you not see that?*

But the barkeep, of course, only saw the money that was given to him that could buy as much cheap whiskey as anyone could possibly hope to drink. Maggart paid for one more shot, then, whistling a tune he had never heard before, something low and profane that made him wither inside, he stepped from the saloon and back out into the streets. A few minutes later, he was watching the crowds that watched the snake-oil salesman. But, mostly, he watched the children.

They made him feel hungry inside.

He screamed in his skull, but only the witch heard him, only she could understand the depths of his torment. Her laughter echoed through his mind. She whispered and his body obeyed and he was powerless to stop what it did. The boy it found. The money it gave him to help load a wagon. How his hands gripped the boy's throat and held him until his face was blue, then put him in the sack.

It was only when he led his team out of town that she released him and by then, it was too late, just too late.

23

Since there were things that needed doing and no one else who could do them, Katy Three-Hands took it upon herself to save a heathen whom she did not like nor completely understand in his wicked, wicked ways, but felt compelled to save despite the fact.

As she packed her things for the journey, she thought, *Ah, he is not worthy, oh Lord, yet in mine heart there is pity for he knoweth not what he has trafficked with.* So she would help. Though she did not consider herself necessarily a Christian nor of any conceivable faith, she understood the concept of Christian mercy as it was written, if so very, very rarely practiced by the frauds who praised Jesus in one breath and courted the blackest sin in the very next.

When her belongings were packed out in the wagon, she rode into the center of Epsipalia where those who did not know of her stopped and stared at the crazy old woman in the creaking wagon, which was decorated with a menagerie of dangling hides and snakeskins, rattling bottles and jars, bones and wolfskins and buffalo skulls. Those that did know her, who and, possibly, *what* she was, turned away. Some crossed themselves and pulled their children indoors. Others, who remembered special curatives and charms they had gotten from her, looked down in shame for their dealings with her (and for the fact that they dared not admit in their Christian charity that she had helped them in the first place).

No matter.

Katy did not think less of them (in certain cases, such a thing would not have been possible). They were upright animals pleased by their shiny, well-groomed pelts, deceiving themselves that they were the favored children of the creator that supposedly made them, believing that godliness consisted of showing their dour faces at church each Sunday rather than practicing the tenets of their faith. They were monkeys stroking their shiny fur and peacocks displaying their plumage, all bluster and appearance on the outside, but scuttling mice and scaled serpents under the skin. And when the simple confines of their faith or their rudimentary understanding of medicine could not help them, they turned to her for amulets and charms, forbidden knowledge and witchery as old as Babylon to cure their children and fight the evils of illness and infirmity. But in their black hearts they would never admit to the same.

Shaking her head, she thought, *Turn my eyes from looking at worthless things, and give me life in your ways.* Onward she went with her wagon and team, ignoring those around her, the gossiping women and vile-hearted men, for they were all dust to her, worms of the soil feeding upon the carrion of their lives.

She came to a log store called Burke's Mercantile and stepped inside. She was not unaware that the clientele abandoned the premises upon her entry. The proprietor watched her warily. His name was not Burke, but Steinbull, a man who had once visited her seeking a remedy for impotence, which she sold him in exchange for a store of bacon, flour, and beans (and one that proved a wise investment for him, in that he fathered three children within two years with a randy wife half his age).

"Must you come here?" he said. "There are other stores, other—"

"Silence thy tongue and tend to my needs, or thou shalt be visited by the curse which once plagued thee," she told him. "I seek provisions which are listed upon this paper. Provide them, mine friend, at a reasonable cost or thy manhood will forever shrivel into a boneless mealworm."

"Yes, ma'am," he said, trembling.

He took the paper and filled her order. As he did so, Katy helped herself to a glass of iced apple cider from the barrel in the corner. She drained it and had another.

He wrapped her parcels in linen and paper, secured them with twine.

"Have all you want," he said.

"I shall, and I thank thee."

He quickly packed everything up and brought it out to her wagon. When he returned, he stood there in mute silence.

"Speak what is on thy mind, proprietor."

He swallowed. "Just noticing it looks like you're going on a trip."

"Aye, it is so. A mission of mercy, one might say."

"Will you be back?"

She laughed. "Ah! So that is it, eh? Will the old hag return and roost once again in our fair town? She certainly might if the good Lord favors thee."

"I put lemon drops in with your goods."

"Thou recallest the sweetness of my tooth."

"Yes."

"And how bide thy manly duties?"

"Quite well. Thank you."

Katy helped herself to another glass of the most excellent cider and then went back out to her wagon. To her amusement, a group of children had gathered. They watched her with wide eyes, equally fascinated and frightened by the witch of lore they had heard so much about suddenly appearing in their midst. She studied them beneath the brim of her campaign hat, feeling a tug of remorse at her core. It was a regret well tended in her heart that she had never had children of her own and that the only man that she had ever loved and thought worthy slept in a buried box beneath the spreading branches of an oak tree at the churchyard.

"I regret that I have no black cat nor broom of hazel to entertain thee with, my fine young moppets," she told them. "But ... wait! Watch with thine eyes."

Facing the wagon, she let out a gasp of air and floated four inches off the ground, levitating before their amazed eyes. Three of the children screamed and ran away, two did not.

"It's a trick," a girl said.

"Of course, my child." Katy laughed. "Now it will be up to thee to figure out how I did it."

She left them with that bit of simple magic in their lives, climbing up into the wagon and moving on down the street. There were dozens of simple parlor tricks she could have amused them with, but there was no more time. She needed to reach Sam Bouchard before it was too late, if it wasn't already.

24

The deceased was a white female of approximately 28 years, examined in situ. She was supine on the floor near the hearth of the sitting room, face to the wall, left arm extended, right arm close to the body. Legs were drawn up. Physiognomy indicated extreme duress at, or shortly before, the time of death. Surface decomposition had commenced and it is estimated the body lay undiscovered for three to four days after death.

The body was greatly emaciated and no food was discovered in the stomach. Due to the lack of blood internally, it is suggested that the deceased died of extreme exsanguination of a degree I have never previously encountered. There were many scars and contusions on the belly, breasts, and arms, as well as ulcerated sores and a highly peculiar squamous condition to the skin.

On the throat and breasts, clear-cut punctures were discovered. They were deep with a downward deviation. They were delivered post mortem, possibly by the teeth of an unknown animal.

Examination of the internal organs clearly indicated an inexplicable necrosis.

The abdomen was laid completely open, possibly by a surgical knife. Again, this is believed to have been done post mortem. The intestines, completely severed from their mesenteric attachments, were discovered several feet away from the body. From the pelvis, the uterus and its appendages had been entirely removed. No trace of them has been found. The incisions were cleanly cut, avoiding the rectum, and dividing the vagina low enough to avoid injury to the cervix uteri.

The work appears to be that of an expert, one, at least, who had such knowledge of anatomical or pathological examinations as to be enabled to secure the pelvic organs with decisive incisions. The appearance of the cuts confirmed the opinion that the instrument had been of a very sharp character. The mode in which the knife had been used seemed to indicate great anatomical knowledge.

Dr. Joseph Petard, Coroner,
East Baton Rouge Parish

Addendum: The deceased has been identified as Madelyn Borcheaux of 207 Lafayette Street

25

Gutierrez found bones.

Circles of bones. There seemed to be no rhyme or reason to any of it. He found them in open grasslands, the mud flats of river cuts, dry stream beds, and in buffalo wallows hemmed in by Indian grass taller than a man.

When he discovered the first circle at the foot of a bridge spanning the Verdigris, he paused on his mare, studying it, more than a little puzzled. He dismissed it as possibly an altar of some local tribe, the meaning of which no white man could ever fathom.

Then he found another.

And another.

Both many miles apart, but nearly identical. At the center was a jawless human skull, boiled white and quite fresh by the looks of it. It was surrounded by a ring of bones—femurs, ulnas, tibias, rib bones, and vertebrae. Some were the bones of men and others clearly those of diverse animals: wolves or dogs, coyote and rabbit, birds and reptiles. There seemed to be no definitive pattern. Only that the ring around the skull would be circled by another, larger ring in a concentric pattern.

But what did it mean? What was it saying?

Though he was essentially on a manhunt, he became more than a little concerned about the bone totems (if that's what they were). And what troubled him greatly were the dead animals between the rings. He found rattlers and rat snakes, mice and voles, hares and woodchucks, hawks and warblers. Even a full-grown bobcat once. Though it seemed more than a little fanciful, he began to wonder if any animal that passed into the rings died. His common sense—which was beginning to fray at that point—told him the idea was ridiculous. Yet he could not entirely dismiss it.

But if that could not be, then how did the animals get within the circles?

Were they killed elsewhere and brought there as part of some religious ritual? Or was he putting too much thought into something that was merely the work of an unbalanced mind? Whatever the answer was, he noticed that at each site it was an ongoing affair: while many of the animals had been dead for days, others were quite fresh, recent additions.

He came upon an Indian man fishing on a creek bank with a stick and twine. Though he looked old, it was really hard to say. Sometimes you could never tell if they were thirty or seventy because a life spent in the wind and baking sun had a way of prematurely aging them. He was dressed like a white, in cord trousers and an old flannel shirt, so it was hard to guess which tribe he was affiliated with.

"You wish something of me?" the old man finally said, his body language making it apparent that he was not comfortable being alone with an armed white.

Gutierrez climbed out of leather, holding the reins, doing his best to appear harmless. "You speak the language, sir."

"I speak it."

"Will you answer a question?"

"If I can."

"Downstream, about three or four miles, I found bones. A display of bones and dead animals."

The old man had been jigging his line. Now he stopped. "I have see it," he said.

He still hadn't looked at Gutierrez and Gutierrez had a feeling he never would. The question made him nervous. That much was obvious.

"Do you know what it means?"

"I do not."

"It isn't something from the tribes?"

"No."

"You're sure?"

The old man sighed. "Once, long ago, I was a Sauk who knew many things, but now I am just an Indian who knows nothing." He jigged his line a couple times. "I hear stories. The bones mean death to anything that crosses them, so I stay away from them. When you see them, you should do likewise. If you want to live."

"But how can that be, sir?"

"I do not know. As an Indian who knows nothing, I cannot guess. As a Sauk, I would say the medicine of the bones is strong."

"Do you know who built it?"

He shook his head. "No. I have said what there is to say."

Gutierrez went on his way because he knew he'd get no more from him. When an Indian did not wish to speak, nothing could compel him to. Discourse was a white man's art that the Indian had no use for and did not trust.

In the coming days, he heard stories from farmers and hunters, saloon-keepers and drifters riding the grub line ranch to ranch. Some had seen Sam or thought they had. Others were certain they had spotted the Spenning brothers. When they learned there was no bounty on any of them, they quickly lost interest.

In the Oklahoma panhandle, a drunken ridge rider told him there was something malevolent moving across the plains that left death in its wake. That it was tied in with the bone displays. But regardless of how much whiskey Gutierrez poured into him, he would not say how or dare to put a name to it.

Four days after his chat with the Indian, he found another bone totem. It was, again, identical to the others and like them, it bothered him immeasurably and he was not sure exactly why. Anxiety filling his belly like poison, he stood there, his breath hot in his throat, staring at the dead animals from a safe distance.

Funny, he got to thinking, *all this carrion and not a single buzzard circling.* And that made him realize that he had seen no buzzards or crows, flies or maggots on the other dead animals either. That was more than a little unusual. Then he thought, *And funny how these totems seem to always be directly on Sam Bouchard's trail, like arrows pointing in his direction.*

These unpleasant revelations had barely passed through his mind when he saw a bald eagle swoop down, intrigued by the easy pickings. It circled the totem three times, preparing to land ... then it seized up with a terrible, uncharacteristic squawking and fell from the sky, landing between the rings. A dead raven to one side and a porcupine to the other, it shuddered and went still.

Gutierrez was shuddering himself by then. He crossed himself, muttering, *"Jesucristo, protégenos del mal ... amen."* Then he was on his mare, riding hell for leather down a buffalo path, fearing for his immortal soul.

When he stopped that night, he stayed close to the fire, drinking coffee but unable to eat. All night long, the wind blowing through the tallgrass sounded like whispering voices.

26

For many days there was nothing, but Sam did not dare let his guard down. *It's still out there,* he thought. *Do not for a moment think it's not. It's biding it's time. It's waiting for you to relax, then it will begin again.* He settled into a rough-and-tumble Texas panhandle town called Tascosa, which was less than an hour from Epsipalia, and as close as he ever planned on getting to Katy Three-Hands, that *bruja* hell-cat, again.

The beauty—and perhaps, the curse—of Tascosa was that it had no law. It was a violent, crime-ridden hell zone of rustlers, gamblers, thieves, fugitives, cutthroat prostitutes, and evil-eyed predators, most of whom had such unsavory reputations that they had been run out of every decent town for a hundred miles. Murder was a daily event, men and women being gunned down, stabbed, bludgeoned (and even burned alive in one instance) for everything from winning too much at cards to spilling drinks to flirting with the wrong girl. With no government or sheriff, perceived wrongs were righted by hotheads and bullets.

It was a scraggly, dirty little collection of adobes where no one asked questions and if they did, their life expectancy wasn't much more than five minutes.

Sam found a room at a hotel called the Wyatt and considered his situation carefully. He went easy on the whiskey, never went anywhere without his guns, did a lot of thinking, and even tried praying for divine intervention in his desperation. He was definitely living in the very bottom of the well by that point. He jumped at the slightest sound and could not always be convinced that what he saw was in fact real. Emotionally and mentally, he knew, he was close to some sort of breakdown. Physically, he was gaunt from rarely eating, his hands shook and he often lapsed into fugues that could last five minutes or, in some instances, an hour. He woke sweating in the night to a manic itching that felt like there were insects crawling under his skin. He had numerous visions of death. It seemed that there were always dozens of flies in his room. And no matter how many he killed, they just kept coming back.

But he could trust none of it.

He was hallucinating freely, often thinking his skin was yellowing and becoming scaly or that a pervasive stench of decay seemed to follow him about. One night, he woke to a terrible rustling and scratching. Upon lighting his bedside lamp, he discovered that the floor was a sea of rats, hundreds of them in creeping, slithering motion. Within seconds, they were gone. Sometimes the only way he could sleep was with liberal amounts of whiskey and laudanum.

He stepped into a saloon his first day in town, and a Mexican cowhand pulled a knife on him, claiming he had raped his mother. Sam beat him down and bloody and no one even batted an eye. The bar girls stepped over his body while he was out cold, and two desperados stole not only his knife, but his boots.

That's the sort of town it was.

Each night, he waited for the Hell Rider, thinking he heard the sounds of his boots in the corridor or coming up the street. But it was only in his mind. One afternoon, he left a saloon and saw a dead dog rotting in the gutter and was overcome with a gnawing, insatiable hunger that he could barely control. Something inside him wanted him to sink his teeth into its maggoty husk. The very idea made him sick to his stomach. He ran into an alley and vomited out what looked like a ball of writhing scorpions.

So even though the Hell Rider was not there, his presence was felt.

Finally, Sam went to the telegraph office and wired the only two people he knew who might understand what he was going through— Tommy Hawthorn and Frank McKay. Like Shorty Brice, they'd been in Guadeloupe with him, so there was a very good chance they were going through what he was. He told them to meet him in Wichita.

If they were being tormented as he was, they would come. If not, he was completely on his own.

§

Three days later, Sam set up camp on a fork of the Red River, preparing for his jaunt north. He made coffee and bacon over a small cookfire. As he considered trying to eat, he heard a creaking and groaning noise as an old farm wagon came up the dirt track. It was pulled by two Appaloosa nags. He had never seen such a contraption in all his born days. A structure of willow uprights and crossbars was built up from the bed and from it dangled the most eclectic collection of items—animal pelts and mummified rattlesnakes that swung back and forth, rattling chains of bones and what looked to be iron manacles, hollow gourds that knocked together and glass bottles that made moaning sounds as the breeze blew over their open mouths.

That was more than enough to garner his attention, but it was the stick-thin form up in the seat that made his mouth hang open. It was an old woman wrapped in a trade blanket with a beaded campaign hat on her head, a steel-gray braid down one shoulder and a seamed face like baked clay that had cracked open with dryness.

No, he thought. *Not this one.*

She brought the wagon to a halt, things jingling and jangling and clanking. Putting ebon eyes upon him, she said, "Does thy third eye remain open, Samuel Bouchard? Hast thou seen and courted death most unholy?"

27

As she sipped his coffee and nibbled his bacon, Katy Three-Hands stared off into the distance, eyes narrowing, as if she could see something out in the high grass that he could not.

"It is good of thee to feed a poor old woman," she said to him. "Most would leave such as myself to their woe and misery, with a nary a charitable act."

Sam did not know what to make of this latest development. The last he had seen of her in Epsipalia, she had told him there was no help for him, that he was cursed by a terrible black medicine. Yet here she was, and he felt in his gut that it was not by accident. Part of him wanted to know what brought her, and another did not want to know at all.

But it had to be asked, so he did. "I take it you did not come all this way for my company or my coffee."

She chuckled low in her throat. "Questions, questions, questions! How they spill from thee, Samuel Bouchard. I can hear thy thoughts in mine own head." She laughed again. There was very little humor in the terrible sound of her cackling, yet she seemed more than a little amused by herself. "Ah, thou fearest me? An old lady with a wagon full of possibilities and potentialities? What tripe and shit, my boy. I am no danger to thee! I will not have thou raise thy killing irons against me. No, no, no! I can nullify them with my many tricks. Be warned, young man, be warned!"

He sighed. "I'm not about to raise a gun against you."

"Ah, but such a thought was in thy mind. I sensed it."

"What is it you want?"

Katy Three-Hands finished her bacon and packed a clay pipe with rough-cut tobacco. Using a stick from the fire, she lit it, puffing contentedly, her smoke twisting away in the low wind. "Ah, but I am in the late autumn of my lamentable existence, Samuel. There are things I have done which I take no pride in. But in this late hour, I shall do thee a service. I shall counsel thee, for never has there been one in such need of it." She puffed for a few moments. "Soon, I fear, I shall sit at the table with mine gods, and I wish to know that I will be looked upon kindly for helping thee."

"How can you help me?" He dared not hope for such a thing. The idea of deliverance was alien to him now. "You had no interest before."

"Wrong thou art. I took a great interest, but I did not wish to tangle with the concubine of the swine in my advanced years." She sipped her coffee. "But my heart hath changed. My time runneth short. I will assist thee. Oh, be certain of that. But first … I wish to know of thine enemy."

"Her name is Mama Fornay, and she comes from the island of Guadeloupe."

"Oh, by the body of the Christ, a place where the dead walk? I have heard tell of it."

He nodded. "She's powerful. She's old like you, I think, but she can appear young if she wishes."

"Ah, the mother of serpents, I fear. Far older than I, Samuel! And what poisoneth her soul and dwelleth within her is far older still."

He tried to get sense out of her, to make her talk of the things that vexed him and brought ugly, grisly death into the world—not just Mama Fornay, but those things she commanded or, perhaps, commanded her: the Hell Rider that trailed him and the boar demon that stood behind it all and the terrible things between those poles—but she would not. She would not hear of it or assign names to any of it. For the longest time, she stared into the fire as if she had slipped into some fugue of old age where she recalled the joys and hardships of her youth. But he knew that wasn't it. Maybe her eyes were locked with the fire, but he was certain she was seeing something else, looking at vast distances leagues beyond.

Finally, she refilled her pipe, smoke puffing and billowing from her like steam from a locomotive. "So tell me all, Samuel. In thine own voice, speak the truth of how thou offended that voudoun hellcat. Let me hear thy words. Thy cup is empty, I know, but we must fill it. Now is not the time for thou to give up or give in."

So he told her everything that he thought was relevant, from his experiences in the war to his roughshod life living by the gun, which led him to Guadeloupe and the horror he encountered there, which forever stained his life and everything, every awful bit, that had occurred since.

"Ah," she said when he had finished. *"Ah!"*

"What?"

She made strange motions in the air with her skeleton-key fingers, describing things, sketching them out, muttering under her breath. "And thee feelest weak with it all? Thee feelest thy strength steadily ebbing, both physically and spiritually, dost thee not?"

"Yes."

"Of course. For thy life strength is being tapped, drained off drop by drop." She set her pipe aside, laying her hands on his face, his arms, clutching his hands. Her skin was smooth as silk, worn thin by countless years. "Death is very close to thee. Yes, yes, and yes. Thy face begins to take on the countenance of a cadaver … thy skin yellowing and scaling … eyes sinking … thy form rawboned and skeletal—and wouldst thou like to know why?"

"Yes."

"Because another, a terrible elemental, is conjoined to thee, Samuel. It is part of thee." She traced lines over his face. "It is the thing that hounds thee to thy grave, sent by that heathen witch."

"The Hell Rider."

"Ah, yes, apt. Quite apt. This Hell Rider draws off thy strength."

"Can it be stopped?"

"It will only cease if thou cease to exist."

"So I must die to be rid of it."

"Not necessarily, my son. Not necessarily. Somehow, we must cut the tether between thee and it. But to do that, yes, Samuel Bouchard, thou must meet it on common ground and destroy it. There is no other way."

"And where might that be?"

She thought about that for some time. "Thou knowest the place. I can feel it in thy mind."

"I don't."

"Yes. It is there as it's always been there. We must seek it out. Then we shall know."

He knew what she was going to suggest. Perhaps he had known it when he first saw her sitting up in that wagon among the bones and bottles. She tapped out her pipe and returned with the damned gourd, the same one, he thought, that he had initially drunk from at her hut. It was evil stuff. It could do things to your mind, throw open doors that you would well wish had remained closed. It brought suffering and pain, but it also brought revelation of sorts. She gave it to him believing it to be a righteous offering.

"That snake piss again," he said.

"Aye, but there is no other way, Samuel. Thy third eye has begun to close. We must pry it open again, so that thou canst see the unseeable and remember that which has been suppressed. Drink deep, my boy, drink deep."

Sitting by the fire with the gourd in his hands, he had a last cigarette, screwing up his nerve for the journey which he knew would not be an easy one. Finally, he uncorked the gourd. *Gah.* That same awful odor of fermenting fruit and black soil. Narrowing his eyes and clenching his jaw momentarily, he opened his lips and drank deep as she suggested. God, just like last time. It filled his mouth with fire, searing his throat and burning through his belly like a branding iron. Terror washed through him as his mind—the mind he knew—was supplanted by something older, something primal and all-seeing. Sweat that was hot and cold beaded his face. His knees went out from under him and he dropped into the dirt.

The world around him wavered, then faded, and he saw ... he saw what needed seeing. All these many months since leaving Maddie he had been circling and circling, to the east and then west, south then north, cutting back again, revolving and spinning like a child's top, a hound casting for scent ... and now he knew.

When he opened his eyes again, the sun had moved in the sky. He sipped water that Katy Three-Hands offered him. He washed trail dust down his throat.

"Well?" she asked.

"Devil's Creek," he said. "That's where it all comes together and ends."

"I am not familiar with it."

"Neither am I," he admitted. "But that's where we must go. Whatever is out there waiting for me, it waits in Devil's Creek."

Katy sighed. She opened the leather bag at her side and removed a necklace of hooked eagle claws, tarnished opalesque gems like tiny moons, and metallic charms hammered into stars and crescents. Carefully, almost lovingly, she placed it around his neck.

"It is a talisman that belonged to my mother." She shook her head. "Thy belief in such matters is not required. It hath power. Never doubt that. It will keep thee safe for a time. Use it wisely. I wish that I could go with thee, but I cannot. The years have not been kind to me, and I have nary the strength nor willpower for a long ride. I am nearly played out. Let thy third eye guide thee."

He wanted to tell her it was not enough, that he needed her there. That he was not up to the task of fighting that witch on his own. But ultimately, he did not say these things. He couldn't bring himself to.

She smiled, seeming to know, and brushed his face with her hand. "Know only, my boy, that I shall be with thee in spirit."

Ten minutes later, she was gone and he was once again alone, feeling dark forces gathering around him. He thought about Devil's Creek. He would find it or it would find him.

28

Days later, Sam rode into Wichita.

A rain had fallen and the prairie grass was wet with dew, moonlight sparkling off it like bits of silver. The streets were busy with drunken cowhands hooting it up, howling and shooting their irons now that another drive from Texas was at an end.

He went immediately over to Delano, Wichita's red-light district.

He hitched his dappled mare to the rail and right away, something moved in the darkness a few inches from his boot, coiled and rattling. The mare whinnied and Sam pulled his pistols ... a rattlesnake. Just a rattlesnake. He leathered his Colts and spit tobacco juice at it and it slithered off.

Just a snake, he thought. *Sure, they could send snakes ... but not common timber rattlers. What they would send would be far more exotic and far more deadly.*

He found a saloon and started pouring back hooks of whiskey tempered by tepid glasses of beer. All around him, there was noise and confusion, fighting and loving and shooting. Smells of perfume and body odor, tobacco and horseshit.

He managed to polish on a good shine by midnight, his eyes lit and his hands steady, a fine warm heat in his belly.

You're safe here, he told himself. *Things will be okay.*

He had gotten real good at giving himself false hope. It was the only thing that kept his racing, worn mind out of the gutter of dementia ... for it was never a far drop away. He found himself watching the other men, knowing they could not know what he knew and how it was when your guts went to sauce and you lost your nerve. How shadows were no longer shadows but reaching, grotesque shapes with hooked fingers and skulls for faces. How it was when you were pursued by things that lived in closets and under beds, when the dark and grim seeds of primal terror were planted in your head and they gave flower and vine, twining you up and pulling you down into six feet of black, crawling earth.

They could not know this, they could—

"Stop it," he said under his breath.

He knew damn well they could reach him here if they wanted to. He was not going to hide. He was going to fight and make it just as hard on them as he could.

"Well, as I live and breathe, Sam Bouchard," a voice behind him said.

It was the voice of Long Lucy McBride, a veteran whore who'd worked just about every cow town, mining camp, and rail spur in the Territories. Last time Sam had seen her she was turning tricks and shilling drinks at a sporting house in Socorro, New Mexico. Her blonde hair was piled high, her breasts high mountains heaving the hilly landscape of her bodice. She was green-eyed and not un-pretty, but hard-looking from a life spent in the wrong places with the wrong people.

She hugged him and brought him up to her room.

They had been friends, and Sam cared for her but did not love her. Not the way he loved Maddie Borcheaux. Maddie, whom he missed and dreamed about, who smelled of jasmine and French perfume. But Long Lucy was in love with Sam and always had been. And after they had made love and were sipping from a bottle of Kentucky bourbon, she told him as much as she stared into his drawn face, running fingertips over his thin mustache and bony forehead.

Then Sam drifted off.

His sleep—he thought—was heavy and still and dreamless. But then he came awake beaded in sweat, shaking and asking Long Lucy if she smelled something, something like an open grave.

"That must have been some dream," was all she would say, candlelight painting her breasts in flickering yellows.

"Was … was I talking in my sleep?" he asked.

"Talking? Honey, you were thrashing and moaning enough to wake the dead."

But those were not well-chosen words and they made Sam's sweaty face go pale as plaster. His lower lip trembled, his eyes became wide and wet stones set in puffy, red hollows.

Long Lucy had a little leather bag in her hand. "What's this?" she wanted to know, completely at ease going through his belongings. "It smells funny … spicy or something."

Sam licked his lips. "It's a gris-gris."

"A gree gree? What's that?"

"A gris-gris is sort of a good-luck charm the colored peoples swear by, a mojo. Had a fellow down in New Orleans make it for me."

Long Lucy put it back in his coat. "Sam … maybe you should be honest with me here. You're not the same man I knew once upon a time. You're jittery, you jump at every sound … you smell things I don't smell. You're carrying good-luck charms. Is there something you wanna get off your chest?"

And there was, God yes, there was. And maybe it was high time to do just that. He pulled back a slug of bourbon, rolled a cigarette and lit it. He started by saying, "You know how I make my living...."

And she did, of course she did. He made it with a gun. He'd fought for the Confederacy during the war and when it was over, he found the only thing he was any good at was killing. So he worked as a range detective, hunted down horse rustlers and desperados, hired out as a gunman to ranchers and towns plagued by violence and bad men. He'd worked as a mercenary in Mexico and Central America and had been a town marshal in the Arizona Territory. He killed for a living and she knew it. But she never asked about it, his reputation being enough. And he never spoke of it or how it was when he woke up with the shakes at four in the morning, certain his fingers were red with blood.

"Last year," he said, taking a drag off his cigarette, the cherry glowing like a setting sun, "I met a fellow from Baton Rouge way name of Charles DeFleur. His old man owned a big cotton plantation in Livingston County. Had a coffee plantation in Martinique and a sugar plantation in Guadeloupe...."

As Sam told it, they started talking about the war and what had come after it. DeFleur knew all about Sam's reputation and told him so, asked him if was interested in some work in the Caribbean. Pay would be good, climate fine. What sort of work? Well, DeFleur's old man was a major supplier to the American Sugar Company. He had two huge, sprawling cane plantations on Guadeloupe and employed hundreds of locals to chop the cane and run his sugar mills.

DeFleur was very rich and the locals very poor.

Slavery had been abolished in Guadeloupe back in 1847, but it still existed in a way. The creoles that cut the cane and worked the factories were paid pitiful wages and expected to put in fifteen-hour days, seven days a week. Labor unrest began to spread through the masses like wildfire. The flames, DeFleur knew, fanned by a crazy voudoun witch named Mama Fornay who had a hut up in the hills above the east plantation. She was something of a mythical figure to the workers.

"Now, I didn't know much about voudoun before I got there," Sam told her, smoke wafting from his nostrils. "Being from Louisiana, sure, I'd heard of it. Some sort of pagan religion the blacks and creoles practiced in Baton Rouge and New Orleans, chickens and snakes and the saints and what not. A few whites were involved. I knew one that swore by it, that it wasn't just a bunch of dancing and gourd-rattling, but a legitimate religion. Course, I never bought any of that. My people are Cajuns from bayou country. Out there, well, we had our share of witch-folk and the like ... but I never believed in any of that horseshit. I was a Christian. At least, that's how I was raised even if I parted company with religion during the war. Then came Guadeloupe...."

Sam and Charles DeFleur took a clipper ship from New Orleans to

Pointe-a-Pitre on Grande Terre, one of the main islands that form Guadeloupe proper. First thing he thought was that he had never seen a more beautiful place in his life. The Caribbean was crystal blue, the trade winds warm, the islands lush and green surrounded by white sand beaches. Paradise. It was just like the sort of place he'd dreamed of as a boy, reading adventure stories of pirates. Pointe-a-Pitre was lined with tall, white French colonial-style buildings with wrought-iron balconies. The people were black and French, Creole and Carib Indian ... and mostly a combination of them all. Cinnamon-skinned women in colorful Creole dress sold bananas, oranges, and soda bread from market booths. There were sidewalk cafés where the white planters drank their afternoon rum punches.

As they rode by carriage out to the DeFleur plantations, Sam was in awe. The dense stands of jungle and lush fern forests, cocoa palms and rugged mountains. And, yes, the sugarcane. Endless acres of cane rising up higher than a man, rustling in the wind, rippling like some secret, fathomless sea of green and yellow.

In the distance, he saw the towering chimneys of the sugar mills, heard their clanking machinery. There were rum distilleries on the hillsides and he could plainly smell the yeast, alcohol, and cane juice that went into the vats. The air was sweet and damp. Ox-drawn wagons cut up the winding roads, bringing the cane to the factories. Lines of creole, Hindu, and Chinese laborers waved to Charles DeFleur with their machetes, cradling their sweat-stained straw hats to their chests out of respect.

The DeFleur plantation house sat behind heavy stone walls. It was a rambling place with pillared porches, wide verandahs, and red-tiled roofs. The grounds were carefully landscaped with bougainvillea and palms, vibrant orchids of every imaginable color and some that could not be imagined.

For the next few days, he did little but lie around drinking rum, flirting with the creole servant girls, and eating. The meals were extravagant and filling—lobster and turtle, red snapper and stuffed crab, roast wild goat and broiled dove, stewed conch and jugged rabbit. All with that mouth-watering, utterly unique blend of creole spices.

Everything seemed idyllic ... how could there be trouble in such a place?

"But there was," he explained to Lucy, "and a lot of it. You see, running a sugarcane plantation takes a lot of hands. You need armies to chop the cane and another army to process it. When the cane is chopped, it's taken to big mills where these huge rollers grind it down to extract the cane juice. Now, the workers figured they were being taken advantage of and they certainly were. DeFleur was paying them pennies a day for grueling slave labor. And with what Mama Fornay was spouting, wasn't long before they left the fields, refusing to work...."

But planters like DeFleur, Sam said, were not stupid. And they were not about to let their plantations go to seed. They began bringing in indentured immigrants from India, mostly Hindus. Those boys had worked cane fields for the British back in India and they knew how it was done. Suddenly, the creoles weren't needed. Eventually, they rose up against their French masters, began burning the cane and killing the Hindus. More Hindus were brought in, as well as Chinese, and even black workers from Martinique and Haiti. DeFleur and the other planters hired armed men to patrol the cane fields on horseback.

Some of them were killed, most found less dangerous occupations. The planters decided what they needed were professional soldiers, gunmen who could hunt the marauding creoles down and beat them into submission.

"It was Mama Fornay that got them going," Sam confided in Long Lucy. "She started the whole goddamn mess. I mean, hell, I didn't and don't exactly blame the creoles. They were being misused. But the planters were very rich men, Lucy, and you can't fight rich men. I've learned that the hard way. Those planters could've brought in thousands of soldiers and wiped out every creole in Guadeloupe without straining their bank accounts. They were *that* rich. Last thing any sane man wants to do is get between a rich man and his money and that's exactly what the cutters were doing, because all that cane, it was ready cash sprouting from the soil."

Sam told her that the whites never understood the peoples they enslaved and the enslaved peoples never understood their masters. It was a familiar story and an old one. The Apaches and Sioux out west, he said, were learning that very lesson. They didn't understand white man's greed.

They didn't realize that whites could be extremely relentless and violent when it came to other races keeping them from money.

And the creoles on Guadeloupe didn't understand that either.

For every white they killed, a dozen of their own went to their graves.

"And all because they wanted to be treated like human beings," Lucy said.

"Yes. Exactly. Old man DeFleur hired a dozen professional shootists in addition to myself," Sam said, the memory of it all making his breath come in ragged gasps now. "Real hard, desperate men that had fought in the war and were handy with pistols and killing. Some had fought for the stars and bars like Johnny Pierce, Al Monk, and Tommy Hawthorn. And some had been Union boys—Frank McKay, Shorty Brice, and Mike Bolan. No matter. Reb or Yankee, we got on fine. We were hired guns is all. Our old loyalties had faded. We had a new loyalty and that was to folding money and as much as we could lay our greedy little hands on.

"After we were thoroughly sunned and fed, we began riding the cane and the hills, hunting our quarry." He let out a long sigh. "The cane, the cane. If you never been in it, you just can't imagine what it's like, Lucy. Christ. It's hot and windless. Full of snakes and hopping lizards, insects and spiders. And the heat … maddening. You ride through it, your face wet with sweat and all around you it's crisping and rustling, even when there's no wind. You wonder when those growing, dry stalks are going to close in on you and squeeze the life out of you. It's cut by narrow roads and little weedy footpaths, none of which ever seem to lead anywhere but back into themselves. Just a maze, a constricting maze.

"And the workers … those poor bastards. They cut cane from first light to sundown. The cane was their life. Their whole world. You'd see little clearings and brakes filled with huts and then you'd realize these people, they never got out of the cane fields. They lived out there week after week in that growing, crowded world of sugarcane, that black dry heat. I was never so glad as to ride out after a day's patrol … but the workers? They never came out. Some just disappeared right into the cane and nobody ever saw 'em again…."

Yes, the miles of sugarcane were hell.

But as Sam rode it and made friends with the workers and began to understand what it was all about, he began to understand voudoun. How the dirt-poor cutters relied on it for their spiritual sanity. Up until then, what he knew of voudoun were stories mostly perpetuated by French Catholic missionaries, stories designed to belittle the religion in favor of their own. Stories of human sacrifice, cannibalism, devil-worship, and sex orgies. At first, with what Sam saw, he was inclined to agree. In the cane, there would be shrines, little circles of animal bones set off by human skulls, eviscerated goats strung from trees as sacrifice. But he just didn't understand. None of these things were offered to the gods lightly. They were very important and, sometimes, even painful offerings, but necessary to contact spirits, to get their blessings and receive their protections.

But he learned.

And as he learned, he heard about Mawu Lisa and Agwe, Dambala and Ogou Balanjo. He learned the customs and listened to the folklore. Wild tales of evil spirits and jumbees, serpent cults and sects of the black goat, werewolves that devoured lambs and human babies, bloodsucking ghosts and walking dead men, the *corps cadavre.* In the cane, at a cutter's cottage, he heard about *zumbies,* as the locals called them—for the first time. About them being summoned from the tomb to serve their masters. How the locals took such things very seriously, burying their kin under heavy slabs of masonry so that the bokors—voudoun black magicians and witches—could not get at them. They interred their loved ones at crossroads where the traffic was too heavy to perform the secret ritual of resurrection and often stood guard over their tombs. The cutters insisted that there was a French planter on the other side of the island—Henri Charrone—who worked his cane exclusively with dead men.

"It was fascinating stuff, Lucy, but it wasn't why we were there. It wasn't long before we killed our first bunch of guerrillas." Sam swallowed down hard at the memory. "Pitiful is what it was...."

A group of creoles and blacks wielding cane knives and machetes came charging out at him and three of the mercenaries—Pierce, Monk, and Bolan. They were half-starved, dressed in rags, eyes wide and raging. They had absolutely nothing to lose. They broke through the cane and charged the men on horseback. Less than a minute later, the mercenaries were clutching smoking pistols and the cutters were heaped in a bullet-ridden pile. And it was just the beginning. In the coming weeks, as the insurgents grew more bold, the mercenaries began to learn about them. How they operated, where they hid. There were nighttime raids that left dozens of guerrillas dead, many more injured. Within that first month, the mercenaries cut down no less than sixty of them.

When they interrogated the survivors, the story started coming out.

Mama Fornay was behind it.

Sam and the others figured as much, but finally they had proof. Mama Fornay was part-revolutionary, part-spiritual leader, and part messiah. But the most interesting thing they learned was that the cutters in general were terrified of her. She had the power, they said. She could cure the sick and bless the crops, look at a pregnant woman and tell what sex her baby would be. She could tell fortunes and give lucky numbers … and she could also bring down terrible curses on you and yours if you crossed her.

"See, Lucy there's two types of voudoun magic—*rada,* which is good magic and *petro,* which is black magic. The *rada* priest is called a houngan and the *petro* priest is called a bokor. Sort of a witch doctor, I suppose. The kind of person who likes to control people and can help you get back at your enemies–"

"But that's just superstition, Sam," Lucy finally broke in, tired of a certain fine man she'd once known becoming the fearful, charm-carrying wreck before her. "Maybe the colored folk can accept those things, but you and I … we're white, we're Christians. Those pagan gods have no power over us. None whatsoever."

"Don't they?"

"No, they do not."

Sam seemed amused by her dismissal of it all; but maybe it wasn't amusement, but envy. "Let me tell you one more thing, just one more thing. I need to get this … *insanity* off my chest before I die.…"

Old man DeFleur and the other planters decided there was only one true way to stamp out the insurrection once and for all: Mama Fornay would have to be killed. The creoles and blacks followed her like sheep, terrified of her powerful black medicine. Once they were shown that white medicine was infinitely stronger, well, they would fall in line.

It sounded reasonable.

So day by day, intelligence was gathered and within a few weeks, they knew where the witch lived. Sam led the raiding party on her place one dark night. Mama Fornay lived up above the cane in the wild, rugged hills, deep in the rainforest. The raiders found her hideout without too much trouble—every path seemed to lead there. They picketed their horses in that wet, stinking jungle and attacked Mama Fornay's encampment. Forty or fifty men and women were gathered around fires, dancing and pounding on drums, shaking rattles and holding snakes above their heads. Armed with Winchester repeating rifles, the raiders encircled the camp and started shooting.

Like shooting clay pigeons, was how Sam remembered it.

The raiders pulled triggers, levered, pulled triggers, reloaded and repeated the process. Within ten minutes, dead men and women were scattered everywhere. Roosters were crowing and pigs squealing, the air thick with smoke and death. Those that had not been killed outright, ran off.

Sam was one of the men who entered Mama Fornay's hut—a little cottage thatched with cane straw set in a stand of flowering shrubs and climbing vines. The cottage was her temple. Sam kicked the door off its hinges and went in low, Colt pistols in either hand.

The place was filled with incense smoke and flickering candles, seemingly hundreds of them. There were chickens in reed cages and snakes hanging from the smoke-blackened beams overhead.

Standing before some sort of altar was a naked, heavy-breasted creole woman with eyes like hot steel. Sweat was beaded over her naked torso and her face was sharp and bony, more skull than flesh. She bowed to Sam, muttered something, and scattered dried corn kernels at his feet.

"Welcome, Samuel Bouchard, welcome to my house," Mama Fornay said, her accent cultured and smooth like whipped cream butter.

A few of the other men—Bolan, Monk, a couple others, hard men who enjoyed killing—came in behind Sam, staring wide-eyed at the voudoun temple before them.

And, Sam admitted, it was some kind of place.

The centerpiece was an altar crowded with candles and animal bones, ceremonial cloths and human skulls, jars of powdered insects and dirt. There were pictures of Christian saints and grotesque onyx carvings of pagan devils. Flanked by two hanging baskets of mummified birds, there was an African fetish doll, a *nkisi* figure. It was a grotesque thing about two-feet tall, made from wood and leather and cane straw, its head like a demonic, leering skull. There were pins and needles, nails and knife blades jabbed into it. Something that looked like blood dripped from the numerous perforations.

And above this, adorned with snakeskins and feathers and beads, an effigy of Jesus Christ on the cross. The nails pounded into his hands and ankles were painted red and Sam was not so sure it wasn't real blood, as if Christ had just been nailed up there. The Lord's face was a despairing mask of horror and agony … it was so awful to look upon, Sam had to take a step back.

Mama Fornay plucked a black rooster from a cage and slit its throat, shaking the blood around and chanting some weird melody that was positively profane to hear. She dropped the bird at her feet and sprinkled a barrier of cornmeal around it. Fingers bloody, she painted crosses on her chest, cheeks, and forehead.

"Samuel Bouchard," she said in an eerie, whistling voice that sounded like wind blowing through a cave mouth. "Samuel Bouchard, I have expected you these many days. Samuel Bouchard of Louisiana bayou country. Samuel Bouchard, whose soul is perverted and wretched and depraved by the taking of lives. Samuel Bouchard, whose very aura is grim and haunted and smells of graveyards. Yes, Samuel Bouchard, who is pursued by the lost, hungry souls of those he has murdered. And, yes, Samuel Bouchard, at the hour of your death they will be waiting, waiting in the netherworld to claim you—"

"Shut your goddamned mouth," he finally said, his flesh crawling. "You know why we're here. Best make peace with your gods, because you're soon in their bosom."

But Mama Fornay only laughed. "Why, Samuel Bouchard, why is it that you, who does not believe in gods black or white, would give me this time? And better, yes, better: why is it you have come here?"

"I came to do a job," Sam told him.

The witch nodded, seemingly unhappy at this. "If you were a smart man, you would run away and get off this island. You might live in peace then—" and Mama Fornay began to grin "—at least until the time of your death."

Behind him, Monk spat tobacco juice onto the floor. "You gonna listen to this fucking bullshit, Sam? You don't kill this wench, I will."

But Sam ignored that. "You're getting your people all riled up, Mama, and we can't have that." He brought up his pistol. "That won't do at all."

The witch smiled and that smile was sharp as a razor. "My people are not slaves, not any longer."

"Maybe not. But they can't keep carrying on like this. It's not gonna work, you riling 'em up with this hoodoo horseshit."

"Is that so?"

She sat down then in the circle of cornmeal, scattering kernels around again … except they weren't kernels, but teeth, human teeth. "When I was in my mother's womb, Samuel Bouchard, my mother was mounted by the *loa,* the spirit of Dambala the Serpent. He touched me, planted a seed within me, decided that I should become a bokor like no other. Would you, Samuel Bouchard, care to see what it was he planted within me?"

Sam said he wasn't sure what happened then.

But suddenly the witch's face began to ripple and flow, it oozed like melted wax, the bones falling in and thrusting forth again only to dissolve back into a slow-churning muddy pulp of blood and meat. She became a coiled, knotted serpent and then an immense swollen rat with fleas the size of bullets jumping in her greasy fur. And then, even these images flew apart, exploding into a hollow-eyed storm of ghost-faces that grinned and leered and Sam cried out because he knew that all of them were men he had killed—in the war and after—and they wanted to drag him screaming into abyssal tomb-depths and bury him in black silt and concrete silence.

And that was bad enough, but it was hardly the end. The ghost-faces blew apart like dandelion fuzz and gathered in an undulant, fleshy compost heap of swarming meat flies that solidified into the image of a distorted wild boar that stood upon two cloven-hoofed feet. It was a monstrous creature, snarling and hissing and drooling from massive tusked jaws. It had beady eyes like blood blisters, bristles jutting like sharp spines, its flesh leathery like the boiled leather of a barbarian. In a snorting, squealing sort of voice, it said, *"At the hour of your death, Samuel Bouchard, I shall be with you...."*

But he was no longer listening.

He started shooting until his pistols were empty. But the bullets did not touch Mama Fornay. They passed through her as if she had no more substance than smoke, punching holes into the altar, shattering vials and wooden bowls, but never touching the sorceress herself.

Sam felt hands pull him out of there.

Kerosene lanterns were tossed and soon the entire hut was blazing, but Mama Fornay, engulfed by flame, sat calmly, her eyes yellow and triumphant.

"We figured she died in the fire," Sam said after a time, his hands trembling on the whiskey bottle. They shook so badly now, he could barely get it to his lips. "But the next day, we went back ... the temple was burned flat. We found lots of charred bones, but I think we all knew that Mama Fornay's were not among them."

Long Lucy had been patient through it all. She loved Sam Bouchard. Loved him and respected him and it hurt her deeply to see him reduced to the quivering thing that sat before her.

"Sam," she said very softly. "The jungle is a bad place. Fevers and the like. You've had a rough time of it, but you can't really believe that anyone can live through bullets and fire."

"I don't know what I believe anymore."

She got up, stared out the window. "And that's what happened? That's how it ended?"

But Sam shook his head. "One by one, the soldiers died. Some took their own lives. Others went mad and ran off into the cane. Monk was burned alive in his bed. Burned to a crisp, Lucy, only the sheets were never so much as *scorched* ... can you explain that? Can you explain Bolan who suffocated, his lungs filled with insects? Or Pierce who died vomiting blood? They opened him up and his belly was full of poison

TIM CURRAN

frogs. Can you explain the walking dead? Devil babies in leather sacks? And can you explain the snakes...."

"The snakes?"

Yes, he told her, the snakes. Out in the cane there was an especially fearsome serpent called the fer-de-lance. It was, along with the bushmaster, one of the most deadly snakes in South America and the Caribbean. He told her it reached eight feet in length, had golden eyes, and triangular blotches on its back. It was called a two-step snake because if it bit you, you took two steps and died.

"They came into the cane after rodents," he explained. "Now and again, a cutter would get bit. But they didn't come into houses. They never came into houses ... yet that's what happened. Maybe a single snake, maybe several of them, came into the DeFleur plantation house and bit the remaining soldiers ... save for me, McKay, Hawthorn, and Brice. And each of them were dead in an hour. You don't find that a little coincidental?"

It *was* crazy, she knew. The snake or snakes not attacking anyone but the soldiers, but there had to be a rational explanation. But Sam assured her there was not and could never be. It was voudoun. The bokors could control snakes.

"Brice, Hawthorn, and McKay left the next day. It was enough. You cannot fight the unknown, the impossible, and the unseen. They were going to stay with me and fight on, but something happened, something horrible...."

"What?" Long Lucy asked.

Sam told her that Tommy Hawthorn woke him in the middle of the night to show him something. "It was a hex, it was witchcraft and voudoun and black sorcery. Somebody had come into Tommy's room in the darkness and tied a leather sack on a string over his bed. When I got there, it was swinging back and forth. By then, Shorty Brice and Frank McKay were there, too. None of them knew what the sack meant, but I had a feeling it was some sort of conjure bag."

Sam cut it down. By lantern light and the rays of the tropical moon coming through the rattan blinds, he slit it open with his knife.

"We had no idea what might be in there. Being from the bayou,

157

I figured feathers and dead insects, some graveyard dirt ... the sort of voudoun shite I'd seen in New Orleans. But this was nothing so crude nor primitive...."

Inside, was something that looked like a sort of membranous transparent pouch of fluid and curled up in it was a fetus ... sort of.

"I slit it open and the stench was unbelievable," he told her. "That fetus ... a little manikin or pygmy, God only knows what ... it was like something from a sideshow jar, sort of pink and gray, not completely formed, shriveled and evil-looking ... its eyes like bulbs waiting to open, the little slit of a mouth opening and closing ... and it was breathing—"

"That's enough, Sam. Dear Lord, that's enough," Long Lucy said, visibly shaken at the very idea.

"We burned it. And when we gave it to the flames, it cried out, Lucy. It mewled like a kitten." He wiped sweat from his brow with the palsied, knotted hand of an old man. "That's what drove them away. But I stayed. Yes, for two more days until something else happened."

Long Lucy looked pained when she said, "And what was that?"

It took him some time to continue and by then the whiskey bottle was empty and his eyes were red and sunken. "I took a last ride through the cane. The workers stopped cutting and hid at my approach. The Hindus and Chinese fled. When I got back to the house, the creole servants wouldn't come within fifty feet of me. In my room, I found something. In the heat, I smelled it long before I saw it: a corpse. The rotting corpse of a white man dressed in my clothes and nailed to the wall."

"Jesus, Sam, it—"

"I buried it, stripped my clothes off it. Because I knew, you see, I knew that a corpse in my clothes was one of the most serious of voudoun curses ... that it wouldn't be snakes for me, but something a hell of a lot worse."

He didn't tell her any more.

Not that night.

Not about Baton Rouge or Fort Smith or Texas. None of it. She thought he was insane and maybe he was. It was the pity in her eyes that finally made him turn away in bed, fall into an uneasy sleep. Because she could not understand any of it, could not know that they were still hunting him.

Several times during the night, Long Lucy was certain she heard something sniffing around the door like a dog. Just before dawn, there was a scratching out there as if something wanted in. Whatever it was, it squealed like a boar.

She didn't dare move until the sun came up.

PART THREE: THE CURSED

29

At night, as they sat around their cookfire, eating biscuits and beans and tinned meat, the Spennings discussed it to death and arrived at no set conclusion. Sam Bouchard was certainly moving like a hunted animal, the only question was why.

"Maybe what we ought to do is just go on back to Junction City," Race suggested more than once.

"And do what exactly, you idiot?"

"Something. Anything."

"There's nothing there for us."

"And what's out here? So we find Bouchard and kill him. How's that fill our pokes? How's that give us prospects?"

Damn. Denver had to give that oaf some credit. When they'd set out after Bouchard, they'd been whiskeyed up and not thinking very clearly about the future. The hate had been enough for a time. But after all these many days being led on a wild chase on the hard trail, that had waned. *We kill him … then what?* It had never crossed Denver's mind, but it bore some thinking about. He wondered if what they shouldn't do was go chase some bounties. At least it would pay.

One night, not long after, as he slept away in his bedroll, dreaming of whoring and drinking, Race shook him awake.

"What?" he said. "What the hell is it?"

Race whispered, "Someone out there, circling our camp."

"Bouchard?"

"Somebody," was all Race would commit to.

"Injuns?"

"Heard something moving in the grass."

Denver sighed. Why, of course there were things moving in the grass. Wild things came out at night. Bobcats and coyotes, pronghorns and bear. He was going to tell his idiot brother that … but he couldn't seem to find his voice. It was cool and black and silent out there, the moon breaking through banks of clouds from time to time, making the grasslands seem to glow with ethereal luminosity, then go black as tar as it disappeared again. Nothing moved out there as they waited with weapons in their hands.

But there's something out there, Denver thought with rising apprehension. *I know it. I feel it.*

Race shifted position. The fire had burned low, only a few weak flames flickering among charred wood and dung. Denver heard a rustling. It seemed to be behind them, then off to the right. A shadow sneaking through the encroaching tallgrass prairie that hemmed them in from all sides. Race grabbed a stick and tossed it on the fire. The flames licked up, throwing guttering light over the stands of bluestem. And then, precisely as the fire grew brighter, they both heard something like the guttural lowing of an alligator coming from the darkness.

Denver felt chills run up his back. Such a sound. This wasn't Louisiana. There was anything around here that could make such a sound.

Race threw another dry hackberry branch on the fire and it blazed up again, brighter now, casting its light deeper into the grass. And for one second that was barely even that, Denver thought he saw some hunched, elfin thing watching them from the shadows with huge dead-white eyes. Then it was gone. He turned to his brother, but Race was still staring at the fire. He hadn't seen a thing and maybe it was just a delusion, the light playing on the shadows, turning an old stump into a monster.

While Denver was more nervous than ever, Race seemed to have calmed. He seized up a burning stick from the fire and stood up, the double-barreled Parker in his other hand.

"What you doing?" Denver whispered.

"I'm having me a look."

Denver was thinking of telling him not to, that it was a fool's gambit, but he didn't. Despite the fear that threaded him like lace, his selfish brain was working again and he figured if that idiot could draw what was out there to him, he could get a shot at it. So he let him go, taking aim in the direction of his retreating form with his Navy six.

Race moved in a circular pattern, dispelling the gathering shadows in the high grass with his burning stick. He kept widening the circle, pushing deeper into the grass. Denver wanted to call out to him, to ask him if there was anything, but his voice was caught in his throat.

Race paused once or twice, pointing the shotgun at something, then moving on. Then in the zone of illumination, Denver saw something not three feet from him. He blinked his eyes, thinking it was another mirage. But then the moon came out, sketching it in light white as salt—a small figure again, a boneless, anneloid shape that seemed to slither in the grass, slime-glistening and stealthy. It followed Race ... then stopped, peering back at Denver as if it knew it was being watched. It had stringy long hair and grub-white eyes. It stared at him a moment, then disappeared.

Denver sat there by the fire, his heart pounding, the pistol shaking in his hand.

Seconds later, Race returned. "Nothing," he said. "Ain't nothing out there."

He dropped his stick into the fire, stretching out on his bedroll with the Parker at his side. Before long, he was snoring again. Denver did not sleep. His mouth was dry, his body trembling. He kept the fire burning until first light. Just before dawn, as his eyes grew heavy, he heard a high, angry yowling from deep in the grass.

30

For Katy Three-Hands, the haunting began. She had felt it gathering strength on her ride back to Epsipalia and within a week, it had gained an awful, dire momentum. Even surrounded by the many charms and apotropaics of her hut, it crowded in on her from all quarters. She could not sleep. She had no appetite. Voices whispered around her and she sensed things moving in the corners.

Evil had come to roost. It was irresistible and relentless as it filled itself with life, sent by that creole witch, Katy knew, because she had dared intervene on behalf of Samuel Bouchard.

Sooner or later this had to happen, Katy told herself as she alternately shivered and sweated fevers. *You have made a terrible enemy in that one, an enemy far darker and more powerful than any you have yet faced. She will best you, but you must make it difficult for her.*

Carefully, she drew a circle in the dirt around herself, only closing it when she had those things she needed—a selection of old talismans, a leather-bound spell book, her Bible, a few jars and stoppered bottles of powder with which she drew arcane figures around herself.

Let it come to pass, she thought.

Malign influences and slithering forms that she could not sense with her five senses, but detect with some much older form of divination moved around the circle, seeking ingress. In time, she knew, the circle would fray and they would enter, but not just yet.

She picked up the gourd that Sam had drank from twice now and sipped the concoction within. It was a foul-tasting brew that made her gag, but she held it down, feeling it burning first her guts and then inside her head, melting away the real world and showing her another reality of things that had been and would soon be. Despite the panoply of images that crowded her brain, she forced her well-disciplined mind to concentrate on the image of Mama Fornay. That she had never seen the woman did not matter—she knew her spirit, or the rank pestilence that passed for one.

She saw a vague, smoky image of the woman that would not gain clarity. She knew it was because the witch was purposely fighting against her, protecting her image from Katy so that it could not be harnessed to do her harm. Yet the generalities were there. Who she was, what she was, a sense of something stark and immense that stood behind her.

Her mother was a whore, her father a conjure-man, and both trafficked with unholy forces they summoned through ritual. While she was still in her mother's belly, a corrupt and unclean spirit had entered her, shaping her into a foulness that would pollute any and all she came into contact with. That much Katy saw. Just as she saw the witch's mother preparing to give birth to her and as she saw this, a voice boomed in her mind:

HIS TAIL SWEPT DOWN A THIRD OF THE STARS OF HEAVEN AND CAST THEM TO THE EARTH. AND THE DRAGON STOOD BEFORE THE WOMAN WHO WAS ABOUT TO GIVE BIRTH, SO THAT WHEN SHE BORE HER CHILD HE MIGHT DEVOUR IT.

Yes, Katy knew, *yes*.

That was it.

That was the seed.

The child that would become the creole witch was promised to the serpent by her parents; her soul was emptied from her, poured into the sand, so that she was an empty vessel for a discarnate entity that crawled from the cellar of creation. Yes, the child was the egg, but the meat that filled it was a malevolent spirit, something that should never have been born.

SHE HAS BECOME A DWELLING PLACE FOR DEMONS, A HAUNT FOR EVERY UNCLEAN SPIRIT, A HAUNT FOR EVERY UNCLEAN BIRD, A HAUNT FOR EVERY UNCLEAN AND DETESTABLE BEAST!

Now knowing her as well as it was possible to know such an abomination, Katy could see her face. Out of some unbodied, dark dimension, Mama Fornay was staring out at her with eyes like purple blood blisters, her grinning mouth mocking and cruel.

She knew that Katy was no true threat to her, not now, not in her in weakened, depleted state. Age and illness had taken the edge from her and her abilities were trifling. She would soon be dead.

Katy knew this, too.

Her entire body was shaking from exertion as she came out of the trance. She was drenched with sweat, her teeth chattering, her muscles aching, her mind threatening to close like a door. Oh yes, oh yes, dear God, here was the darkness gathering, threatening to enfold her. She could hear the piper and sense the approach of the Angel of Death. But these were of the natural order and she did not fear them. What she feared was the witch and her familiars that were circling her like hungry wolves as her circle of protection dissipated.

In her mind, which was fading to a seamless fog of gray, her voice called out one last time, *DELIVER MY SOUL FROM THE SWORD! MY LIFE FROM THE POWER OF THE DOG! SAVE ME! OH LORD SAVE MY PATHETIC SOUL! DO ... NOT ... LET ... HER ... FEED UPON IT....*

Now terrible hands were laid upon her, hands that were hot and grave-cold, withered and unpleasantly fleshy. But as they seized her lifeless husk, what was inside her had already fled.

31

When Sam woke the next day, Lucy had a pail and a scrub brush in her hand. It took him a moment or two to remember where he was and why he was there, but when he did, he jerked upright, asking where his guns were, his gris-gris.

"In the nightstand drawer, Sam," Lucy said. "I'll get you some breakfast."

Sam found them, allowed himself to relax by degrees. He poured some water from a china pitcher into a bowl, splashed it in his face, a mask that was all lines and hollows. "Getting caught up on your cleaning?"

"Yes and no. I got up this morning and I found something outside the door."

Sam's fingers froze on the cigarette he was rolling. He looked over at her carefully. "What did you find?" he managed.

"Oh, it was nothing."

"Tell me!" he snapped. "Goddammit, woman, tell me!"

With a pitying look in her eyes, she explained that it was nothing to get excited about, nothing at all. Just a handprint, a little muddy handprint like that of a boy. But if it meant nothing to her, it was a portent of doom to him. His face went tight and gray, his lower lip trembled. He seemed to be having trouble breathing.

"I thought," he said in a weak, airless voice, "I thought I would be safe here ... that they couldn't get me here."

"Sam ..."

But he shook his head. "You don't understand, Lucy, by God, you don't."

And she didn't. A handprint. It meant something, all right. There was always the possibility it was perfectly harmless, but he did not believe it. Could not believe it. A handprint ... and of what? Mud? Feces? Both? To him, it could only have one possible meaning: *marked*. He was marked. And *they* were telling him they knew exactly where he was.

Long Lucy left with her bucket of water and Sam sat there, thinking, wondering where he could run to next. He listened to the traffic out in the streets—carriages, wagons. He lit his cigarette and studied his Colt Peacemakers, his gris-gris.

He thought: *Jesus Christ, this is what it has come to. Guns and mojos.*

He had told himself that he wasn't going to run anymore, that he was going to stand and fight. But he had no idea how to even wage such a campaign. Only that it would begin in Devil's Creek.

Lucy returned sometime later. She brought him a breakfast platter—coffee, bacon, homefries, biscuits. A lot of food. More than he'd eaten at any one time—or any one day—in weeks and weeks, if not months. He drank some coffee.

"I might have to leave," he said.

"Because of what I found?"

He found that he could not meet her eyes. "You think I'm crazy and I don't blame you. I wish it were that easy, that simple."

"But, Sam—"

"I don't do any of this lightly, Lucy. If I stay here, they'll come after you. They'll get to me through you."

The news brought great pain to her, but he was powerless. He had no choice. Dutiful, caring, she began to put his things in order while he sat and smoked, staring at all that food but not touching it. She packed his bags, made sure his shotgun was with them, his extra boots.

"At least," she said, "let me get this coat pressed for you."

He did not argue. There had been a time when he took great pleasure in his appearance … but that was long ago now. His Prince Albert coat was wrinkled like an old trade blanket. He had tossed it over a chair and she picked it up now, going through the inside pockets, removing a handkerchief, his wallet, a fifty-dollar gold piece … and a small box tied with black silk.

"Ah, a gift from a lady friend," Lucy said, half-joking.

And Sam, who had not been watching her, but staring out the window, smoking, turned now and saw Lucy pull the ribbon free and open the box. His voice stuck in his throat and it took a great force of will to bring it out, for the box was not his.

Lucy gasped, "What in the hell—"

And then something came up out of the box, something large with legs like needles. Before Lucy could do more than let out a strangled cry of disgust, the spider was on her arm and she screamed.

Sam brushed it away, stabbed it to the floor with a letter opener. Its legs bicycled madly and then it went still. Lucy clutched her chest, breathing sharply and fell over onto the bed, her eyes wide and shining.

It was beginning again.

§

She died that evening.

Sam was with her at the end, holding her hand. She had been in a coma since that morning. He watched as Dr. Rennel pulled the sheet up over her face, stood there scratching his chin.

"Damnedest thing," he kept saying. "No spiders around here are killers. We have some large trapdoor spiders that can give you a nasty bite, but they surely do not kill you. Allergic reaction, perhaps."

But Rennel was a fool and Sam knew it. He was okay for cuts and broken bones, but helpless before anything even remotely more exotic. He stood there looking at the spider Sam had brought in. He had it in a little glass dish. It was maybe four inches long, black in color, its body very slender, its legs long. Of course, now it was curled up and nearly split in two from the letter opener, but it was obviously built for speed.

And fast it had been.

"Can't say I've ever seen a little devil like this one. A nasty set of fangs," Rennel said, prodding it with the tip of a pencil. "Perhaps it came from the south with a shipment of fruit, maybe—"

"It's a banana spider," Sam said in a dead voice. "Some people call it a traveling spider. You find 'em in Guadeloupe, the West Indies. South America probably."

"You've seen them before?"

"Oh yes, yes I have."

§

The next evening, after the funeral, Sam went back to Lucy's room.

The spider had been meant for him. If he hadn't have come to Wichita, she would still be alive. And that was something he had to remember. Stay away from people he cared about or they'd get sucked into this horror with him.

There was a knock at the door.

Sam pulled one of his pistols, nearly put a round right through it. But he waited. Hesitated. "Who's there?" he said. "You've got five seconds to identify yourself, then I start shooting...."

He heard the sound of footsteps walking away, down the corridor.

He swallowed, felt his heart pounding in his chest, his breath like soot sticking to the back of his throat. Calmly then, as calm as was possible, he walked over to the door, threw it open.

There was no one out there.

But at his feet, there was a little box. Not like the one Lucy had opened, but a black box carved into the shape of a casket. It looked to be fashioned from mahogany or some equally dark, exotic wood. Death waited in that box and he knew it, but he did not panic. The box did not disturb him as much as he thought it might. No, whatever was in there was contained, it was impotent until he set it free.

But the corridor itself ... odd, surreal. The oil lamps guttering on the walls cast weird shadows that were not shadows but a black, crawling ooze that flowed and sluiced. The corridor was in motion, tilting, narrowing, walls pressing in, ceiling rising high then coming down until it brushed the top of his head.

Sam tried to walk out of there, but he fell down and could not rise. It was as if there was some great leaden weight on his back, pushing him into the rug. His breath would not come, a darkness lit by flashing explosions in his brain turned his thoughts to fragments. There was a great pressure within him, as if he were being squashed flat. It seemed like his innards would vomit from his mouth in bloody tangles at any moment.

Crying out, he dragged himself back into his room.

Suddenly, over the threshold, he could breathe.

The pressure was gone.

Trapped, he thought, *trapped*.

They did not want him running away again. They wanted it to end here where they could get at him. Perhaps they were as fatigued by it all as he was. Maybe, maybe.

They're torturing you, you idiot. Do you really, really believe it'll be anything as simple as a spider or a snake for you?

The little coffin box was on the nightstand.

He had not put it there.

There was half a bottle of whiskey next to it. He pulled hard off it and lit a little fire in the wood stove. He would burn the box and whatever was in it. When the flames were glowing brightly, he made to do just that … but the box jumped from his fingers onto the bed. He tried to pick it up again, but his fingers were suddenly numb and useless. He could not control them. They wiggled and shook and try as he might he could not make them work.

He backed away from the box.

He pulled a pocket knife from his coat, knowing they expected him to open it and that he could not disappoint them. He inserted the blade under the lip of the little greasy lid, easing it open and then jumping back when it popped up. Nothing moved in there.

There was only a little doll made of some pale, waxy-looking clay with moss for hair, bits of straw for hands and feet. Just a witch-doll, an *ouanga* and nothing more. He picked it up, held it in his hands. It was warm and pulsing, as if it were filled with some hideous life.

And then it began to move.

Its tiny limbs were undulating, its torso writhing. *Alive, Christ, it's alive.* It moved and squirmed, its clay flesh felt like warm, living tissue. With a scream, Sam threw it into the wood stove, watched the flames engulf it. And as it died, it let out a high, unpleasant wailing sound like that of a newborn infant.

Sam began to sob, then to giggle.

His mind a lukewarm mush, he waited for what came next.

32

Gutierrez told himself again and again that he should turn back, that every mile and every dark twist of the trail brought him deeper and deeper into the geography of hell. Nothing good would come of it. He was a town marshal. He belonged in Junction City. He had a job to do there. When he left, he felt confident that his office was being handled by men of integrity and honor. That they would not besmirch all that he had built there. He still felt that way and knew it to be true. But the longer he was on the trail of Sam Bouchard, the more he began to believe that he was completely out of his element.

There were things stirring here that were not of this world and the unease he felt during the day with this knowledge was nothing in comparison to the terror he knew when the sun went down.

He found a few more of the bone totems and, again, always pointing in Sam Bouchard's somewhat meandering trail. He picked up enough bits and pieces from people along the way to be certain he was going in the right direction and the bones confirmed that.

But, as always, every minute of the day, there was the question that seemed to have no answer: what did it mean? What did any of it mean? Because as unnatural and disturbing as it all was, he had lived long enough to believe that coincidence was rare, that all things had a system and a reason if you only looked deep enough to find it.

As he rode through the endless high grass, he came upon a rotting little village of gray, splintered shacks that creaked in the wind. Its boundaries were marked by death—heaps of yellowing buffalo bones tangled in growths and creepers. It looked abandoned. He did not expect to find anything living there ... yet, as he approached it, he saw buzzards circling high above and he knew that there was not only death there, but recent death.

He was not mistaken.

He could not say when the town was abandoned. Many years before, he guessed, but a group of squatters had taken up residence there and he found them in the dusty road that snaked through the leaning structures. They were sprawled about, limbs stiff with death, bloated things covered with flies and ants. It was hard to know in what manner they had died, but it was obvious that it had been sudden and violent. Some of the bodies were headless, others were torn completely in half. Buzzards were pecking away at them, and several pigs they had kept had gone feral and were eating their bodies.

It was horrible, but Gutierrez expected horrible by that point. He told himself that as a man, he should have shot the pigs and scattered the buzzards, buried the remains with some Christian decency ... but he did not.

After finding the bodies, he rode to the edge of town and found yet another atrocity. Four men had been nailed to wagon wheels with railroad spikes pounded through their arms and legs. They were naked, and a cluster of greasy, gray, and well-fed rats were eating them. The rats had chewed most of the meat from their legs and feet, gnawing deep to red bones and sinew. And when he arrived, they were in the process of tunneling into their bellies, feasting on organs and entrails. One of them was chewing the tongue out of a man's mouth.

It was revolting, but the worst part was that the rats did not scatter at his approach. They continued to feed. All that he knew of rodents told him that they always fled when men approached. It was a simple survival mechanism. They should have run off as a man would run from a larger predator like a grizzly bear that had taken an interest in a deer he had shot.

But they did not.

It was not only unnatural, but aberrant and grotesque. It was indeed a grisly matter in and of itself. But then he realized that one of the men was still alive. He opened one bleary eye and a crusty moaning came from his throat.

Gutierrez, stifling a cry, pulled his Hopkins .44 from leather and shot the man in the head. He killed five rats before the others scattered.

He rode quickly from the dead village until he was well away from the stink and could breathe again. If he had doubted it before, he was now certain that there was something far worse than the Spenning brothers trailing Sam Bouchard. And whatever it was, as that ridge rider in Oklahoma Territory had said, it left death in its wake.

It was closing in on Sam.

There could be no doubt of it.

And if Gutierrez kept tracking him, one of these nights, he was going to meet it face to face.

33

Around midnight, Sam heard the sound of distant wind blowing with a mournful howling sound and he trembled as the walls of his room seemed to dissolve around him like melting paraffin. He was out on the prairie suddenly. It was a hallucination, a haunting sent to torment him, but that did not make it any less terrifying. The sky was a terrible, rolling blackness split by red seams like gashes that looked as if they would rain blood at any moment. He looked out across the barren plain and saw that nothing lived out there, that it was a lifeless cemetery expanse of dead grass and deader trees, nothing but bones strewn in between. In the distance, he could see a decrepit little town.

The sight of it made him scream.

And then he came out of it, pulled from it by the sound of his own wailing voice. There was a bottle of whiskey on the nightstand. Though he was trying to limit his drinking, he pulled long and deep off the bottle, until he began to cough and retch. He vomited a thin gruel of bile to the floor. Things were crawling in it, but he refused to look at what they were. There was a hope of sanity in avoidance.

He sat back down, trembling. It took him nearly five minutes to roll a cigarette. Nothing was easy now. His mind and body were disconnected. Every time he felt like reality had returned, that the earth was solid under his feet and there was stability, the horror came for him again and again.

That witch, he thought then, lighting his cigarette with a hand that jumped and spasmed. *I have to find her. And this time it won't be a gun. I'll burn her and chop up what's left.*

For a moment, that made him shake so uncontrollably he dropped the cigarette. Then he heard her thin, brittle laughter. It was only in his mind, of course, but that made it no less terrifying.

This is it. You stand at the threshold of a very ugly death. You can either accept it or you can find her and put an end to this and an end to yourself.

He did not doubt that he could find her. For many weeks and probably months, he had been drawn from place to place by some awful magnetism he could never understand. If he really wanted to find her, he knew, all he had to do was open up his mind and connect. That was all there was to it.

Drawing off his cigarette, he calmed himself the best he could. Then he concentrated. As she could find him, he could certainly find her. The tether between them worked both ways. He could follow it as she did. He stubbed out his cigarette and stretched out on the bed. The time was now. He put his hand to the talisman around his throat that Katy Three-Hands had given him. It was warm. By God, warm like the thing was alive. The nightmare he'd just had—vision, prophecy, whatever in the hell it had been, the talisman had reacted to it.

He gripped it in his hand and opened the third eye in his head.

Now I seek you out.

Once again, the room dissolved around him and there was utter darkness, a blackness beyond anything he could imagine. He was trapped in it, covered in it, sunken in it. He was—

Oh, dear Christ, buried alive.

Yes, there was no doubt of it. He was imprisoned in a box and he could not move. The walls of the coffin pressed in tightly from either side and drooping casket silk that stank of earthen rot hung down, just brushing the tip of his nose. He could nor raise his knees or free his arms. His hands could move a few inches, but that was it.

Water was dripping.

Dank, filthy water strained through many feet of dank soil. It plopped on his chest. And as it did so, he could feel insects crawling over him. Ants ... beetles ... they worked their way into his shirt and pants, nipping and scratching at his skin, digging into his flesh, tunneling deep into soft tissues and glutting themselves on his anatomy.

He cried out, trying to move, to work himself free, but it was hopeless. They continued to feed on him. They covered his face and neck. They bit at his lips when he tried to keep them out and crept up his nostrils, worrying at his eyelids.

You ... you've made contact with her, a demented voice in his mind said. *You wanted it and now you've got it.*

He began to scream, shrieking out his mind until his throat was raw.

The water continued to drip. *Plop, plop, plop.* It struck his chest with a maddening, skin-crawling repetition, droplets of lukewarm casket slime spattering his chin and lips with a foul sewer smell, running down his neck and into his shirt. And still the insects glutted themselves with jagged pincers and tiny, hungry mouths. He could feel them moving like beads beneath his skin.

He fought, straining at the confining box, but it was hopeless. It was a vise that held him in a tight, sepulchral embrace, his arms locked to his sides. Already water was filling the coffin. He laid in an inch of it that soaked through his clothes and filled the dwindling air with a noxious stench of corpse rot. It was gagging, suffocating and damp.

Plop, plop, plop.

The water was dripping faster now, bringing clods of mud into the box ... and something else, dozens and dozens of cool, squirming, noodle-like forms. Grave worms dropped onto his chest and slid into the water. He could feel them lacing his fingers together and sliding up the sleeves of his shirt with oily gyrations. One of them teased his bellybutton, a knot of them wriggled at his groin. Another slid up his ass like an icy finger.

Not real, not real, he told himself. *You must remember that none of it is real. She's doing it. Trying to drive you out of your mind.*

But if it was a hallucination, then it was much more than a mental aberration. The pain of the gnawing insects in him was very real. It was organic and agonizing. As his nerve endings were strummed by icy fingers and sawed by blades, so was his mind pushed beyond the limits of endurance as the box filled with coiling, ravenous worms. They were an inch deep, then two and three and four and finally, five, flooding over him, burying him in their wriggling depths.

This is how it ends, a voice in his head taunted him as the worms infested him, crawling through his hair and slithering in through his eye sockets and filling his gasping mouth. *This is how it will end for you, how she will take her ultimate pound of flesh.* And in his head, his voice shrieked with madness as the grave worms slid down his throat and looped through the butter-soft folds of his gray matter, where they laid snotty clusters of glistening eggs that bloated with obscene life, bursting in a moist gush of larva.

And then—

He came out of it. Drenched with sweat, breath rasping in his lungs, he was on the bed in his hotel room, moaning, sobbing, his eyes bulging from their sockets. He tried to calm himself, but the absolute terror and revulsion were not so easily dismissed.

You wanted to make contact with that bitch and you did, he thought, thrumming with anxiety that would not release him. *Ever since the island, you've been a walking dead man and she has shown you your future. She has taken your friends from you one by one—Monk and Bolan and Pierce, then Shorty Brice and probably McKay and Hawthorn for all you know. She destroys everything you care about. She got Long Lucy and probably Maddie, too. You can almost be certain of that because the heathen witch knew you loved her best of all. She's trying to break you down, crack you like a chestnut, reduce you to a groveling, spineless worm that will beg her for death. And that's what she wants more than anything else: for you to deliver yourself to her, broken and emasculated, a writhing worm she can step on.*

Yes, that was the sacrifice she wanted, wasn't it? Complete self-desecration as he offered himself at her feet.

The thoughts broke off in his head, blurred, becoming nonsensical. He suddenly could not breathe. There was an immense, crushing weight on his chest. It was the black, cadaverous form of the hag herself squatting on him, digging her thorny claws into his flesh, riding him into death, pressing him down into the grave. Her piss-yellow eyes leered at him, her rank breath stank of tombs.

"Give that unto me which is mine," she hissed. *"Offer your life and soul or I shall take it. I shall pull it throbbing and bloody from your very core."*

His head thrashing back and forth, Sam refused even as his oxygen played out and black dots exploded in his vision as he slowly asphyxiated. He had absolutely nothing left to fight her with, yet he *did* fight even as she screeched at him with rage and possibly even pain. She had crawled up from hell to receive what was hers and it was denied. Her wrath made the room seem to shake. She impaled him with her long nails, digging trenches into his chest, her skeletal fingers sliding deep inside him, followed by her hands and arms as she slid beneath his skin, filling him with herself in a pulsing black pregnancy. She was an incubating nightmare whose blood was poison sap flowing through his veins and corpse gas in his lungs, a malignant succubus that envenomated him and sucked his life force dry like an infant suckling mother's milk.

And then his insides erupted with pain and there was a shrill, piercing scream as she lost her hold and was expelled.

Sam fell off the bed, striking the floor. He threw up, droplets of sour-smelling sweat dripping from him. He had driven her off. And he had done so, he knew, by sheer willpower and the undying strength of his spirit.

Slowly, shakily, he pulled himself to his feet.

The talisman was burning hot now. It actually singed his throat. *That's why the witch screamed. She couldn't overpower you because of the talisman.* Many times in the past days, he had felt foolish wearing it, but he did not feel that way any longer.

This was their first true clash, but it would not be their last and, somehow, he needed to ready himself for the next one.

§

He had never been so lonesome or hopeless before. His mind was blanked, his soul barren, and there was no direction he could turn for help. It was as if everything he had always known and held to be true was a blatant lie. As he walked the dirt streets of Wichita, seeking a friendly face or a sympathetic eye, he realized that he was an outsider. Not just to the town, but the race of men in general. He had seen things they could never see and understood evil truths that they could never comprehend.

There is the world they know, he thought, *and just beneath, another plane where terrible forces hold sway.*

He went to every hotel, rooming house, saloon and brothel in town, seeking McKay or Hawthorn, but there was no sign of them. No evidence that they had ever received his telegrams. No letters had arrived for him, no wires. He had hoped they would come and they could fight that creole whore together, but, finally, he came to the conclusion that he was alone and whatever happened, he would face it alone.

Feeling crushed and broken, he went into a saloon called the Oasis and ordered a beer and a shot of whiskey. Sitting at the bar, he sipped them slowly, the world around him barely existing. It was about that time, as he finished his beer and another was poured for him, that he distinctly felt eyes upon him. Not just on him, but boring into him. He looked secretively around using the mirror above the bar. Nothing seemed wrong, at least, not in the way he was used to things being wrong.

Then he saw it.

A kid over at the faro table was eyeballing him. He looked to be in his early to mid-twenties, scruffy and unpleasant in dusty trail clothes, a rakish smirk on his face and a derby hat tipped forward on his head. His eyes were beady and dark.

Sam, having seen his share of such young men pretending to be something they were not, knew he was going to make trouble. *He either knows you or knows of you and he's decided to test his mettle against you because he's looking to make a name for himself.* There was no doubt in Sam's mind. Some hapless, gangly kid with a large amount of imagination and a small amount of common sense. Sam could picture it all just fine. A sodbuster's son who read yellowback novels and saw himself as a professional gambler and a deadly gunman. He was trying to live out his dreams in a hard country that had no use for dreamers.

Now he'll make his way over to you. His heart is pounding and his hands are shaking, his palms damp with sweat. He is contemplating the fact that this might be his last day on Earth, but refusing, in his youth, to believe it.

Sam knew it was true.

How many times in his checkered career had he been in a situation like this? Faced down by some nobody trying to be somebody? It never ended. Stupid kids like this one who could not accept the limitations of their existence and were convinced they were going to be a legend were common as scrub weed. He had known a few legends in his time and none had ever planned on being one. He would let this play out, but he would not draw on the kid even if he was called out.

Look, he's on his way over now. He's moving slowly because he's in no hurry to die. The fear is thick on him. That pistol in his belt ... see how his hand inches toward it? How his fingers tremble? He knows this is either going to be the greatest day of his life or the worst mistake he's ever made. In the next sixty seconds, he'll either come to his senses and walk away or he'll convince himself that this is his destiny.

Sam sighed because he realized the kid was going to go for the glory. Well, let him. Let him remember the day he shot down Sam Bouchard. Let it make him feel more like a man. Sam would not fight. He would happily let the kid kill him because it would be a clean death, much better than what fate had in store for him in the form of Mama Fornay and Devil's Creek.

Here he comes. His time is now.

Sam watched him move up behind him. He was quivering as if he was filled with springs. His fingers were nearing the butt of the pistol. A single bead of sweat rolled down the side of his face. He was the most dangerous predator of all—a young hothead who was out to prove that he was not afraid to take a life.

"Speak your piece, son," Sam told him.

The kid cocked his head. His eyes were wide and white. His Adam's apple bobbed up and down as if there was something caught in his throat. He was so young, Sam thought, so damned young to throw it all away like this.

"Seen your face before," the kid said. "On a wanted dodger maybe."

"You've mistaken me for someone else, *junior*," Sam told him, carefully baiting him. "Now turn around and walk away, lick-finger."

That's it. Now you've hooked him.

Oh, the kid was practically boiling now, face red as a beet as the men at the faro table laughed at him. All that hot blood was surging through him. He was a killer, a professional shootist, not some punk to be talked to like that.

"You best turn around when you talk to a man," he sputtered. "You know what's good for you."

Sam put back another shot of whiskey. "Ain't talking to a man, son. I'm talking to a *boy*."

"I'll kill you."

Sam laughed. "Will you really?"

"All right, all right," the bartender said. "I won't have this. Not in my place."

Now the gun came out. It shook in the kid's hand. Sam had not seen one like it in years—a .36 French LeMat, a cap and ball pistol that held nine rounds rather than six. He remembered Confederate officers carrying them during the war. Probably belonged to the kid's daddy or an uncle. Either way, it was plenty of firepower for the job at hand. Sam had found his executioner.

He swung around on his stool, eyeing the kid like he was no more threat than a shivering lost puppy. *Keep his dander up. Work him.* Sam smirked, chuckling again.

"And what the hell are you going to do with that, you little piss-mouse?"

Grimacing as if he had been kicked, the kid brought the gun up. Nobody was laughing now; they had all seen situations like this turn very ugly.

"You put that away," the bartender said, but there was very little conviction in his voice. He knew trouble when he saw it.

The kid turned on him. "You shut up! You hear me? You just shut up! I got the gun! I make the rules! You don't damn well tell me what to do!"

Now Sam stood up. He did not want his killer wasting needless bullets on the bartender. No, that was not how this was supposed to play out. The kid had but one task and that was to put him down in cold blood. Getting himself in front of the bartender to shield him from flying lead, Sam said, "Well, shoot or go suckle your mama's tit. Get to it already."

The kid had his finger on the trigger, but he was hesitating. That wasn't acceptable. Sam moved in on him, crowding him, forcing his hand. He stepped fearlessly right up to him and slapped him across the face.

"Get out of my sight, you worthless pudding-gutted squeeze of shit," he told him.

The kid bristled, raging and terrified at the same time. He kept his gun on Sam, but he was afraid to take the final step. He could not understand Sam's complete lack of fear. It made no sense and that was obvious from the look on his face.

"I'LL KILL YOU!" he shrieked. "I SWEAR TO GOD, I'LL KILL YOU!"

But he wasn't going to and Sam knew it. He was petrified, spitting and swearing, simply out of his league. He backed away as Sam strode forward, full of anger. Here he had finally found a way out of this misery and this silly little turd didn't have the guts to see it through. The kid, trying to save face, warned him again and again to stay back, but Sam would not.

"Then shoot, you coward! Pull that trigger, you little toad, you fucking spineless mama's boy—"

And the kid did.

Finally, amazingly, he did.

Sam felt the bullet pass within inches of his left wrist. The kid fired again and this one went over Sam's shoulder. Exasperated, foaming at the mouth, drenched in his own fear-sweat, the kid emptied the pistol, cocking and firing, cocking and firing. Rounds drilled into the bar, shattered bottles of liquor beneath the mirror, and even punched into the ceiling … but not a one hit Sam.

Did you think it would be that easy? he asked himself in a wounded voice. *Did you think that witch would allow you the easy, pure death of a man? She has plans for you. You will die in the dirt like a dog.*

But could she have that much power?

The craft to reach out and stop bullets from afar?

No, he realized, she probably didn't, but *what* she worshipped most certainly did.

And that made anger jump in him again, a wrath that was limitless. He went after the kid with venom, slapping him with broad, powerful blows until he dropped the gun, backed up against a poker table, a broken and sobbing little boy who had now pissed himself with the sheer terror of a man that could not be killed. Regardless, Sam slapped him again and again. But it wasn't really the kid he was hitting, but himself—the naïve, glory-seeking, mindless little fool he had been at eighteen, who was, in many ways, like this kid. The easily led and easily manipulated, immature and gullible hot-headed Sam Bouchard who had fought for the stars and bars in a war he could not begin to understand and lost his innocence on one blood-soaked battlefield after another.

"That'll do, mister," a voice said. "That's enough."

A deputy sheriff stood there, a dour-eyed, humorless sort of man whose mouth was hidden by a shaggy walrus mustache.

"I never pulled on him," Sam explained, regaining his composure.

"I know, I know." The deputy sighed and yanked the kid to his feet. "He's been helling around town the past week, just looking for a fight. It was only a matter of time before something like this happened." He shook the kid roughly. "You can be thankful, you little peckerwood, that this man did not kill you. And that you couldn't hit the ground with your own feet."

The kid was shaking and crying. "But the bullets … the bullets wouldn't hit him! *They went around him! They went right around him!*"

The deputy shoved him toward the batwings. "Destruction of property. Discharge of a firearm in a public place. Maybe even attempted murder." He shook his head and turned to the bartender. "Bob, you can have his gun and horse, anything else he's got to cover expenses for the mess he made. He won't be needing any of it for the next six months."

Sam watched them leave through the batwings. If he hadn't known it before, he knew it now—he would die, but only when his enemies decided it was time.

34

When the creole witch was done making with her blasphemous sorcery and pagan words, she pointed at the dead child with a burning stick pulled from the fire and made three circular passes over it.

"Now," she said, "it is ready for our purposes. Pick it up."

Maggart was shaking. "Oh, please, not that, not that...."

"Do as I say. We have an agreement."

Dear Christ, he thought. *Dear Christ.*

But he knew there was no longer any channel between him and the Christian god. He had sold his soul to something evil beyond words. Shaking, feverish and weak, he scooped up the corpse of the child. It dangled limply in his arms like a broken marionette. He could not bring himself to look at it after what she had done to it. By God, it looked like a skinned squirrel, pink and flayed. One eye was missing, the other stared up at him like a glass ball.

"Bring it to the wagon," she commanded.

For a few brief fleeting moments, he felt defiance rise in him, but it died away soon enough. She had the boy. She held his life force, his soul, his vitality ... whatever it was, she held it and she could torture him eternally if she wished. There was no limit to what she could do and the horrors she could command. Maggart was at her mercy.

"Do as I say," she told him.

Mindlessly, whimpering in his head, he carried his awful burden to the buckboard.

"Set it next to the box."

He did so. "What will you do with it?"

"Why do you ask?"

"Because I want to know."

"Do you?"

But he knew he did not. Her maleficent ways offended him deeply. He felt them eating away at what was left of his mind and his soul. If he was a good man, he knew, a decent man, he would have pulled his pistol and killed her. It would have been a simple matter if her back was turned.

He could put a round right through her head and end her wickedness for once and all. But not if she was looking at him. When her eyes were on him, she filled his head with diabolic magic and he was helpless. He had tried once to kill her and the .36 Patterson in his fist had become a rattlesnake. He knew it was a hallucination … yet it had sunk its fangs into his wrist. His arm had swollen up and he could barely stand the rest of the day.

Out of her bag she took the eldritch doll of the boy. It was made out of cloth sacking with black beads for eyes and stuffed with straw. Like the toy of a child. Yet it was no toy. It was an effigy of the most hideous sort. It had a jagged mouth drawn with red crayon. She held it tenderly in her arms, rocking it back and forth as if it was a living infant, cooing and making strange guttural sounds deep in her throat.

Turn away, Maggart told himself. *Do not watch this. If you don't, what happens next will haunt you to your grave.*

He looked away. He studied the fire, the shadows jumping in the grasses, the stunted trees. He looked up at the crescent moon above which hung like a great white hook in the sky, the clouds scudding past it. The light it threw was unnaturally bright, suffusing the landscape with a cold lunar glow.

He could hear the witch doing things with the doll. Stroking it, whispering to it. He could hear her unbutton her dress and step out of it and then climb up into the wagon bed.

Do not look, dear Christ, do not look.

Yet of course, he did. And whether that was out of some deranged morbid curiosity or she had compelled him to, he looked all the same. In the moonlight, she stood not four feet from him. He gasped. His heart rattled in his chest. Once again, she was no longer the darkly seductive creole woman, but a withered old hag with silver hair lying on her shoulders like moss. Her face was suckered to the skull beneath, a maze of wrinkles and ruts like ancient, scarred sutures. Her flesh was that of a petrified animal, yet glistening with oil, some rancid unguent she had greased herself with that made his stomach crawl. Her breasts were huge and full, swollen like those of a pregnant woman.

He tried desperately to turn away, but he was rooted to the spot.

She had the eldritch doll pressed between her breasts. She reached out with her other hand and placed it on the lid of the box wherein the remains of the boy lie. Her fingers were long and twisted, the nails like the talons of an owl. Slowly, she scraped them over the surface. Initially, it seemed random, but then he saw it was not random at all—she was making precise, patterned scratching movements over the lid, tapping and clawing in elaborate, repetitive motions.

Maggart began to feel faint and sick in his belly. Everything about her repulsed him, yes, but this was beyond that. The air around him which had been slightly chilly grew warm and he could feel the shadows sliding around him in some hallucinogenic phantasmagoria. Something was happening. Some terrible diabolical alchemy was taking place, some shift in the atmosphere around him as if the ether had been gutted, turned inside out.

The witch looked into the sky and made a hissing, reptilian sound and the moonlight seemed appreciably brighter. The back of the buckboard seemed to glow as if she had called down the light of the stars.

Maggart felt his skin crawl, his scalp tighten with a strange prickly heat. She took the doll and touched it to the top of the box, then the bottom. She drew it along its surface, speaking coarse words under her breath and then she began to circle the box widdershins, her hips swinging, her body gyrating in some weird pagan dance, tossing her head back and forth so that her hair flew with what seemed dizzying speed. All the while, she held the doll high above her where it became luminous like the moon itself.

Maggart could barely stay on his feet. Cold sweat poured down his face and his guts were twisted in a knot. His eyesight was lucidly clear, but his head was filled with cavorting graveyard imagery.

"Wake up," the witch whispered. *"Now you must ... wake ... up."*

She stopped dancing and threw herself atop the lid of the box, her hips bucking, her breath coming fast. Then squatting atop it, she brought the doll to her lips and kissed it on its scrawled mouth.

Maggart uttered a small, choked cry as he felt the dark energy in the air around him suddenly ramp up, rising until it felt like there was a burning white-hot seam in his brain and his breathing became an asthmatic wheezing.

He heard the pathetic cry of an infant.

And then something terrible happened.

Something impossible.

The doll began to move. Its limbs began to writhe. Its body contorted with muscular contractions. It was no longer made of sack cloth, but pale gray-white flesh that gleamed and pulsated. The witch held it to one swollen breast and its puckered mouth began to suckle the nipple with juicy, slobbering sounds.

Maggart felt the seam of heat in his head blaze up and a scream lock in his throat. The doll was *alive*, it was a living thing, a slug-like parasite that clung to her like a leech, milk dripping down its chin. Adhered to her like that, she reached out and opened the lid of the box, and a rank odor of putrefaction filled the air.

"Awake," she said. *"Follow my voice."*

And what was in there, grave-rotted and maggot-riven, became alive, sliding around in the box, breathing with a congested, wet sound.

As the doll lived, *it* lived.

The witch cackled and the doll made a low mewling sound and from the box there came a like sound. She placed the doll inside and took up the body of the child Maggart had brought. With a knife, she slit its throat and black blood poured into the box and what was in there thumped and slithered. It made gulping, licking sounds as it fed.

And two graying hands with ragged, sloughing sheets of skin reached up into the moonlight, skeletal fingers clicking together.

Maggart fell over, striking the cool earth. Moaning in his throat, feeling unclean and corrupted right to his core, he let out a broken scream and blacked out. In the bed of the buckboard, voices began to speak....

35

Long after midnight: the smell of mass graves and rotting tombs. It blew in through the window, seeped under the door like oil. About the time it got so strong that Sam's belly began to creep up the back of his throat, the doorknob began to rattle. Somebody out there was turning it, testing it ... and that somebody was wormy and decayed.

This is how it comes, he thought then. *Not as a scared kid with a gun, but as a horror.*

The door trembled in its frame, shook, groaned, creaked. Then it blew in, torn right from its hinges and a huge nebulous shape stepped forward, its breath coming hard and moist-sounding like mud sucked through a pipe.

One of Sam's Peacemakers was in his hand. He jerked the trigger twice, but it had no effect on what had come to destroy him. It ate the bullets. They punched through it as if it was made of some inert material like cold clay.

It was death.

Yes, but a death beyond anything he expected. Death made intimate and personal.

Oh God, a voice whimpered in his head. *Oh dear sweet Christ, not this ... not this ...*

The shape was a giant monstrosity. It carried a big machete of the sort cane was cut with. It was dressed in filthy rags, clots of grave earth still dropping from it, a composite horror whose body was that of a giant creole threaded with cemetery fungi but with the head of a white man grafted to its neck. Sam cried out as he recognized who it had been— Frank McKay. His head had been sutured onto the walking corpse. It dangled to the side like that of a hanged man. His face was a bloodless, marble gray, his eyes black, empty holes drilled into his face, his mouth hooked in a sardonic smirk, the lips sewn shut with black strings of gut.

He shambled forward with a pained, dragging gait.

Sam dropped the Peacemaker and took up his short Belgian shotgun by the pistol grip. He gave the zombie both barrels, knocking it back and away, spraying the wall with glistening, creeping things. The dead thing made a phlegmy, bubbling sound in its throat, attempting speech through stitched lips. Sam picked up his other Peacemaker with shaking fingers and drilled the creature through the forehead. It went stiff as a plank and fell straight over.

It shook and went still.

Within minutes, people were filling the corridor, curious to view the carnage of what they thought was yet another violent exchange between armed men. But when they saw what Sam had shot down, they got out of there as fast as they could.

Within twenty minutes, the sheriff showed. He was a big man with a lazy eye, very methodical and careful in all things he did. He looked Sam over, asked what he was doing in town and listened silently to his version of events. Then, he studied the cadaver on the floor, swearing under his breath.

"So you saying this … individual was walking?"

"Yes."

"I see."

He was understandably incredulous as he kneeled down and examined the carcass in some detail, noting the burnt cavity in its abdomen from the shotgun blast, the flesh mottled with mold and furry ridges of fungus, wrinkling his nose at the horrendous stench of the thing.

"Looks to be dead some time," he muttered. "And you say this … *man* came after you? That you had to shoot it so it didn't use that big knife on you?"

"Yes."

"The corpse of a black fellah, by the looks of it, with a white man's head sewn onto it?"

"Yes."

The sheriff nodded. "Well, that's real peculiar, Mr. Bouchard. Yes, that's certainly one for the books. I'm guessing the body, at least, has been dead two or three weeks if not a month."

And it was peculiar, all right.

"I … I got into some bad business down in Guadeloupe, an island in the West Indies. They practice a terrible magic there called voudoun," Sam explained, knowing it was pointless, but doing so anyway. "They have the ability to call dead men from their graves, they can use them—"

"Mr. Bouchard, you're out of your mind."

"I know how it seems."

"It seems like you are a madman, sir. That you belong in an asylum."

He shook his head. "You seem lucid enough, but obviously you've had some sort of breakdown. Now, I'll see to it that this … *thing* is disposed of. But I want you out of my town. Do you understand? I want you the hell out of Wichita. Do I make myself clear?"

"Yes."

"Because if I find you here tomorrow or the next day, I will have you in irons and shipped off to the insane asylum."

The sheriff left and Sam just stood there, looking down at the carcass. He packed his bag, paid his bill (ignoring the looks of fear and pity he received) and went over to the livery for his horse. Numb, hopeless, he led his horse out into the street. It was all over with now and he knew it. He had been holding out hope that he could hook back up with McKay and Hawthorn, that they could fight Mama Fornay together, maybe come up with some way between them to end the curse and put that evil hag down.

Now he knew that was not to be.

McKay was certainly dead and he figured Hawthorn was, too. It was like closing a book in his mind. There were no longer any avenues of escape. He had told himself many times—and mostly to keep himself going—that he would no longer run, that he would stand and fight. But that option seemed gone now, too.

He bought a bottle of whiskey, some beans and bacon (even though he couldn't seem to stomach food any longer) and rode his dappled mare well outside Wichita. He made camp in a stand of honey locust where he was not going to run into the sheriff.

There.

That was it.

He pulled the talisman out of his shirt. It was cool now. He clutched it in his hand and slowly, slowly opened the third eye again. Devil's Creek. He thought about Devil's Creek. That's where he would meet the Hell Rider and find the witch. Something blinked in his mind and he saw the town. In fact, he knew where it was—New Mexico Territory.

For the sake of his soul and his sanity, he had to go there and face his ghosts, as Katy had once said. Though the idea terrified him in many ways, he did not cower from it. The witch had taken everything from him. He knew without a doubt that she had killed Maddie. The hate he felt for her was pure and unsullied. He'd chase that bitch straight into hell if he had to.

36

Denver Spenning woke just before dawn, climbing out of his bedroll frantically, a deep terror rushing through him. He could not explain it or hope to completely understand it, but he had the most awful feeling that danger was near, that it had been circling him as he slept like hungry wolves.

A few feet away, his brother slept on.

I should wake that idiot, he thought. *Before it's too late.*

But too late for what? This was the question he could not understand. The fire had burned down to a few glowing embers and by its light, he put on his spectacles and unleathered his Navy six.

It's close, it's very close now. What's been following us is closer than ever.

He could not put a name to it, but the terror was real. He could feel its icy breath at the back of his neck and its cold hands around his throat.

He could not truly comprehend it, at least not with the usual five senses, but he had the most ominous feeling of impending dread. It lived inside him, breathing, pulsing with the beat of his heart, crawling over his bones.

The Navy six trembling in one white-knuckled fist, he thought, *it's out there right now, watching you. Studying you. And at any moment, it will pounce.*

Yet his eyes saw nothing, his ears detected nary a thing. Whatever it was, it had come without form, with deadly intent, but made no sound, left no tangible signature of itself. What he was feeling, he believed to be instinctive. He had heard of such things. Much as a rabbit feels the approach of a hawk, he could feel that ... *other* out there, moving in.

He shook his brother awake.

"What? What the hell is it?" Race wanted to know.

"Quiet," Denver told him. "There's something out there."

Race reached for his shotgun. He was alert within seconds, eyes wide, scanning the shadows with his Parker. If anything dared move, he would kill it.

"Do you think it's—"

"I don't know."

For the past few weeks, something had been making itself known. They could not say exactly what it was. It came at night out of the darkness. It camouflaged itself with shadows as it crept ever closer. Twice now, Denver had seen some worming, goblin-like shape moving through the yellow Indian grass. Race claimed he had seen someone following them in the distance on horseback—a man-like shape snipped from darkest shadow. That its eyes were a brilliant red like fresh blood. And on more than one occasion, they had both heard the high, enraged squealing of a hog.

Denver threw a few more sticks on the fire. The flames grew brighter, pushing the shadows (and whatever haunted them) further back.

There were at least two more hours until sunrise and experience had taught him that they could be a very long two hours with something out there, stalking them.

Race swallowed. "None of this happened before we went after Bouchard—"

"Shut up," Denver whispered. "By God, don't make a sound...."

He could hear the dry panic grass out there crunching as something, something big, moved through it. A stick cracked loudly. Then there was silence again. No insects whirred. No birds called out in the sky. No frogs croaked down by the creek. The volume of the night had been turned down.

Denver's mouth was dry as gravel. His heart jumped high into his chest. All of his senses were intensified, his nerves strung tighter than the strings of a bow fiddle.

Something moved out there ... first off to the left, then the right. Now just behind them. The horses whinnied and strained at their pickets. At any moment, what was haunting them would show itself, an inhuman monstrosity that sometimes left the cloven footprints of a beast and sometimes those of a man.

"There!" Race cried out, bringing up his shotgun and firing. The sound of it echoed across the prairie like thunder.

A warm wind blew out at them, bending the grass and kicking up a whirling tempest of chaff. There was a smell to it, one that Denver remembered from the war, from the killing fields of Antietam: the stink of the unburied dead, of corpses heaped upon corpses slowly decomposing into a slime of putrefaction that was leeched by the hard, hungry earth.

It was sickening and hot in his face.

Race made a gagging sound, the shotgun falling from his hands. He pressed a dirty neckerchief to his mouth.

The flames of the flickering fire rose up in the wind, scattering ashes and hot coals. It threw light for ten feet. And just beyond its range, a shape appeared, born from the night-black shadows. Race fumbled to get the shotgun in his hands and Denver, cold sweat beading his face, let out a high, childlike cry and brought up his Navy six.

The awful fetid wind seemed to be cycling from the shape. It stood there, flapping like graveyard cerements in the blow—an ebon form of black hides and threadbare skins, pistols holstered at its sides, what might have been bandoliers of ammunition crisscrossing its chest like gleaming teeth. It stared out at them with searing, lambent red eyes.

Both Race and Denver began to blast away at it.

Though they were both near-hysterical, their aim was true. They hit it with every shot. Twelve-gauge buckshot and .36 caliber rounds punched holes in the shape, bits of it splattering into the grass and flying off in the wind. But it did not go down. It didn't even flinch.

Screaming, Race pulled his huge butcher knife and threw it at the shape with everything he had. The knife, smaller than a machete by bare inches, spun end over end and sank into the shape's chest. Still, it did not move. As if it was made of mud or wet clay, the knife slid down its torso and dropped into the grass.

Seconds later, there was nothing there.

Just the knife lying in the grass. Neither man spoke. They stayed by the fire until the sun came up. When it came time to pack up camp and get on the trail, they did not talk about it. Though in their hearts they wanted to ride for Junction City, they did not. They followed the trail of Sam Bouchard because, by that point, they really didn't have a choice.

37

As Gutierrez edged into the High Plains of Texas, he began to come across the remains of the great herds. Among the switchgrass and black, gnarled trees, buffalo bones were scattered in every direction. Huge skulls and jutting staffs of ribs, scattered vertebrae and massive femurs and hips. All baked chalky-white by the blazing sun.

By day, groups of bone-pickers scavenged them and by night, packs of starving wolves could be heard howling like jackals. It was an eerie, unsettling place where death was not just a hard reality, but a thriving business.

The pickers were numerous now that the herds of buffalo were nearly decimated. All along the endless ribbon of railroad tracks of the Kansas Pacific, there were bison bones, gigantic heaps of them scattered in every direction. Hunters had dropped thousands of the animals, shooting from passing trains and, in the process, breaking the backs of the plains tribes that depended on them for everything from food to clothing. The bones brought in the pickers, that sold them to firms out east, for fertilizer and bone china.

It was a desperate existence, but no worse than many others on the frontier.

Wagons drawn by oxen were piled with bones. The pickers were a wretched lot dressed in dirty skins and mangy buffalo coats, breaking up the huge bison skeletons with axes and hammers, tossing them into the wagons. Entire families were at it, crawling through ossuary forests, scavenging like wolves. Failed farmers, most of them, trying to eke out a living. While adults smashed the largest bones into manageable fragments, children swam through the great litter piles of them like eels. Dressed in grimy shifts, powdered with chalky-white bone dust, they were ghosts that haunted the bison's graveyard, in constant industrious motion, arms filled with the white staffs of snapped tibias, ulnas, and carpals.

Gutierrez rode among them slowly on his mare, but none of them would look at him, let alone speak to him. They were a clannish lot. The sour smell of marrow hung over them like a shroud.

There was a time, he knew, when the prairies were black with buffalo. He remembered seeing a herd in central Kansas that went on and on, fading into the horizon. It was beyond belief. And now the majority of them were gone. It made him sick in his belly when he thought of the destruction of these animals. There was something positively sacrilegious about it. But none of it, of course, was by accident. The government wanted the buffalo exterminated because as soon as they were gone, the tribes like the Sioux that lived off them would be brought to their knees.

The first sign of true habitation he found was a place called Sorreno, a pathetic little mud-walled village of sod houses and weathered brick structures that seemed to be sinking into the earth, slowly crumbling away. The town had a dingy, dark-looking church, a livery, a dry goods store, and even a saloon. The latter was where Gutierrez went. After buying a few warm, flat beers and a couple shots of whiskey that smelled like varnish, he put the usual questions to the barkeep and the miserable men slouched over the plank bar.

"Funny," said one of them. "Was a fellow in here not an hour ago, asking the same questions. Name was Maggart. Strange sort." The other men at the bar looked uneasy at the mention of his name. "Not the sort you wanted to get too close to, if you understand my meaning. Had hisself an old buckboard and team, said he was looking for that Bouchard fellow, too."

Gutierrez thanked him and off he went. He was more than curious than anything by that point. Who was this man? What was his connection?

Just beyond the outskirts of Sorreno, he spotted the buckboard.

He saw pretty quickly why the men at the bar, rough and hardened though they were, found Maggart more than a little intimidating. As he approached, there was acid in the man's gaze that burned holes right through him. Gutierrez had faced down some of the worst human trash the plains had to offer—everything from kill-happy gunmen to desperate highwaymen and noxious scalphunters—but never had he come upon a man like Maggart. He was a particularly unpleasant wretch with the narrow, hollow-cheeked face of a well-starved corpse, a mouth that was a scrawl of hate, and eyes just as black as creosote.

If ever there was a man haunted by his own ghosts, Maggart was it. Just looking upon him, Gutierrez found himself taking an involuntary step backward, his belly filled with sour milk. Maggart eyed him suspiciously, lips pulled back from peg-like teeth. It was as if some enormous struggle was going on inside him, demons of the darkest variety fighting for possession of his soul, and he kept them at bay with sheer willpower.

"You are Mr. Maggart, I presume," Gutierrez finally said. "I was told you would be here, sir. A man in a wagon with a box in the back."

Mention of the fact made Maggart scowl with deep-hewn intensity and loathing that looked as it had been cut into his face with a chisel. "And who told you that?" he asked in a gruff voice.

"Men at the saloon."

Maggart's hand spider-crawled to the butt of the big Colt Patterson .36 at his hip. It was sheathed in a well-worn homemade holster.

"And what is it you wish of me?"

Gutierrez dared get no closer to him. "I understand we both seek the same man, sir. Samuel Bouchard. Is this true?"

"Who and what I seek is my own affair."

"I see."

Maggart swallowed. "Are you a lawman?"

"Yes. And I plan on taking Bouchard in to stand trial."

Maggart uttered a guttural laugh. "Mister, turn around and go back where you came from. You have no idea who or *what* you are seeking."

"I shall seek him regardless."

"Then you're a fool. But I will give you a second hard-learned piece of advice—stay well away from me. Hell follows in my wake and death gathers around me."

Gutierrez, of course, was not surprised to hear that. "May I ask what that box is for?"

Maggart pulled a buffalo rug over it. "That is kin being taken for burial and no business of yours."

He would say no more.

He climbed up in the wagon, grabbed rein and led his team off into the endless grasslands of the High Plains.

Gutierrez, slowly relaxing, decided he would heed the man's advice and keep a good distance between them. At least, for a time. But sooner or later, he knew, on the trail ahead, in some bleak quadrant of the frontier, there would come a grim intersection of their fates with that of Sam Bouchard and the devil that followed him.

It would all come together soon and, on that day, a terrible magic would be made for all.

38

When Sam reached Devil's Creek, the wind was moaning and the sand was flying. It was a dingy, shuttered little village on the edge of the New Mexico desert, and the first thing he saw, marking its boundaries, were skeletons—the fully articulated skeletons of huge tusked boars. They stood like sentries, blown by sand, ragged bits of hide hanging from them in threadbare ribbons, flapping in the wind. There were dozens of them ringing the town, and he knew that whichever direction he approached from, he would see them.

What sort of madness is this? he wondered.

And in his head, the voice of Katy Three-Hands answered. *We have arrived at the perimeter of hell. The hell-witch has brought thee here: prepare for the foulest of abominations, for she will now play her final hand.*

The voice was so lucid, it made him start in his saddle. He actually looked around, thinking that she would be riding next to him. She wasn't, of course. But where had the voice come from? It was so clear it was as if it had been spoken into his ear.

He swallowed, peering through the blowing grit. The third eye. He had to open the third eye. It had become easier with practice. What it showed him was her death, the witch tormenting her into the grave. *Her ghost. That was her ghost speaking. How many lives am I responsible for? How many people have I killed?* But even as he thought that, he could hear her voice again, telling him he was ultimately responsible only for his own.

As he studied the skeletons, wondering what it was that held them up in the blow, he thought more than once that he heard the sound of drums. But that might have been his imagination. But what wasn't was the smell of putrefaction carried on the wind. It was hot and gut-turning.

He sat there with the reins of his mare in his hands. In his mind, he could hear Katy Three-Hands' collection of hanging bones and gourds and bottles rattling and jangling and setting his nerves on edge.

Now, said her voice, *forward, Samuel, for there is no going back for thee.*

He rode slowly into the town. It would be sunset in an hour or so and what the dirty light showed him was a warren of crowded little houses and false-fronted buildings, all weathered colorless, most boarded up, some falling right down, fences collapsed, windows shattered, all of them leaning and creaking in the wind like haunted houses. A few dead trees lined the intersecting dirt roads, a rotting church in the distance. Sand was whipping down the streets, tumbleweeds making for cover, the air a churning, blowing mass of sticks and grit and weeds.

This was a terrible place, and he knew it. He could feel its magnetism drawing him deeper and deeper into its marrow. Katy was right—there could be no going back. He knew the town would never let him leave. He was trapped now.

He peered out into the raging, windy dimness and saw a form standing on the boardwalk down the street. A flapping, leaning form that did not shield itself from the blow.

He took his eyes away for a moment, and it was gone.

He kneed the mare forward in a walk. She snorted nervously. He saw the form again. This time it was standing in the middle of the street. The wind and whipping sand did not just blow around it, but through it. He caught a glimpse of gusting scarlet hair, and his heart dropped in his chest.

Maddie. Oh, dear sweet lovely Maddie. Please not you, not you....

He thought about Baton Rouge, how much he loved her, how he wished he had realized that long before Guadeloupe. But mostly, he wished he had never contaminated her life with his evil. Because she had paid dearly for that, and he knew it. The knowledge of her end, which was not known to him but deeply intuited, was a blackness that rotted his core. He was physically ill with the idea and had been for many weeks. And it was also the hate that fueled him and gave him the strength for what he knew would come next.

The wind blew, doors banging open and shut. Each time one did, he expected to see the creole witch leering at him, but all he saw was emptiness and the desolation of the town, which turned his insides like a screw.

He brought the mare to a barn that still stood and tethered her in there, out of the blow. He stroked her, trying to calm her, what little good it did. Then it was time. His Colt Peacemakers at his hips and the Belgian shotgun in his hands, he made ready for the final act.

39

The Spenning brothers entered Devil's Creek with guns in their hands because they felt the menace coming for them from every direction. Like Sam, they had seen the boar skeletons, and even their simple minds recognized blatant evil when they saw it. Like livestock, they had been driven to this place. They liked to tell themselves it was to take revenge on a man named Samuel Bouchard, but by that point neither believed it.

Denver kept his Navy six in his hand. The fear that worked its way incessantly through him was debilitating. The air was warm and dry. He could smell death on it, recent death and a death that was ancient and somehow much worse for it. His entire body was taut as a telegraph wire. His nerve endings seemed to buzz.

Race said, "You hear something? You—"

But Denver told him to shut up. He heard a rumbling sound, a pounding as if from the hooves of a hundred horses, like some invading army was pushing in. And not from one direction or even two, but seemingly from every direction at the same time. And in the blowing dust and sand and the dimming light, he knew they would not see what it was until it was right on top of them.

Listen! Oh, by Christ, what is that?

He figured they were roughly in the center of the wreckage and ruin which was Devil's Creek. All around them, leaning and rotting structures creaked and groaned. They were at a crossroads of sort where two dirt streets intersected, and he remembered a tale from childhood of the Devil collecting souls at such places.

"Maybe we should go back," Race suggested. "Ride right on out."

Denver laughed. He didn't mean to, but the laughter just came out of his mouth, echoing into the shadows. Why, what a perfect fool his brother indeed was. *Ride right on out? Is that what he said?* Why, the idea was certainly ludicrous. Once you had entered hell, you did not leave of your own free will.

"Hell you laughing at?" Race said, growing angry. That, combined with an edge of terror, made him grip the Parker shotgun on his lap that much tighter. Denver knew without a doubt that his brother was thinking of murder at that moment.

No matter, no matter.

Such things would soon no longer matter, and he now saw why: hogs. *Hogs.* Yes, from every direction they were coming. Race and he had become an island in a sea of hogs and they were like no hogs he had ever seen before—they were the pale white of grubs, hulking, squealing, thick with muscle and layers of fat, their eyes just as red as setting suns.

"Ride!" he cried out.

But the advancing horde was so terribly loud, that his voice was instantly drowned out. The school of hogs flowed forward and Race, his horse rearing up, emptied his shotgun foolishly into them and it was the last thing he did. The ferocious beasts took his horse down and him with it. He screamed with agony, his own cries barely audible above those of the hogs and the death whine of his horse. Blood sprayed up into the air as both of them were torn apart, rendered to basal anatomy by clawing hooves and tearing red-stained mouths that bit and chomped and ripped. Jaws clamped down on bones, gnawing and splintering them, crushing skulls, and glutting on horse flesh and soft pink human meat. The rising blood cloud blew on down the street in a whirlwind.

Denver screamed, trying to ride in one direction after another, but the hogs closed every avenue of escape. They hit his horse like sharks, breaking its legs and opening its belly and he was thrown onto their backs where he leaped from one to another, skating uneasily over their blood-greased hides and falling to the ground.

The hogs charged and he leaped to his feet.

A doorway.

He threw himself though it and slammed it shut behind him. He expected it to buckle and collapse under their attack, but it didn't. In fact, there was not a sound coming from outside. He could hear the low moan of the wind, sand scraping along the outer walls of the building, but that was it.

There was nothing else but silence.

He was in a saloon.

An oil lamp glowed behind the bar, reflecting dusty bottles. He crawled across the floor, filthy and blood-spattered, his eyes wide and white and filled with madness.

"Wondered when you'd show," a voice said.

Denver looked up and saw Marshal Gutierrez from Junction City. Denver shook his head, because it certainly wasn't possible. It *couldn't* be possible, any more than there could have been hundreds of hell-hogs rampaging outside and now there was only the silence of graveyards.

"How ..." He swallowed. "How can you be here?"

Gutierrez had a .44 Hopkins in his hand. It was aimed at Denver. There was a shotgun on the bar next to a bottle of whiskey. "Same way you're here, hunting the same man."

None of it made a lick of sense in Denver's mind. Thoughts were leaping into his brain, which was already crowded with nightmare imagery and bleak madness. Nothing was and nothing could be and he wasn't really here, he was screaming his mind away in a madhouse somewhere, because he had never really seen the awful things he thought or his brother ripped apart by hogs—why, it was all a dream, a fever, a sick, sick, sick fucking joke, and that's what made him laugh uncontrollably until Gutierrez came over and slapped him across the face not once, but two and then three times. And when he broke down sobbing, the marshal poured whiskey into him.

"We had the right," he heard his own voice say, squeaking and trebly like that of a child. "We were ... was was ... *yes,* we was hunting that murdering sonofabitch that killed our brother and we were within our rights. Ye ain't got no jurisdiction here!"

Gutierrez fed him more whiskey until he calmed a bit. "You and I, Denver, are not the only ones hunting him. There are others, and I fear that many of them are not even human."

He said it. Denver heard him say it. That was good. That was encouraging because it meant he had seen them, too. The imp, maybe, and the terrible shape with the burning red eyes. He swallowed, listening to the eerie sound of the wind outside punctuating the silence.

Gutierrez, who had never held anything but contempt for him and his brothers, poured him another whiskey.

Denver accepted it with a shaking hand, swallowing it. He was beginning to feel warm inside, solid, no longer like some cold, tatty thing that might blow away at any moment.

"There were hogs out there," he said. "They killed my brother. They killed his horse. They tore them apart. I saw it. I really saw it."

"We're going to see lots of things this night, I fear," Gutierrez admitted. "We'll definitely see Sam Bouchard ... but I'm afraid he is the least of our worries."

"I'll kill him."

"You'll do no such thing."

Denver began shaking and cackling again. He wiped slobber from his mouth. "He brought this on us! Don't you see that? *He's the Devil! He's a witch or a warlock, some thing from hell."*

At that moment, the door swung open. Denver nearly fell over. His heart felt like it was going to pound out of his chest. He clung to the bar.

Sam Bouchard stepped into the saloon. His eyes were hard, his mouth set. "You two," he said, framed in the threshold, the door swinging open and shut behind him in the wind. "First thing I have to ask myself is if you're real."

"We're real," Gutierrez told him.

"Second thing is: what are you doing here?"

"That's a bit of an involved story," Gutierrez said. "If you may recall, sir, the last time you saw me, you shot me."

The hard, suspicious look on Sam's face softened by degrees. "I haven't forgotten. I'm glad you survived. It would be more than a little complicated to explain that situation, that what I shot at was not you. At least, that's how it appeared."

"He's a killer, Marshal! That's all he is," Denver said.

"And why did you bring this rodent with you?" Sam asked.

Denver felt his cheeks redden. He hated this sonofabitch ... yet he didn't dare draw on him. Not just yet.

"We didn't come together," Gutierrez assured him, as if the idea was offensive.

Clenching his jaw, Denver listened to the exchange between them. His entire body was trembling. He saw in Sam Bouchard not only the man that had murdered his brother George, but brought about the death of Race, causing every awful bit of bad luck and nefarious happenstance in-between those two events. *Devil? Witch? Warlock?* No, just an animal—sick, violent, frothing at the mouth—that needed to be put down. Denver's hand begged to be filled with the weight of the Navy six at his belt. The only thing that stayed it was Sam's reputation as a fast, deadly shot and cold-blooded killer. Denver had no desire to join his brothers in the cemetery.

Still, the need to kill him was like a hunger in his belly. He was a starving man, and Sam's bloody, violent death was the juicy slab of meat that would sate him.

Yet he waited, cautiously, patiently. *Ye'll know when the time is right*, he told himself. *Then ye can empty yer pistol in his back*. And that time was coming, oh yes, praise Jesus, it was certainly coming. But until then, he listened to that haughty fool Gutierrez tell crazy make-believe tales of bone circles and dead animals, men slaughtered by a nameless horror that crept in the night. To which Mr. Sam Bouchard added high randy tales of a place called Guadeloupe where the dead walked and demons cavorted with wicked hags at voudoun altars.

But you believed it all a minute ago—devils and demons and that rot.

Yes, but now he knew better.

He refused to give credence to any of it, because as much as he had built up Sam in his mind, he was just a man. Witch tales, ghost stories, and kiddie spook yarns were silly. Regardless of what he had witnessed on the trail of Bouchard, he now refused to believe any of it. Sure, it was just hallucination and delusion. All manner of fancy ten-dollar words existed to explain away such things. His mind was very simple: it clicked on and off like a gas valve. When he decided he believed in something, he believed it all the way. And when he told himself it just wasn't so, no one could convince him otherwise.

"So where does this leave us?" Gutierrez asked.

Sam lit a cigarette, exhaling a cloud of smoke. He was rough-looking, trail-weary, and desperate, Denver thought. His duster was dirty and torn, his disheveled hair hanging to his shoulders, his face unshaven and drawn. He looked close to death, and Denver would see to it that he was soon even closer than that.

Sam said, "It leaves the two of you in a dangerous position. You've gotten yourself tangled up in something beyond what you can imagine. This is my fight, not yours. You need to get out of this town fast as you can."

"But the hogs," Denver said. "The streets were full of them. They killed my brother."

"Nothing out there now."

Denver pushed past him, throwing the door wide. The wind caught it and slammed it against the gray, splintered façade of the saloon. The sun was near to setting, but there was plenty of light—murky, shadow-riven, obscured by flying dust and grit, but enough to see by. He took in the shuttered buildings across the way. A bare hitching post. A horse trough filled with sprouting weeds. A broken-down wagon sinking into the earth. A few tumbleweeds rolling up the street.

There was nothing else.

No hogs. No sign that they'd ever been there.

Denver stood there, shaking his head back and forth. Had the hogs been another fever dream? He stepped outside and immediately saw a collection of bones, horse *and* human, not twenty feet away. Real. It had been real. Those demon hogs had been real.

Then … then … then, his mind stammered, *had the rest been real, too? The imp? The horrible red-eyed haunter? All of it? Oh dear Christ, ALL OF IT???*

A tormented, God-awful frisson had been building in him day by day and week by week despite his best common-sense efforts to the contrary. The only thing that leveled his sanity was the idea that he had dreamed all those aberrant nightmares … but now, now his mind was faced with the reality of the unseen, the unreal, and the unnamable, and it broke loose of its moorings.

"YOU!" he shouted at Sam. "YOU ARE THE CAUSE OF IT ALL! YOU ARE THE DEVIL! YOU NEED KILLING! YOU ARE A FOUL EXPIATION TO BE LAID AS BURNT OFFERINGS BEFORE THE LORD!"

"Stop it," Gutierrez told him. "We can't afford this now. We need to band together."

But Denver did not see that.

Already, the Navy six was in his hand. Again, it begged to be put to use. He was not about to band together with such a man as Samuel goddamn Bouchard. His childhood biblical learning came back to him, mixing up in his head, confusing him even further. Sam Bouchard was a monster, a foulness, a demon like Jesus had cast out at Galilee. And Denver would not join with scorpions and vipers, nor pagan devils that had invaded the filthy bodies of hogs. Pestilence, he knew, must be burned out and a scourge must be eradicated.

"Denver," Gutierrez said. "Listen to me. You have to get control of yourself."

But his voice spoke with a crooked tongue, and Denver could no longer hear it. He saw only Sam Bouchard at the bar, sipping whiskey, calm as a midnight pool, nary a ripple on his surface.

And that enraged Denver even more. His guts filled with cold jelly, his limbs quaking, drool coursing from his contorted mouth and his eyes bulging in their orbits.

Kill him, the voice of a woman chanted in his mind. *Kill him, kill him, kill him! Shoot the heathen down and remove the blasphemous charm from around his neck so we can begin the Lord's work upon him.*

"Yes," Denver said under his breath. *"Yes ..."*

Sam poured himself another whiskey, swallowing it, then pushing the flap of his duster back so the Colt on his right hip was unhindered. He was known for his icy calm before an engagement. As many times as he had been in this situation, and that was beyond numbering, he never lost his nerve. His spirit, of course, was badly frayed from months of nameless horrors and creeping dread, yet he fell easily into his well-practiced role of shootist. He was tranquil, his soul serene, his manner unruffled.

He thought: *He's been thinking of killing you ever since you walked in, and you know it. You saw it plainly in his eyes. The only thing that stopped him was the fear of dying. But that's gone now. His mind is broken. It's fractured from what he's seen since he took to the trail after you. All of it has come home to roost in his diseased mind, and now he's insane with it.*

Denver took two or three shambling steps forward that were involuntary and stiffly mechanical, like those of a wind-up toy soldier. And Sam knew at that moment, from his twitching mouth to his glazed eyes and clockwork movements, that it was more than simple mental degeneration that had taken hold of him. The witch had him. She was possessing him, working him from within, controlling him with her hands on the reins as if he were but a beast of burden, a puppet.

Sam made ready.

That ruthless bitch was going to force him to take another life. There was no way out of it. And this time, the bullets would indeed hit him, not to kill him but to debilitate him. He would be easier prey that way.

"Denver! Stop it! Goddammit, man!" Gutierrez cried out.

But it was far too late.

Denver cocked his head to the side, listening to an inner voice, and fired at Sam, who threw himself to the floor a split second before the trigger was jerked. The round was a clean miss that shattered the dirty mirror behind the bar, splinters of glass flying like shrapnel. Gutierrez ducked, covering his face.

Denver shrieked like a scalded cat, bringing up his Navy six again, fanning and firing three more times, seeking out Sam with each bullet. One of them drilled into the floor. Another into the bar above Gutierrez's head as he went for his own gun. The third punched a hole in the table Sam jumped behind.

"Stay still!" Denver absurdly shouted. *"You stay still and die like a man!"*

He charged forward, firing wildly, and Sam popped up from behind the table and shot him directly in the chest. Denver screamed and emptied his pistol into the ceiling.

Sam did not fire a second time.

Something happened. The air around him went freezing cold, then suffocating and hot with rolling heat waves. His third eye peeled wide and it was not Denver Spenning with a hole in his chest that he saw, but something invidious, unnatural, and far, far worse—

It was the swine.

The boar demon that was a sow that was a boar. Swine Peter. Yes, that was its name. It had been known since antiquity by other names, but here and now in this hellish shape, it was called Swine Peter—a grotesque, palpitating monstrosity of quivering gray flesh and rippling girth and bulging, obscene musculature. It had the cloven hooves of a devil-beast, human hands, and stood like a man. Clock springs of greasy gray hair sprouted from it, along with black bristles. Its huge, bobbing head had massive yellowed leonine tusks jutting from both the upper and lower jaws. Its red eyes gleamed like blood rubies. And its heart boomed, fleshy and drumming.

Thump ... thump ... thump ...

Its flattened snout wrinkled back from bloodstained, nubby teeth made for the grinding of bones. Its upward and downward curving tusks gleamed, ready for disemboweling.

"At the hour of your death, Samuel Bouchard, I shall be with you...."

Thump ... thump ... thump ...

The third eye closed and it was just Denver standing there, grimacing with the agony of the .45 caliber slug that had augered a hole in his chest and sprayed the bar top with blood and clots of pink-gray lung tissue. He dropped his gun, pressed hands to the wound, blood blossoming between his fingers. He made a wet gobbling sound and more blood gushed from his mouth. He teetered, then went face-down on the floor,

shuddering in a red pool of his own making. He made one last whistling gasp and went still.

"I had no choice," Sam told Gutierrez. "*She* made him do that and she'll take hold of your mind, too." He leathered his pistol and took up his shotgun. "Stay here. Do not come after me. I tried to take your life once, and now I'll try to save it."

"But you can't go alone."

"I must. Promise me you'll stay here until it's over."

"Yes."

"If you don't, what hunts me will hunt you."

With that, Sam pulled his neckerchief over his mouth and nose, disappearing out the door into the blowing night.

Sam moved up the center of the street, drawn by forces he could not quite comprehend, knowing it was where he had to go. There was no longer any hesitation in him. His thoughts were not erratic, his movements not indecisive. Whether it was the talisman around his neck or the third eye or the lingering ghost of Katy Three-Hands, he seemed to know exactly what he needed to do and where he had to go.

He thought: *I will not survive this battle, but neither will my enemies.*

Stalwart, hard as iron on the outside even if he was terrified on the inside, he moved forward, the Belgian shotgun in his hands. He was ready not just to kill but to be killed, but mostly he was ready to bring this nightmare to heel and grind its memory into the soil with his boot.

He saw a shape move through the shadows and blowing dust ahead of him. It was the same hulking, impossible form he had seen upon first entering Devil's Creek, an apparition that appeared and disappeared, there, then gone, cloaking itself in the storm.

He heard a low, guttural croaking noise that became a squealing of many pigs. It seemed to be all around him and then, from the crooked doorways and broken walls of the town, he saw hogs. Maybe the ones Denver had been rambling on about.

He did not run.

He faced them.

They were bloated pale things, some terrible hybrid of human and swine. He was repulsed by them, yes, but he was not convinced of their physical reality, so his fear at the sight of them was kept at a low simmer. It seemed that dozens of them had gathered now, encircling him, grunting and shrieking and puffing out hot clouds of sulfurous smoke. It blew out of their mouths and snorting nostrils, issued like steam from their pores.

And in his head, he heard the voice of Katy Three-Hands again. It was weaker than before. *Yes, Samuel, there were once people in this town, squatters that occupied it, called it home. They gave themselves to worship of the boar demon, and this is the result.*

Slowly, the circle tightened. Why they did not rush in and overwhelm him, he did not know. It would have been easy with their numbers. Yet they did not and he had the feeling that somehow, they feared him as he feared them. Then he knew why: the talisman around his throat was growing warm again.

They were afraid of it.

Afraid of the old woman's magic, for lack of a better word.

They inched forward, approaching him as a bird might approach a snake, sensing that its form was deadly, but not certain to what degree.

A few moved closer still, hesitant, but the unquiet evil in them would not be abated. Even though they trotted on all fours like beasts of the field, they were still disturbingly human-like. Maybe it was the way they carried themselves or their all-too human hands or their grinning, feral mouths. Regardless, it was there as they edged in closer, watching him intently with black-red eyes.

It seemed like they were whispering to one another in human voices.

Sam hesitated no longer.

One of them got too close, and he raised the shotgun to destroy it … but something stopped him at the last second: the beast had become a dead thing, a skeletal husk hung with strips of brown flesh like cured leather. Meat flies as fat and round as large, juicy blueberries began to lift from its carcass, circling around it like moons orbiting a dead world. One of them landed on the back of his hand, jabbing him with a needling proboscis. He slapped it away and blood squirted over his knuckles.

It had been sucking his blood.

Now others flew at him, buzzing in his face, whirling around his head. They landed on his neck, forehead, and hands. They jabbed him, and he could feel them draining his life drop by drop. He slapped at them, pawed them away. For each one he smashed, three more took its place. Each time he tore one away—and they wriggled bonelessly like worms—their mouths pulled free with wet, smacking sounds.

Thou must distinguish between the real and unreal, Katy's very worn voice said. *Thou must distinguish diversion from that which is crucial and know when thou art being misdirected.*

Yes, Sam knew it was true, and in that moment of revelation he wasted no more time—he fired. The flies instantly vanished, and the hog was no longer an animate rack of bones like those that circled the town. The blast, at such close range, evaporated the beast's head into a pulp of blood and meat. He took out the next one just as fast.

He suddenly felt fearless.

Invigorated.

And it was as though they could sense it. Again, they could have easily inundated him in their numbers and ferocity, but they did not. They scattered as he strode purposely forward. Their ranks parted. He loaded his shotgun, fired, reloaded and fired both barrels again. It was like a shooting gallery, and they did not dare challenge him. The talisman around his neck was not only warm now, but hot. Any hotter and it would have scorched his skin.

He thought: *By God, they fear me. They actually fear me. They scatter before me like sheep from a wolf.*

Only he soon realized that wasn't it. At least, not all of it. They had scattered, yes, ringing around him at some distance, as if to corral him, but there was a much darker reason for it.

He's coming for me, Sam thought. *Here and now.*

There could be no doubt. The Hell Rider had been dogging him for a long time, and now, here in Devil's Creek, there would be a showdown. He smelled something like ancient pelts, blackened hides, and mortuary spices. Out in the storm, there was the thudding of heavy boots, the jangle of spurs, the creaking of split leather.

Sam had run many times from the Hell Rider, but he did not run this time. Their meeting was fated. Funneling steam blew out of the dust storm, a nauseating stink of burning sulfur.

Sam waited with his guns.

He was ready to die.

A shape as black as coal stepped from the furnace of steam and smoke. A gigantic figure with holstered pistols and braces of cruel-looking skinning knives, bandoliers of ammunition wound around him, necklaces of dried human ears at his throat. "Samuel Bouchard," the Hell Rider said. "I have come for you."

He stepped forward, creaking and slithery, a demon dressed in draping human leather and rotting animal hide. Beneath a wide-brimmed hat wound with bands of rattlesnake skin, his face was like a skull carved from black wood, cracked and splintered, eyes burning red.

And then, without hesitation, perhaps tired of the game and fatigued by the hunt, the ghoul pulled its pistols and fired in Sam's direction. The shots went wild, drilling into a boarded-up building behind him. Sam threw himself to the ground, despite the fact that every muscle in his body cried out in agony. He winced, rolling through the dirt as the Hell Rider fired again and again, .44 caliber slugs ripping up the earth around him.

He jumped to his knees and fired both of his Peacemakers simultaneously, punching holes through the Hellrider, who stumbled backward. The holes were clean. No blood came from them, just boiling black smoke. His fright mask of a face was hitched into a scowl of rage and agony.

You hurt him, a voice said in the back of Sam's head. *You've actually hurt him.*

That was the amazing thing—that he could actually wound this walking nightmare. But he had. The Hell Rider recovered slowly, bringing up his guns again and Sam was certain that his hands shook as he did so.

The Hell Rider fired, the big bore Colt Walkers in his hands letting loose a booming report that echoed out into the storm.

Again, he missed.

And again, Sam fired and did not.

One bullet slammed through the Hell Rider's chest; the other blew a section of his shoulder away. He roared like an animal, shrieking with volume.

Sam threw himself to the ground again, keeping distance between them, rolling behind a dirt-filled water trough. The Hell Rider's rounds hit it, shards of wood exploding into the air, and Sam jumped up and fired again. The Hell Rider seemed to break apart like clay. He was hobbling now, moving with an uneasy seesawing sort of motion as gouts of foul-stinking black smoke issued from him.

And was it Sam's imagination, or did the red glow of his eyes seem dimmed like lanterns running low on oil? His shambling progress was jerky and spasmodic like a puppet worked by untrained hands.

This Hell Rider draws off thy strength, Sam could hear Katy telling him.

Yes, that was it.

It had to be it.

When the Hell Rider first showed, Sam was feeling weak, unsure, the abuse of his body telling. He felt near death … but now, *yes,* now he felt oddly reinvigorated. The aches and pains had lessened. His eyesight was noticeably clearer. His hands did not shake. He felt strong, something at his very core revived.

That thing has been drawing off your strength like Katy said, weakening you, sipping your life force like a spider sipping the blood of a fly—and now you're feeding off him.

There was no other explanation for it.

As the Hell Rider brought up his guns, something which looked like it took great exertion, Sam emptied his pistols into him, blasting more holes through him. He dropped his guns, caught in a vortex of that sulfurous-smelling black smoke as if he was burning up from the inside out. Sam's final rounds had not only cored more holes into him, but broke away great pieces. He was shattering like glass. His left arm was blown from its socket. The Hell Rider screamed, not so much with wrath, but pain and possibly even terror, as he struggled to stay on his feet.

Sam made to reload his weapons, but he knew he wouldn't have time. The Hell Rider, despite his fragmentary, depleted condition, had pulled one of his long skinning knives and he made one last manic charge at Sam, the blade raised to split him wide.

What Sam did then was automatic.

The talisman felt red-hot at his throat. He remembered Katy saying to use its power wisely. He took hold of it, burning his hands. With a cry, he tossed it at the hulking form of the Hell Rider and when it struck him, there was a thunderous explosion and a blazing flash of blue light.

When Sam recovered, the Hell Rider was a black, twisted, smoldering mass on the ground, incinerated and breaking apart in the wind, a whirlwind of debris rising from it.

Breathing hard, stunned, but still very much alive, Sam watched the carcass blow away until there was literally nothing left.

Loading his pistols, he got to his feet.

The peculiar thing, he realized, now that his mind was lucid from the injection of strength from the Hell Rider's death, was that though the sandstorm still raged, rising and falling, the sun had yet to set. It hung there like a hazy coin; Devil's Creek lit dimly, but never actually going dark.

Sam.

He stopped, whirling around. That voice. It sounded as if it had been spoken just behind him. Not the voice of Katy Three-Hands, but another female voice that he instantly recognized, but at the same time was completely alien. And evil. God, the most wicked thing he could imagine in that desolate wind-blown street of dust devils and rolling tumbleweeds.

Oh, Sam ... help me. I'm all alone.

He stood there, shivering, hurting deep inside on a very intimate level. He could not be hearing that voice. It was impossible, yet it called to him again and again.

The storm lessened and he could see the rotting old church he had seen when first entering the town. It was just before him, a boarded-up clapboard structure weathered gray as a tombstone, the steeple leaning precariously to the side as if it might fall at any moment. Great holes were eaten through the roof, buzzards perched atop it, hissing like snakes.

Sam, I need you. Come to me. Oh please, come to me, my darling.

He kept shaking his head, hoping to dispel the madness that boiled in his brain. He could not be hearing the voice of the woman he loved so dearly. Not here in this place, in this shunned town. In a perfect world that he did not believe in, Maddie would have been back in Baton Rouge, waiting for him. But he knew she was dead. She had lost her life in a very terrible way simply because of her association with him. This he believed, but he did not believe she was here.

Yet despite the fact that he knew the devil-witch was playing with his mind, he followed the voice because it was the one thing in this awful world that he could not ignore, and Mama Fornay knew it.

The sinister shadow of the church was cold as the grave. It was like stepping into a black pool. He could feel the noxious atmosphere seeping out from beneath its askew door, a pestilential miasma that seemed to get under his skin, invading him and filling his belly with tacks. He shook. He perspired. His heart pounded. If the entire town was unhallowed ground (and he was now certain that it was), then this was its epicenter, its spiritually rancid core.

His hands shook on the shotgun as he pushed the door in. It creaked, then groaned like spikes pulled from rotten wood.

You'll lose your mind in this place, he told himself, but still, he entered. And right away, the atmosphere seized him, held him in place with cold claws, sucking the will from him and making him feel empty and hopeless inside.

It was only through sheer determination that he was able to move forward. It was dark in there, a nest of writhing shadows. What light there was came in from the gaping holes in the roof, and it provided but scant illumination. The pews were broken and worm-holed, the walls bowed. He could smell rodent droppings and wood rot, the rank, pervasive odor of animal dens. But there was something else, too, something beyond the decay and mouse piss—a spicy, sharp odor like tanned hides. The way a dead body might smell if it was embalmed by heat and arid wind, sand and desert air.

He was drawn forward, stepping over debris and splintered beams to what waited for him on the altar. It was wreathed in shadow. He could make out a distorted form up there, but not in any detail. He brought up the shotgun, ready to fire.

It could have been the creole witch.

It could have been Swine Peter.

It could have been many things, but what he saw in dust-filled beams of light was the very worst thing of all. He'd taken more than one slug in his checkered career as a gunman, but none of them had hurt like this, none of them made his nerve endings feel like they were being peeled raw.

He went down to his knees before the chancel, his stomach twisted up and his mind swimming in a soupy brine. The shotgun slid from his hands as if it had been greased. His vision focused sharply, then blurred, his mouth filled with the taste of pure physical horror—rust and copper, blood and vomit.

As his head shook from side to side, a pathetic voice crying out, *oh Christ oh no ... not this, please not this,* the world spun wildly on a wobbling axis and his brain felt like it was dripping in his skull.

He went out cold.

His mind momentarily blanked.

Then his eyes flashed open and it was still there, up on the altar—a hunched-over, misshapen human doll, a grisly mannequin, a patchwork canvas of putrefying animal hides, scaly gray rat skin, and puckered pink hog flesh stitched into a common whole and stretched over a jutting, crooked rack of bones, a buckled and contorted skeleton of excrescent staffs and ridges and spoking ribs. This was what he saw. A scarecrow held together with a black suturing of catgut. Its rawboned arms were splayed out, corpse-white hands reaching for him, the fingers like pallid hooks.

The mummified carcass was like the *nkisi* fetish doll he had seen in Guadeloupe, only human-sized, and like it, it was stuck with countless needles, pins, nails, and knife blades. Around its gnarled feet were gathered dozens of squealing, squirming fetal pigs, the children of Swine Peter, suckering hungry mouths anxious to suckle the withered and lopsided breasts that dangled above them.

It was all horrible, of course, but the thing that put Sam to his knees was the head projecting forward on the bent neck ... it was Maddie's.

Her shiny, lovely scarlet hair hung in greasy loops and filthy knots from a scabrous, piebald scalp. Her beauty had been erased. It looked as if her face had been slashed open with surgical knives, then sewn back up … poorly. One eye was stitched shut, but the other opened and leered at him, no longer sky-blue, but the green of mildew.

Oh Christ, oh my dear Christ, he thought as the strength ran out of him. *They made a fetish out of her. And those squatters who lived here worshiping Swine Peter, jabbed blades and nails into her for good luck, for prosperity, to bring them the favor of the boar demon.*

She had been nailed to the altar, crucified like a pagan Christ. She hung there like a semi-human spider.

And then her contorted, crooked mouth peeled back from yellowed teeth with black grit packed between them. *"My darling,"* her voice said.

Sam wasn't sure of anything after that but the wheezing expulsion of air from his lungs. He jumped to his feet, stumbled backward down the aisle, tripping over wreckage yet never falling. He ran out of the church into the blowing dust, fighting forward until he ran into a hitch post across the street. Then the air bled from him, and he went to his knees again, gasping, trying to breathe.

His head spinning, he tore the neckerchief from his mouth and vomited into the dirt.

40

Gutierrez told Sam that he would stay in the saloon until it was finished, that he would not interfere in what was to come. That was his promise. And although he was a man of his word and a man of honor as befitted a traditional Spaniard, he could not let any man simply go to his death like that.

Even one who tried to shoot me down, he thought.

Pulling his neckerchief up over his mouth so he wasn't breathing sand, he started off into the raging dust storm. It was like being in a fog at sea. Everything was obscured, cryptic forms and nebulous shadows seeming to move around him. He could not be sure precisely where he was in the

town. Like Sam, he was unpleasantly aware that the sun had not set, that it still hovered above the horizon in the haze.

He moved down the street with the Hood shotgun in his fists. There were sounds all around him, things creaking and groaning in the blow, loose boards and planks and whatnot. The town was literally falling apart in the storm.

He was undeterred.

He went another twenty feet when he heard a voice somewhere behind him. The voice of a woman singing, of all things. It was the most incongruous thing to be hearing in Devil's Creek: a voice that was oddly sweet yet profane, discordant and shrilly off-key.

He peered in every direction with the shotgun. He thought he saw an amorphous, ghostly shape pull back into the storm more than once, but it vanished as quickly as he looked.

"Is someone there?" he called out into the wind.

The only reply was the terrible singing that filled him with terror. Its out-of-tune melody had the same tonal quality as a skeleton key scratching in a rusty lock. The singing, which was incomprehensible, was closer now. So close, he knew, that its owner would step into view at any moment.

And this was the very thing that made him uneasy, because he could actually *hear* it out there, moving steadily in his direction with an awful grinding noise that his imagination told him was the sound of bones rasping against one another.

The singing was so loud now, it seemed to echo in his skull.

Fear moved slowly through him like molasses. A hot, repulsive odor blew out at him, and it reminded him of a tannery he'd known in Catalonia as a child—the pungent stink of decaying flesh, chemicals, and animal pelts treated with cow urine, quicklime, and salt hanging from drying racks.

Dear God, what is this? What is this?

A shape emerged from the blowing dust and low, moaning wind, something absolutely monstrous and abnormal. He took one frightful glance at it as it sang his death song, fired the Hood and ran off into the storm. Something hit him as he did so. There was a sudden impact and an agonizing pain in his arm, but he ran until he saw the shape of a building and threw himself through its door. There was a bracket to either side of it. He slammed it shut and slid the plank into it, bolting himself in securely.

Breathing hard, his arm thrumming with pain, he set the Hood on a dusty table, making for the oil lantern hanging from a hook on the wall. He scraped a match off his boot and lit it up.

Better.

He was in what looked like an old gambling hall. There were still a few chairs extant and a heavy oval table thick with accumulated dust still waited for cards to be dealt.

By the light of the lamp, Gutierrez examined his arm.

Mary, he thought, *what is this?*

Sticking out of his arm just above the elbow was a needle. It was silver and gleaming. Gritting his teeth, he took hold of it and pulled it free, dropping it to the floor where it rattled and went still. It was about four inches long and looked like the sort for stitching buckskin.

He wrapped his arm with a strip of cloth torn from his sleeve. The wound throbbed, but the pain was gradually subsiding. He hoped it wasn't poisoned, but given the thing it had come from, he wouldn't have been surprised.

As a town marshal and a former Spanish soldier who had fought Cuban revolutionaries during the Ten Years' War, danger was nothing new to him. He knew very well how devastating fear could be once it gripped you. It had a way of controlling a man rather than the other way around. He had always been able to manage it. If not best it, then use it to his advantage, let it heighten his instinct and hone his intuition to a razor's edge.

But not this time.

What he'd seen out there had reduced him to a shivering white wreck. He had no doubt that what he had come across these past weeks was evidence of supernatural evil. Being raised in a stern Catholic household, the transition to acceptance of such things was relatively easy for him. But to see such a thing, to actually *see* pure diabolic spiritual malevolence take physical form, was devastating. The sight of what stepped out of the storm nearly finished him.

He clung to the grimy wall of the gambling hall, not daring to leave the circle of light thrown by the lantern. Sweating, shaking, his thoughts collided in his head, tripping over one another, coming together in a hysterical jumble of belief, common sense dismissal, and half-remembered prayers from childhood.

You have to come to your senses, he told himself again and again.

But it was no easy matter. He was not just trembling on the outside, but on the inside. The inner man which had always powered him was now a sniveling coward, a scared child. Trying to control his frantic breathing, he listened to the wind outside moaning like a phantom, the rattle and groan of the building itself as it shuddered around him.

He picked up his Hood, making sure it was ready and checking the load of his .44 Hopkins.

When death comes, he thought, *I'll meet it.*

And then it did.

He heard something like a low, baleful growling that made the fine hairs on his neck stand up. It was somewhere between the squealing snort of a wild pig and the guttural snarl of a wolf. He could hear the demon out there sniffing around the door like a dog. Then it began to claw at it, scratching violently as if it was trying to dig its way through.

The door was battered.

It shook in its frame as it was hit again and again with tremendous force. The growling increased in volume. Whatever was out there was driven into a rage and the door groaned as it was hammered constantly, splinters of wood and paint chips flying. Cracks appeared in its surface. They spread, connecting like branching lightning.

Gutierrez, praying frantically under his breath, got behind the table and set his Hopkins on it for easy access. He knew the creature would get in. Nothing could stay its demonic fury. As if in evidence of that, the door cracked wide open, one of the panels falling free.

"Jesus," he cried, blasting away at the form he glimpsed beyond the door. And when this had no more effect but to make it shriek louder and louder like a screaming woman, he emptied his Hopkins into it. He tried to reload, but his shaking fingers dropped the bullets one after the other.

Long white claws burst through the door, ripping it apart in a flurry of slashing, completely severing the bolt that held it closed.

Without further ado, the monstrosity smashed the remaining planks out of its way and stepped into the room.

41

As Sam crouched by the hitch post, sand blowing in his face, he heard the weakened voice of Katy Three-Hands speak to him one final time. It was a dry, airless sort of voice worn thin by countless years.

Thou must do the proper thing, Samuel, it said. *The proper and just thing. Do not let thy lover suffer joined to that blasphemy. Free her. Thou must free her.*

Yes.

Yes.

He stood up shakily. He had been through too much to roll over now. Maddie was trapped in that living husk, a prisoner of malefic forces. He could not abandon her now, when she truly needed him to set her free. It was the right thing to do, the proper and just thing. *Oh, Maddie. You're the only truth I ever knew.*

Resolute and determined, but not without fear, he moved toward the church. "I'm coming, my love," he whispered. "I'm coming for you."

Despite the conditions, he found the church easily enough. He walked in what seemed a straight line, and it appeared before him like a ghost ship coming out of the fog. It towered above him, stark and forbidding, its door thrown wide like that of a desecrated tomb.

He moved up the steps with a Colt Peacemaker in each fist. If the bullets would not kill it, there were other ways, and he was a man who knew what they were.

He walked up the aisle to the chancel as calmly as possible and stopped there at the railing, which was threaded with cobwebs. His heart skipped in his chest.

The altar was empty.

He could see where the nails that held the effigy in place had been pounded in, but nothing more. He knew it had been there. No hallucination had the power to do to him what that thing had. It had escaped, and now it was on the prowl, probably waiting for him out in the storm.

As he turned to go and seek it, his eyes fell on a heap of shattered pews that had been broken up, apparently for firewood. A double-headed axe lay there.

Leathering his pistols, he picked it up and was pleased to find that it was quite sharp. Grabbing up his shotgun that he'd dropped earlier, he went out into the storm.

It was time to free Maddie.

42

"Soon they will come to us," the creole witch said. "And at that time, we shall make a joyful merriment of their suffering."

"And my boy?" Maggart asked.

Up in the wagon, she stroked the box lovingly. There was a narrow smile on her face. Her bosom jiggled as she breathed hard, nearly overcome with some disturbing form of ecstasy. "Then he shall come to you as I promised. He shall be resurrected. He shall once again walk and speak with you ... isn't that what you wanted?"

He nodded, even though he was not so sure anymore that it was. Every day, the simple act of living, of surviving, was painful for him. He had done terrible things. He had sold his soul to a hog abomination and had sexual congress with a soul-eating witch. He had wanted the boy back so badly that he had committed nefarious crimes not just against his fellow man, but against God. Black sin was wound around his throat like a noose and every day it became tighter, making it hard to breathe.

The boy is dead, he thought, *and I should have let him be dead. Then he would be with his mother in a better place ... not trapped in that box, his mind and soul tethered to that breathing meat in there. There are worse things than dead. Far worse things.*

Maggart cursed himself silently, for the pain and suffering he had not only brought into the world but nourished by his acts and allowed to flower. His mind was slowly failing now as was his body, his soul burnt to black ash.

"That which is dead," he said under his breath, staring at the box, "should not live again."

The creole witch looked down on him from the wagon. "What is it you said?" she asked.

Maggart tensed. Had he spoken it out loud? It was meant only to be a thought. It was getting so he did not know the difference in his mental decline.

"Nothing of importance."

But he knew she did not believe him. He could feel her eyes burning into him. Sometimes she could read his mind quite plainly, but usually she just sensed the rebellion in him. He would not look at her. She had ways of punishing him, creating horrible hallucinations if she chose to. And if she was of a mind, she could take control of him, make him do things he did not want to.

But right then, with Samuel Bouchard so close, she dared not expend the energy and weaken herself. She hated the man … yet Maggart was nearly certain that she also feared him. More than once, he'd heard her mutter to herself—particularly in her exhaustion after sending foul spirits to haunt him—that Bouchard was a worthy adversary. And when he asked her what was so damn special about him, she said, "He is not easily controlled like some … his spirit is lively."

She stepped down from the wagon. "I told you once that those of the true faith would be called upon to serve. And you have served well. Do not turn from me now that our time of retribution and rebirth is at hand."

"Will it be soon?"

She circled around the wagon. "Very."

Though Devil's Creek was being assailed by a relentless dust storm that Maggart knew she had called up, it did not bother them. They were in a calm pocket at its center, the very eye of the hurricane, waiting for Bouchard.

"Now," she said, "he will be coming and we must make ready for him…."

43

When Sam saw the shattered door, he stopped dead in the street, the wind buffeting him and sand blowing over his boots. It was like a voice in his head, clear and distinctive: *Here. This is the place.* Not Katy's voice. He knew he would never hear her again. No, it was his own voice. He turned toward the doorway; the feeling growing stronger in him. He saw light glowing within.

And then he heard the booming of a shotgun.

He stepped inside. The Maddie-thing was in there. So was Gutierrez. He was behind a table, backed up against the wall as she came for him, the children of Swine Peter trailing her in a squealing pack. There was a smoldering hole in her side, stuffing hanging out, tendrils of smoke rising from it.

The Maddie-thing held its claw-like hands high for the kill, her fingers opening and closing like the mandibles of an insect.

"SAM!" Gutierrez cried. "DEAR GOD, SAM! HELP ME!" He fired three more rounds into her from a Hopkins pistol. She jerked as the bullets passed through her, but they did no real damage. She turned and looked at Sam, her one working eye flashing like a lightning bug.

My lover, my darling, my tender heart, her voice called out in his mind, a grim mockery of Maddie's. *Come to me. Let me embrace you. My heart yearns for your touch....*

Sam shook with horror, but he did not back down. He knew that Maddie was imprisoned in that walking carcass and the righteousness of what he must do filled him with strength and determination.

She seemed to sense his purpose and hesitated. He could hear her scraping voice in his mind, making obscene promises of eternal love and devotion, seething with contempt and limitless black hate.

Now she moved in his direction, her gaping mouth spilling drool and black blood, her hacked and stitched face wrinkling up in a scowl of deranged fury. Gutierrez emptied his pistol into her, but she did not even flinch. Her moss-green eye was fixed on Sam with the stupid predatory hunger of a spider. She let loose with an unearthly shriek as he emptied both barrels of his shotgun into her. The buckshot punched holes into her torso of sutured animal and human hide. Things leaked out—not blood, but burning straw, black mud, and what looked like swollen yellow seeds like those of a pumpkin.

But she was hardly finished.

She came at him with renewed frenzy and he emptied both Colts into her. Things squirmed and rustled inside her. She made a rattling, grinding sound, her voice hissing like snakes. Her breasts swayed from side to side, terrible leathery pouches, one set up much higher than the other from the crude, lopsided stitching that mated human flesh with animal skin.

The axe.

Sam knew he couldn't destroy something like her with guns. He could shoot dozens of holes in that shambling anatomical monstrosity, but they wouldn't kill her any more than they would a rag doll.

He grabbed the axe, and the moment he did, she screeched with an ear-piercing cry like mating cats. Three, then four needles were ejected from her, sticking in him like poison darts. The pain was excruciating. She ejected several more that barely missed his head, thudding into the door frame. He knew she would nail him to the wall long before he got in range with the axe.

Then Gutierrez intervened.

He stole up behind her, bashing the gourd of her head with the stock of his shotgun. Her skull cracked, the gut that held her face together unraveling.

She spun around, mewling like a kitten, lashing out with her claws and knocking the shotgun from his hands. The impact of which threw him against the wall.

But it was the diversion that Sam needed.

He charged in despite the burning of the needles in his legs, left arm, and ribs. He swung the axe in both hands, and the blade cleanly split her face in half, sinking into the skull beneath as if it was made of rotten cedar.

The fetal pigs at her feet swarmed around her, squealing with pain, connected to her.

The Maddie-thing howled, spraying inky blood.

And Sam went after her again, swinging the axe with powerful strokes, chopping into her like a stump soft with green decay. *WHACK! WHACK! WHACK!* He thought for one insane moment that he heard Maddie—the *real* Maddie—cry out with a weird and wavering combination of passion, pain, and exhilaration.

The Maddie-thing fought and clawed, shredding his duster and laying his arms and face open. But Sam kept at her, severing a hand and snapping an arm like a stick of green willow. She screeched stridently, spilling blood and fetid discharge.

WHACK! WHACK! WHACK!

The axe kept coming down, cracking her open, splitting her worming body. Yellow globs of tissue hung from her, slime gushing and marrow dropping free.

WHACK! WHACK! WHACK!

It was like chopping into the soft, moist wood of a rotting tree. Whatever she was made of flew in chips and splinters as she writhed in pain.

WHACK! WHACK! WHACK!

And now she literally split in two like a dead tree, her termite-holed flesh collapsing from the bone beneath, peeling away in chunks of bark from the pulsating, pumping red-black, blood-oozing organ within—a throbbing mass of purple-veined muscle that beat rapidly like a drum. Its convulsive, agonal pulsations echoed through the ribcage as the Maddie-thing—a horribly animate hybrid skeleton—shook and vibrated, stuffing hanging out in ribbons and rags.

Drenched in sweat and putrescent-smelling blood, Sam saw exactly what he needed to do and brought the axe down in both fists with every bit of strength, weight, and life-force he possessed. The blade cracked through ribs and cleaved the thing's heart in two. Watery blood that was black and brown and vividly red shot up from it into the air like a bladder emptying itself with one last spasmodic expulsion of liquid waste.

The fetal pigs died, stiffening and blackening. The Maddie-thing uttered a final choking, eldritch cry and fell over, breaking apart as she hit the floor as if she was made of dry clay, a soupy gum of blood blowing out of her along with a sea of worms, slugs, lice, and wood leeches.

Yet the refuse still wriggled like maggots.

It was Gutierrez who finished it. He grabbed the lantern and shattered it over her remains, engulfing her in flames as the kerosene splashed everywhere.

He had to help Sam out the door. He was nearly finished. Back in the storm as the building burned behind them, they plucked needles from themselves. It took some time before they could speak. They helped each other up.

"Now," Sam said, aged well beyond his years, "let's get that fucking witch...."

44

She felt them coming.

Her sensory network ran through every fiber of the town of Devil's Creek. Their approach made her nerve endings buzz with excitement. Now, finally, ultimately, her vengeance would come to pass, and more so, she would have Samuel Bouchard, he of the indomitable spirit and fiery will. He would present himself to her as it had been prophesied that dark day many months before in Guadeloupe.

She had trailed him across the Territories for a long time, torturing him day by day and week by week with a cruel and inhuman patience, gradually tapping his strength and eroding his will, directing him, herding him to this very spot at this very time for the final harvesting of his essence.

Her hunger for him was both spiritual and carnal, an appetite of the flesh, mind, and soul. The idea of this final, lasting climax made her quiver. She slithered free of her confining calico dress and rubbed her body with the fatty unguent whose composition was a secret of her nameless cult, handed down for generations, mother to daughter ... though its primary ingredients were the blood of an unsullied virgin, belladonna and snakeroot, and the silky fat of infants strangled in their cribs.

She passionately greased her breasts, working the salve into them until they began to burn. Samuel Bouchard would suck the nipples into his mouth until her hot milk squirted down his throat and filled him, enslaving him, and then she would drain him dry. His life force would be her own and it would prolong her own span another hundred years.

Then his soul would be offered to Swine Peter as promised, and the bargain would be signed in blood.

Sitting astride her web like a black widow spider, she waited for them and the ultimate consummation of her desire.

45

Gutierrez in the lead, they stepped out of the moaning dust storm into the zone of calm where they saw the wagon and horses. Gutierrez recognized the old battered farm wagon. He'd seen it last outside Sorreno. The box was still in the back. What he didn't see was the odd, intimidating man who drove it: Maggart. He had wondered at the time why Maggart was trailing Sam, but now he figured he knew. At least part of it—Maggart was with the witch.

And there she stood.

The architect of this madness.

She was a handsome woman completely lacking in vanity or airs: naked, long-limbed, black hair thrown over one shoulder. Her almond skin was oiled and shiny, her breasts gleaming, a smirk on her sensual mouth.

"Samuel Bouchard," she said. "Approach me. Lay yourself at my feet."

Sam moved toward her, unleathering his Colts in a swift, decisive motion. "I will not."

"You will beg my mercy."

He brought the Colt up. "More likely I'll send you to hell."

By then, Gutierrez had his Hopkins .44 in hand. He had exactly four rounds left and he planned on putting them into her. She stood there proudly, comfortable with her nakedness like an animal. He found himself simultaneously excited and repulsed by her. But the latter won out. She was a reptile.

He took aim, making ready.

Then the cold barrel of a pistol was pressed up to the back of his head. "Drop it or I'll punch a hole clean through your head," a familiar, grating voice said.

Having no choice, he did so.

Maggart shoved him away. "Now stay out of this or I'll kill you."

"Ah, so now things fall into place," Gutierrez said. "You are the consort of this hell-cat, sir. And what has she offered you to make you crawl in the dirt on your belly like a worm?"

Maggart's face was etched into a permanent scowl, his eyes black and fathomless. "The life of the man who killed my boy."

Sam did not even pay attention. He was completely focused on the witch. He wanted her dead.

"Then pull the trigger," she said, laughing. "If you can."

And the ritual began.

Sam discovered that he could not.

Now that the time had finally come to cross swords with this monster, he was utterly powerless. Mama Fornay stared at him with the glistening eyes of a toad. And as she did so, the strength ran out of him. The Colts dropped from his fingers and he didn't even have the willpower or presence of mind to reach for the knife at his hip. His limbs were locked in place like those of a statue.

He could not move.

He could not seem to think.

He was sculpted from ice.

A weak moan escaped his mouth and his eyes blinked rapidly, but that was all as her menacing gaze seemed to drill deeper into his mind. His thoughts became liquid, his consciousness melting into fever dream. And worse, much worse, he had a frightening, disjointed sense that all he was was gradually splintering, that his mind was no longer anchored to his body.

He heard his voice from some distant place, raging and terrified, screaming with one last cry of anguish and defeat. It echoed off into nothingness. He could no longer feel his body. Those elemental things he had known his entire life—the unique rhythms of his body, the beat of his heart, blood rushing in his veins, the ambient humming of his nervous system—were suddenly gone, blown out like a candle.

And then a black vortex opened up, and he was sucked out of his skull, his body, his everything, pulled into some silent chasm of utter darkness, propelled through some revolving dead-end cosmos, gaining velocity, and then—

§

Gutierrez saw Sam freeze up and felt something happening, something rumbling in the air, building around him with thrumming, energetic waves. He smelled a sharp, acrid odor like ozone right before a devastating lightning strike. Static electricity crawled over the backs of his arms.

It was the witch.

She was doing something.

Turning the atmosphere of the bubble within the dust storm inside out. He felt instantaneous moments of exhilaration, gnawing anxiety, and bottomless dark despair.

He screamed.

Maybe it was the terrified primitive within him hoping that a loud, disruptive cry would derail what was happening. But it did not. The witch stood up in the bed of the wagon, making arcane motions in the air with her hands, shouting words that were ancient, ugly, and perfectly vile to hear.

The very sound of them made his guts feel like they were being pulled out of him and bolts of pain explode white-hot in his brain. He felt physically ill, seized by an ominous bleakness that made him want to put a gun in his mouth.

As the ritual continued, he went out cold.

Or was made to.

46

She had him.

She finally had Samuel Bouchard.

He was now her toy, her plaything, and she could now exploit him as she pleased. The ritual was a success. Now she would bleed him, suck him dry drop by drop. But first, oh yes, she would use his essence in a very special way.

Maggart, that simpering maudlin fool, had been pining away for his son.

Well, now he would have him.

In the worst possible way.

47

Sam came out of it and he was trapped in that hideous nightmare of being buried alive again. It seemed the same as before. Again, it was dark and cramped, water dripping. And again, the box was moldering away around him, the black subterranean stink of mildew, soil, and corpse drainage heavy and sickening in the air. As before, his arms were pinned to his sides and he could not move.

But he knew he had to.

Something was compelling him to.

He felt woozy and disoriented.

And oddly, unaccountably ... *small.*

Water dripped into his face, leaving a trail of slime on his lips. An insect crawled over his cheek. The air was thin and foul with the gases of decay. Each time he tried to draw a breath, his lungs felt like they were filled with needles.

Your body, he kept telling himself as his panic spiked, *you must take control of your body.*

It was of paramount importance. He had to move. The witch had done something to him and he had to reconnect with his body, link his nerve endings with his muscles, ligaments, and tendons. If he could only do that, then he would be able to move.

He could do it. He knew he could do it.

Still ... his body felt peculiar. Stiff. Rubbery. Inflexible. And cold. As if it had not moved in a long time. Slowly, slowly, he animated it. He made sluggish worming motions, then an agitated twisting and thrashing.

He managed to free his arms from the oozing muck that was filling the box. He pounded his hands against the sides and then hammered at the lid. It moved, lifted a half inch or so.

But the air was running out in the box. It was fouled. He felt lightheaded and dizzy, the first signs of oxygen starvation. His tongue was thick in his mouth, his hands strangely soft and plump.

As he beat at the lid and gulped in air, his entire body began to tingle madly as if it was finally waking up. He closed his eyes and when he opened them again, it was not with normal vision that he saw, but with the third eye.

And it showed him—

Swine Peter.

Huge, pulsing, bulbous, his gray, mucid flesh crawling with swollen ticks. Steam rose from his greasy skin in plumes and tendrils as if he was burning up inside. A sulfurous stink came off him. He ran distended, fleshy hands over his torso and flyspecked genitals as if he enjoyed the feel of himself. His cloven-hoofed feet stomped, and his heart battered away in his chest.

Thump ... thump ... thump.

He made a cackling noise in his throat, his yellow tusks anxious to eviscerate their prey. He was so close that Sam could smell the rank mud wallow he bathed in, the garbage he fed on, and his hot, nauseating breath like warm vomit. The spines and gray hairs that grew from him quivered. Lice jumped in the whiskers around his flaccid, blubbery-lipped mouth.

"Blood calls to blood as like calls to like, Samuel Bouchard," he said in a smooth, deep, darkly eloquent voice. "Give yourself to me and be rewarded. I offer you a life well spent, the gluttonous sweetness of the well-sated, the beautiful lust of a comely unplowed virgin, and the enchanted blasphemy of the deathless. Would you accept? Would you offer your blood unto me and be made a holy vessel?"

As worms wriggled beneath his skin and meatflies buzzed in his ears, Sam shuddered with revulsion. He sucked a stagnant breath of decomposition into his rasping lungs and gagged out soil and corkscrewing maggots. "I ... will ... not...."

233

Swine Peter squealed like a wild boar, his tusks slashing open Sam's throat in a benediction of blood. "Then you shall be damned," he said.

Thump ... thump ... thump ...

Then the third eye closed, and he was imprisoned in the suffocating oblong box once again. The slime-scummed water rising, grave-worms infesting him, parasites in his skull feasting on his gray matter, he fought to be free.

And with one last push, rising, rising like a burrowing carrion-eater, he pushed the lid open....

48

When Gutierrez's eyes opened again, what he saw filled him with a mad terror because what he was seeing could not be. He pulled himself up, shaking his head from side to side, a hysterical laughter scratching in his throat.

He saw Maggart standing there, eyes wide and white.

He saw the witch down on her knees, mumbling crazily, every muscle in her body drawn tight.

He saw Sam's inert form began to move with jerking, spasmodic motions like a machine, a dirty yellow light in his eyes.

And, oh dear Christ, the worst thing ... the very worst thing ... he saw the lid of the box creak open and something reach up toward the light....

Maggart said, *"My boy ... my boy ..."*

What rose from the box was hunched and deformed, its gray-green face wearing a caul of grave fungus, its eyes like pus-festering yellow wounds.

Maggart screamed.

And the form of his son climbed down from the wagon, moving forward with a shuffling gait. Maggots crawled in his hair. Blood black as the ink of a squid dripped from his crooked mouth.

He moved right past his father and leaped on the witch, wrapping gray, mottled hands around her throat and squeezing as she gagged and gasped, throttling the life from her.

And Sam began to move.

He stepped stiffly over to Maggart, who was literally insane now, drooling and gibbering and pointing. The voice that came out was not Sam's, but the tortured, broken voice of a twelve-year-old boy. *"You should have left me dead,"* it said. Then Sam—or, perhaps his *body*—reached down and pulled the knife from the sheath at his hip and slid it into Maggart's throat.

Again.

And again.

And again.

With spiraling, sickening horror, Gutierrez realized what the ritual had been. Maggart had wanted his boy back, wanted him called from the mold of the grave. That was what the witch had promised him. But what she gave him was a nightmare beyond belief: with her dark witchery, she had swapped their minds—Sam was trapped in the decomposing corpse of the boy and the boy was put into Sam's body.

Gutierrez, his mind hanging by a silver thread, grabbed his Hopkins from the dirt and put a bullet into the head of the Sam-thing as it stabbed Maggart repeatedly. Sam's worn, beaten, badly abused shell collapsed to the earth and the tortured soul of Maggart's boy was finally released from the bondage of the hell-witch.

The boy's worm-riddled, walking cadaver, which was powered by Sam's tormented mind and wretched, cursed soul, continued to throttle Mama Fornay. Gutierrez could take it no more—he put his last three bullets in the boy's head. And as the body pitched forward, he heard Sam's voice say, *"Thank ... God."* It struck the ground and moved no more. Sam was finally free.

But there was still a wriggling sort of life in the Creole witch.

One of the bullets had punched through her chest, and she tried to drag herself away like a crushed spider. Gutierrez knew she had to die. Her killing would be easily justified in light of the horror she had brought into the world.

He picked up one of Sam's Colts, not only ready to send her back to hell, but anxious to exterminate her for once and all.

But then a figure stepped out of the storm—something Gutierrez's disturbed mind would never remember later—and reached for her.

She screamed.

And a voice as soft as cream said, *"Did you fail? Did you promise a gift that could not be delivered? An offering that could not be made? And will you now pay with your own soul?"*

Gutierrez would remember it in his dreams, but only in his dreams. That shape. That horrible shape like an upright, monstrous feral hog. The incessant fleshy throbbing of its black heart. The huge yellowed tusks. The buzzing of the carrion flies that swarmed over it. The squirming parasites that hung from its underbelly. The hot steam and acrid smoke billowing from it that stank of burning hair, vomit, and filth. How it seized the witch in taloned paws and pulled her screaming into the howling, spinning storm.

The sight of it dropped him to his knees.

Bare minutes later, his mind had rejected the reality of it as it would later reject the horror of these many weeks. It was the only thing that saved his sanity.

§

The storm abated.

Gutierrez did not bother with the remains of Maggart or his son. He pushed the box out of the wagon and put Sam's body in there. He led the team out of town for a mile or so and buried him in a sandy hillside where a lone willow provided some shelter from the elements.

He prayed over the grave, but he did not mark it save in his heart.

Later, he led the team out across the dry wasteland beyond Devil's Creek. He did not look back at the town. Once one has escaped the geography of hell, one does not look back. He rode in silence. He did not think. He did not remember. Some things needed to be put in the past and forgotten about, and sadly, the life of Sam Bouchard was one of them.

Buzzards circling above the town in the distance, he pushed on, putting as many miles as he could between himself and Devil's Creek and his memories. He would go back to Junction City now and resume his duties as town marshal.

It was enough, and he never again wanted anything more.

ABOUT THE AUTHOR

TIM CURRAN is the author of *Skin Medicine, Hive, Dead Sea, Resurrection, The Devil Next Door, Dead Sea Chronicles, Clownflesh,* and *Bad Girl in the Box*. His short stories have been collected in "Bone Marrow Stew" and "Zombie Pulp". His novellas include "The Underdwelling," "The Corpse King," "Puppet Graveyard," and "Worm," and "Blackout." His fiction has been translated into German, Japanese, Spanish, and Italian.

ABOUT THE ARTIST

ENnie Award-winning illustrator **M. WAYNE MILLER** still continues his quest to synthesize the perfect blend of science fiction, fantasy, and horror with his work. Primarily focusing on science-fiction and horror imagery for limited-edition book covers, lavish interiors, and numerous role-playing games, Wayne strives for constant improvement as an artist and illustrator through continuous education, training, and pushing the boundaries of his skill set.

A primary goal is to gain work for Magic: The Gathering, a client that has proven as elusive as it is prestigious. His list of clients include Weird House Press, Chaosium, Thunderstorm Books, Modiphius Entertainment, and Pinnacle Entertainment Group.